Love, Chloe

ALESSANDRA TORRE

T0163884

Love, Chloe

Copyright © 2016 by Alessandra Torre
All rights reserved.

No part of this book may be reproduced or transmitted in any form or by any means, electronic or mechanical, including photocopying, recording, or by information storage and retrieval system, without written permission of the Publisher, except where permitted by law.

This book is a work of fiction. Names, places, characters, and incidents are the product of the author's imagination or are used fictitiously.

ISBN-13: 978-1-940941-76-9
Digital ISBN: 978-1-940941-75-2

Editor: Madison Seidler, Marion Archer
Proofreader: Angie Owens, Perla Calas
Front Cover Design: Perfect Pear Creative Covers
Image: Perrywinkle Photography
Cover Model: Brit Allen
Formatting: Erik Gevers

November

I'm blessed. I know that.

1. Booted From My Life

Someone was trying to break in. I sat up with a start, pushing up my sleep mask, the sunlight coming in through the windows too bright, my drunk stumble into bed last night neglecting the blackout curtains. I found my phone and peered at it. 9:48 AM—an odd time for a robbery. There was more pounding, the sound coming from the living room, then the splintering of wood. I yanked at the cord of my cell and unplugged it, gripping it tightly, pushing the covers aside, my bare feet hitting the floor just as my bedroom door swung open, a stranger in the opening.

My search for a weapon stopped as I stared at the man, clad head-to-toe in tactical gear, a walkie-talkie at his mouth.

"Chloe Madison?" he asked.

"Yes?" I said weakly, praying my grandma underwear didn't show underneath my baggy tee, a Versace number that barely hit mid-thigh.

"I'm from the FBI. As of now, this apartment is the property of the US Government. We're going to have to ask you to leave, or you will be arrested."

"But … I own this apartment," I said weakly, my gaze darting around the bedroom, a Monistat box open on my dresser. I closed my eyes in embarrassment, two more men appearing in the doorway.

"Your parents *did*," he corrected me. "Not anymore." He glanced at his watch. "I'm going to need you to get dressed."

There was a time in my life when I found FBI agents sexy. Let me assure you, they aren't.

December

I'd spent my whole life trying to impress people. Maybe that was the start of my fall, the last two decades one plush float into the depths of shallow, insecure, hell.

All I know is that when I hit the bottom, I hit hard.

2. Interview With a Condom Heiress

ChloeMadisonNYU
107 likes
ChloeMadisonNYU Job hunting. #nyc
#winter #fashion
#itsabigcitybutnobodyshiring

I stood in the afternoon sun, my eyes stretching up the Central Park brownstone, counting the stories out of habit. Five. Double-checking the address on my phone, I rang the bell, my toes tapping a nervous beat, my eyes tracing over the decorative *B* that was carved into the heavy door before me. I wasn't used to being nervous. Or anxious.

Or desperate. And that's what I had become. Desperate. It didn't wear well; it itched along my skin like a T.J. Maxx clearance sweater.

I should have been in South Beach, with Cammie and Benta, lying on a beach and celebrating our NYU graduation. They'd flown out yesterday and hadn't stopped Instagramming since. If I could have reached through the Internet and throttled them, I would have. Instead, I gave them the ultimate passive-aggressive snub: no likes.

A pathetic move on my part, but the best I could manage from my reduced social state. Anyone who'd seen a television in the last month knew about my family's downfall. The Madisons—a filthy rich financial advisor couple who pocketed a hundred million bucks from insider trading—were front-page news. My mom had befriended all of the Fortune 500 wives, prying business tidbits from their martini-stained lips and passing them on to Dad. Daddy Dearest had used the information wisely illegally, steering his clients (and our portfolio) through a hundred highly profitable deals. I'd gotten a new Range Rover for my sixteenth birthday and didn't think twice about it. My parents got arrested in the midst of their Christmas party and laughed it off. Told me it was a 'minor mis-understanding.'

They weren't laughing now. Not since last week, when the easy wealth I'd enjoyed my whole, pampered life ended faster than a Taylor Swift relationship. Our accounts were frozen, cars taken, assets seized. Including my NYC apartment. Thank God they had let me keep the clothes. I might be homeless, but I was rocking it in Marc Jacobs.

The biggest issue was my tuition. Half of my last semester was due, NYU being absolutely uncool about it, holding back my degree until it was paid. A month ago, I'd have swiped my AmEx and not thought another moment about it. Now, the huge bill seemed impossible. What good was four years of undergrad without a degree? Worthless when it came to the cutthroat job market that was NYC. So while Cammie and Benta were toasting their futures with mojitos in the sunshine, I was alone in New York, praying that this interview would go well. I'd had three interviews so far, submitted my résumé to twenty-two jobs, and had gotten zero callbacks. I was getting desperate.

The door swung open, and Nicole Brantley stood there.

Nicole Brantley. Sole heir to the inventor of the latex condom. Every time a foil package got pulled out of a pocket, Nicole Brantley got paid. At sixteen, she played a blonde bimbo on a *Party of Five* knock-off and had humped the Lifetime movie circuit ever since. My mother met her at a charity golf luncheon last year, and they'd stayed in touch. Mother promised that "Nicole was a doll" and "would be a pleasure to work for." This all coming from a woman who hadn't worked a day in her life. Regardless, I couldn't be picky. I needed money, and Nicole Brantley had piles of *that*.

"Yes?" she asked, her bright blue eyes skipping over me, darting from my heels to my handbag, a critical appraisal that ended in approval. "Can I help you?"

"I'm Chloe Madison. My mother said you were looking for an assistant? I have an interview scheduled for one." A pathetic opening. *My mother*? But, remarkably, the woman's face curved into a smile, the Madison name still having some pull in the lowly area of hired help.

"Thank God," she drawled, dragging me through the front doors. "This week has been a *disaster*. Come inside and let me track down Clarke." She turned on her heel—a hot blue Louboutin—and clicked a rapid path through the foyer.

I'd been in New York for four years. Enough time to realize the mansions of my Florida youth didn't exist on Manhattan's streets. Pools and guest homes, tennis courts, and country clubs—those niceties were in the Hamptons or New Jersey. In the city, wealth was spoken through garages, Central Park views, and square footage. The Brantleys had all three. I spied a housekeeper, uniformed in the white and black attire that a sliver of the upper-class demanded. Saw the Picasso and Kandinsky in the hall. Noticed the views of the park that dominated the room we moved into, and the man who stepped away from the window, a phone to his ear.

He nodded to me, a curt smile passed over before he refocused on his conversation, his voice sharp as he spoke into the phone. I watched his hand come up to the window and press, the lean of his body against the glass stretching his suit tight across broad shoulders and a tight ass, the drop of his head a masculine, sexual gesture. I watched him and felt a pull of longing, the Chloe romance channel devoid of excitement for a very long time.

"That's Clarke." Mrs. Brantley's voice rang out loudly, no concern given about his call. "Sorry about his lack of greeting," she said airily, snapping at me and gesturing for me to follow, her ability to move in five-inch stilettos admirable. "His hand is permanently attached to that phone." She rounded a staircase and headed up and glanced down at me. "Chanel is up here." She took the steps two at a time, her calves ridiculous, my follow more laborious in execution. I tried to respond and managed a wheeze, glancing around for the elevator that surely existed. *Chanel.* Mom hadn't mentioned any children, and I prayed this girl would be old enough to be potty-trained.

Nicole glanced back. "As far as pay, it's a thousand a week. I'll need you from nine in the morning until four, Monday through Friday. Chanel will be a large part of your job. Does that work for you?"

My breath was short as we finally hit the top of the stairs, my mind working overtime. A thousand a week? That should be enough for food and rent, with a little extra to pay down my tuition until NYU coughed up my diploma and allowed me to get a real job, one that would make use of my real estate development degree. I frowned. My original plan, after graduation, had been to work in commercial and residential real estate, a non-salaried, straight-commission job. A job that—in the wake of my newfound poverty—was now unfeasible. I refocused on the conversation, my mind stuttering a little at the second mention of the child. I'd never been around a baby, my knowledge of infants restricted to sporadic episodes of *Teen Mom*. "Yes, great. That sounds perfect."

She stopped on the landing, holding up a red-tipped finger and pressing it to her lips before turning the handle, pushing open the door to a nursery. I silently groaned at the crib, set in the back of the pale pink room, CHANEL on the wall in block letters. I followed slowly, reluctant to meet the baby. A smile fixed into place, I leaned over, glancing into the crib, and—helpless to stop myself—gasped at the body that lay there.

A *dog's* body.

I stood at the side of the crib and fought to keep my expression normal as I took in the pink outfit that encased a body not weighing more than five pounds. It lay on its side, brown poufs of hair spilling out of each opening in the ensemble, a fur-lined hoodie loose across its back, and snored, little purrs as it stretched out across a duvet.

"She's sleeping," Mrs. Brantley whispered loudly.

Duh. I attempted a polite smile and looked back at the pup. *This* was a large part of my job? To dog sit? Everything turned more appealing, diapers and runny noses no longer part of the equation.

"When can I start?" I whispered, careful to give the proper respect to sleeping Chanel.

She glanced at her watch, a diamond-studded timepiece. "Can you work today 'til four?"

"Absolutely." I smiled brightly.

Mrs. Brantley patted my arm in what seemed to be approval. "Tomorrow, I'll go over my needs. Today, I'd rather you focus on getting to know Chanel and introducing yourself. I've got to hop on a call. If you have any questions, hunt down one of the help."

The Help. A group I was now part of. I nodded politely, watched her exit, and performed a cursory sweep of the room. Decorated in three different shades of pink, the en suite included a miniature treadmill, a puppy closet that rivaled my own, and dressers stocked with supplies and toys. Unsure of what exactly *Getting to Know Chanel* meant, I settled into a leather chair and waited for her to wake up, the gentle snores from the crib creating a soothing lullaby.

I may or may not have fallen asleep. But we could pretend that I diligently watched over Chanel's sleeping form without a single head droop. That was me. Best New Assistant EVER.

At 4:05 PM, I nodded a goodbye to the maid, pulled on my coat and stepped onto the street, the afternoon sun minimizing the chill as I pulled the door tightly shut behind me. *Success.* I wanted to dance—right there on the street, strangers brushing by—in celebration. I wanted to wave my arms and revel in the fact that I, Chloe Madison, was officially independent. I had my own job. Would not become homeless. Would not fail. It was liberating, exciting in a way that my privileged upbringing could never afford. Yes, a thousand a week would barely make a dent in my mountain of debt. Yes, I'd be eating Ramen noodles and taking the subway. But still! I was on my own and, for the first time, it didn't feel scary; it felt manageable.

I moved down the street, swinging my purse from my shoulder and dug for my cell, the phone to my ear by the time I hit Park Avenue.

"Hey beautiful!" Cammie's voice rang through the phone, her greeting seconded by Benta, and I could imagine the two girls, faces together over a pitcher of margaritas, the phone held between them.

"Hey you tan goddesses," I teased. "Enjoying the Florida sun without me?"

"We'd be lying if we said we weren't." In the background, I heard music start. "How'd the interview go?"

I delivered the good news, the girls squealing with an excitement that rivaled my own, a laugh spilling from my mouth at their reaction. "I wish you guys were here to help me celebrate."

"Woman, hop on a plane and get down here! We'll save one of these beautiful men for you."

"Don't tempt me," I warned. "I'm so sick of New York men I could scream." A vision of Clarke Brantley appeared in my mind's eye, his hand against the window, his masculinity screaming through every line in his body. I closed my eyes briefly and fought the urge to check my lower lip for drool. "Anyway, I've got to run. I'm going to check out apartments, try and find a place to live. I just wanted to let you guys know the good news."

"That's great news, babe," Benta called out, her voice overshadowed by the background noise. "Go have fun tonight! Celebrate without us!"

I smiled at her order, said my goodbyes to both of them and ended the call before dropping my phone into my purse and jogging down the subway steps, the mild warmth of the afternoon sun fading as I stepped into the dark underground.

My phone rang as I hit the bottom step, the muted song chiming from my purse. I stepped out of the way, digging frantically as my ringtone neared its end. I followed the glow of the screen, pulling out my cell just in time. My finger froze mid-swipe, and I stared down at my screen at the name.

3. Opening the Ex-File

ChloeMadisonNYU
75 likes
ChloeMadisonNYU
Throwback. #2013
#oldlife #nostalgia

I smirked. Straightened the strap of my gown and looked out the window. "Shh. The driver will hear you."

"The driver's job is to hear me. Now, get on your knees." Vic's hand landed on the back of my neck, pulling me toward him. I twisted away, shooting him a warning look.

He leaned over, whispered in my ear, his breath tickling the wisps of my chignon. "Do it, and tomorrow I'll fly us to Paris."

That *got my attention. I turned, sliding across the seat, his hand immediately traveling up the slit in my dress, teasing the skin on my thighs, my legs obediently parting as he did what he did best and ran his fingers over the silk of my panties. "Private?" I asked, the negotiation eliciting a chuckle from him, his eyes darkening when my hips curved into his fingers, the steal of a digit sliding under my panties turning everything—for one exquisite moment—beautifully black.*

"Yes, we'll fly private, you spoiled woman. Now, let me feel that delicious mouth." His fingers gently played on my neck, a light reminder, and this time, I didn't resist, sliding down, the limo's carpet stiff against my knees, the beaded dress snagging on the edge of the seat before breaking free.

I unbuckled his belt and looked up into his eyes, dragging the zipper down. Heavy and hooded, they stared at me as if drugged, his handsome mouth opening slightly when my hand stole into his tuxedo pants and wrapped around him.

The car took a turn, my left hand gripping his thigh for balance, his finger tapping at the window control, a sliver of cold night air and city sounds pouring through the now-open crack, my eyes narrowing as I placed his cock in my mouth, showing my teeth, threatening him with my eyes.

"Easy princess." He smiled, his perfect grin white in the dark space. "Just adding a little atmosphere. Not enough for anyone to see in. Now, suck."

His order excited me, the dominance in his tone making my thighs clench, arousal growing. Arousal, which, knowing Vic, he'd light into a full-fledged fire by the time we hit his elevator. Arousal he'd put out with his fingers, his mouth, and his body. I closed my eyes and concentrated.

I loved the power of having him in my mouth. I took my time, taking him deep and feeling him stiffen against my tongue, in the course of seconds, my oral ability proven in eight inches of reaction. I smiled around his cock and buried it down my throat.

Fifteen blocks later, only minutes before we pulled up to his Fifth Avenue residence, he moaned my name, his hand tugging at my hair, the shudder of his body the final warning before he thrust into my mouth and came. Hot satisfaction of which I swallowed every bit, the small aftertaste well worth the worship in his eyes as he pulled me into his arms and kissed me senseless.

"I love you," he whispered, brushing the hair off my shoulder, the hair that had

come undone somewhere around SoHo. "Oh Chloe. I love you so much."

And that, in a cum-filled nutshell, was my ex. Vic Worth. His family's name was plastered on buildings all over Manhattan. A billionaire trust-fund baby, we met sophomore year at NYU. Dated eighteen months before I walked in on him mid-thrust into his maid. I dumped him, and he popped the question with a six-carat ring amid a flurry of exorbitant gestures. I said "no" in about four different combinations, most paired with an expletive or immaturely presented middle finger. He wasn't deterred, his pursuit impressive in its effort, a pursuit that I had hoped, with a two-month hiatus since his last contact, had finally ended.

Yet that afternoon, my high from my new job draining with every note of my ringtone, he called. I hesitated, then, despite my better judgment, dragged my finger across the surface and raised the phone to my ear.

I barely had time to speak before Vic's voice came through the cell, his words barking out with some degree of urgency. "Don't get on that filthy thing. The subway? God knows what you'll catch."

I spun around, peering up into the bright white square of sunlight, a swell of bundled New Yorkers pouring over its edge and hurrying down the steps, the vibration of the oncoming train pulsing under my feet. "Are you following me?" I hissed into the phone.

"Hell no. I'm at the Bellagio about to clean house in blackjack. But Jake just texted me that he saw you going down to the six. What the fuck are you doing?"

"Is this seriously why you called me?" The train approached, its brakes screeching as it came to a stop and was immediately surrounded, the crush of bodies swelling like a sea of maggots around a prize. I tapped my MetroCard against my leg, in no hurry to join the party.

He sighed into the phone. "According to Jake, you're in heels—and I know your heels. They aren't built for actual use. Trot your sexy ass up those stairs and get in the warm car; let Jake take you home. *Please.* Then I'll hang up and never bother you again."

"Never?" I challenged, the promise one I'd heard before.

"I'll try my best."

I twisted back and forth, my purse swinging with the momentum, from darkness to light. Though, in this twisted scenario, they were flip-flopped: the dark and dirty wheeze of the subway was where I *should* be going, the light and sunny street the path I should avoid.

"Come on, baby. Let me do this one thing. Just one." The beg in his voice, the crack on the word *baby.* It reached up my skirt and teased my skin, probed into my brain and lured out all of the times his gorgeous mouth had whispered the words.

Come on, baby… his hand pulled me into a coat check closet, parting furs and pushing me back against the wall.

Come on, baby… his tongue, soft on my inner thighs, the scrape of his five o'clock shadow tickled as his hands spread my knees apart and his mouth moved higher.

Come on, baby… his hands up my dress, fingers digging into the meat of my ass, his mouth on my neck as we—tucked into the shadows of a club, music thumping, bodies everywhere—let passion override sense.

Come on, baby…

That was the problem with love. There was no OFF switch.

I ended the call and hurried down the steps into the cold darkness.

4. Girls Just Want to Have Fun

My home was Cammie's couch, a red leather sectional that was super stylish but really uncomfortable. She had offered to share her bed, but I'd heard of the gymnastics that had occurred on its surface… so the couch would work just fine for me. The apartment felt lonely without her, my Instagram strike broken when I drank too much of her wine last night and gorged on their South Beach photos. I flipped through image after image of gorgeous selfies with brilliant blue water behind them, their bikinis depressing when I glanced out her window at the NYC snow. It was official. Being poor sucked.

Vic didn't call back after I hung up on him. Which was a good thing, something that I needed to keep reminding myself. I doodled in the margins of my notebook.

STAY AWAY FROM VIC.

Putting it on paper seemed to help. The caps seemed a bit excessive but did properly emphasize the point. Maybe when I got an apartment, I could wallpaper the walls with that mantra. On second thought, that might scare off potential dates, give a bit of a crazy-girl vibe. I ripped out the notebook page and crumpled it into a ball. If I had any hope of finding love in this city, I needed to put my best foot forward. Outside, there was a short honk and I looked out the window, recognizing Cammie's driver. The girls were flying home, and I was tagging along with the driver to pick them up. I grabbed my purse and cell, tossed my Vic resolution in the trash, and headed outside, waving a hello to the driver as I got in the SUV.

I settled back in the seat, tired from my first week of employment. It was amazing how long eight hours could feel—each day stretching interminably before me, Nicole too busy to teach me anything, my hours spent puppy-sitting Chanel.

Yesterday, I'd spent five hours looking at apartments, my lonely search through the snowy city a complete disaster. Every place was crap, the buildings old, rooms cramped, and neighborhoods sketchy.

I never realized how expensive this city was before, never realized how a majority of New Yorkers lived, never realized how spoiled I was before. I decided to give Cammie's couch a couple more weeks, get my bank account a little more flush, give my mind a little more time—then try again.

There was a loud honk, and the SUV swerved, my hand gripping the center console as I tried to open a text from Benta, my eyes glancing briefly up at the traffic before looking back down at my phone. The text was short, letting me know they had landed and were at baggage claim. Thank God. After a week alone, I was convinced I wouldn't make it in New York without these girls. Life sans them sucked.

Granted, there were a *few* negatives about their return. I'd have to tell Cammie about the dress—her Nicole Miller number that I *might* have snagged slightly during my borrow. And I'd have to disclose the conversation with Vic. They had me on strict probation from answering any of his calls, so I'd be in trouble over that slip.

The SUV rolled into JFK, and I could already see them, their enthusiastic wave barely visible through the snow. Only minutes until their bronzed and relaxed selves would hop inside, and I'd be back in my rightful place: the pasty white stressball in our trio. Granted, I had that title *before* they spent a week sipping margaritas on a Miami beach. Cammie's ethnicity had blessed her with perfect dark skin and almond eyes that made my blond hair and blue eyes look bland. And Benta was from Spain; she looked like a tanned, dark-haired version of me until she opened her mouth and a ridiculously sexy accent flowed out.

"I *know* you aren't welcoming us back glued to that phone." Benta crawled into the backseat, her gloved hand unsuccessfully swiping for my cell.

I held it out of reach with a glare. "I'm still trying to catch up on your Instagram vomit. I swear, you guys woke up each day determined to make me miserable. Give me two minutes to get over my jealousy and pretend to be happy for you."

"Two minutes … ooh, that reminds me. Chloe, when we get to dinner I have to tell you about this 'stud' that Benta hooked me up with. The guy finished before I unbuttoned my shirt." Cammie snorted.

"Is there *more* to that story?" I glanced up from my phone.

"Nope," Cammie said cheerfully. "That's about it. But *ohmigod,* wait 'til you hear…"

I stuffed my phone in my purse and settled in, their excited chatter filling the car, a welcome distraction from my current issues.

5. Kissing a Frog

We didn't head home, our first stop a bar in Chelsea, then a club in Midtown, dancing and drinking until 3 AM when we finally called it a night, stumbling out the doors.

A hand caught mine as we stepped into the street, the pull interrupting my giggle at something Cammie had said. The hand was attached to a tailored suit, wide smile, and flushed face. "Hey beautiful," he said, his breath frosting in the night air. I gently worked my hand free, feeling the flank of my girls rallying beside me.

"Hey." I smiled. "You good?" I stepped back, glancing up the street to make sure we weren't all about to be run over.

"I was hoping for your number, didn't get it in the club. I'm Tommy." He smiled, a grin that probably made his girlfriend real happy.

"Nice to meet you Tommy." I stepped back another pace. "I'm not interested."

He scowled. Held up a hand that swayed slightly, his friends pulling at his shoulder, sending apologetic looks our way while failing to move Tommy. "Awww… come on. One kiss, princess. If it's not incredible, I'll give you a thousand dollars." He fumbled in his suit pocket, pulling out a thick wad of hundreds and holding them out. "Come on. *One* kiss."

I hesitated. Three months ago, I'd have laughed in his face. But with my low bank balance fresh in my mind, a thousand bucks was tempting. *More* than tempting. I stepped closer, Benta's hand wrapping like a vise around my arm. "Chloe," she warned.

I hesitated. When Benta barked, I normally listened. Her authoritative tone was that of the dominatrix variety. But there, on that street, I stood firm.

"One kiss," I repeated, meeting his eyes. "For a thousand bucks."

"You're probably worth it." He shrugged, smacking the cash across his palm as he swayed slightly, the action drawing attention to the shine of his watch, the same brand my father wore. Or rather, used to wear. Behind him, his friends stopped their efforts, suddenly interested in the late-night negotiation.

I examined him closer. He wasn't *terrible* looking. Prep school pretty, I wouldn't depend on him to protect me in a dark alley. I could tell you without looking that his nails were manicured, his palms probably smoother than mine.

I risked death, tugging my arm from Benta and stepped closer, looking up at him. "Okay, Romeo. Give me your best shot."

He stepped forward with a smile, one hand gripping my shoulder, his lips pushing on mine and let me tell you right now, his best shot really, really, really sucked. A thick tongue forcibly rammed itself into my gum line, with a smack of extra saliva as he clamped his chops around my lower lip and slowly pulled away, my lip stretching out before popping free. He tasted like Red Bull and whiskey, sugary sweet with a foul aftertaste. I'd literally had gyno exams that I'd enjoyed more.

I jumped back, shoving off his chest, my hand wiping across my mouth as I glared at him. "*That* was your best kiss?"

He laughed, rubbing his own lips with a smile that reeked of asshole. I held out my hand, wanting the cash, and his eyes dropped to it with a sneer. I suddenly felt sick to my stomach, and it wasn't from the four martinis I had downed inside.

"Let's go, Chloe," Benta spoke quietly from behind me.

"Gimme the cash. We had a deal," I insisted, my palm still extended, my pride at an all-time low. The urge to cry pricked my eyes, and I swallowed hard, begging him with my stare.

"He's not worth it. Come *on.*" Cammie's hand wrapped around my forearm and pulled, my heels tripping over the icy curb, her driver moving to open the back door for us. Before climbing in, I glanced over my shoulder and caught the trio of assholes laughing.

The SUV bumped over a pothole, taking us home. I rested my forehead against the cold window, hoping to get the spinning to stop.

That experience … it had been the first time in my life that I had ever felt cheap. God, the look in his eyes when he'd laughed at me. I must have looked so pathetic, holding out my hand, begging for his cash.

I shouldn't have even turned when he grabbed my hand. I should have listened when Benta spoke. I should have laughed in his face like I would have done three months ago.

But instead, within a month of my trust fund's disappearance, I had prostituted myself for a kiss. And hadn't even gotten paid for it. I groaned against the glass window and felt the gentle pat of Cammie's hand against my back.

Maybe the cultured, confident woman I was before was just a product of my parents' money. Maybe now, with my new life a train wreck, I would discover the real Chloe Madison. And maybe, I wouldn't like her.

Ugh. I rolled down the window and tried not to vomit at the thought.

6. Countdown to Jaw Drop

ChloeMadisonNYU
49 likes
ChloeMadisonNYU Bring on the festive.
#christmas #nyc #prettylights

New Year's Eve. The first holiday season spent without my parents, Christmas normally spent at our Aspen home, a picturesque cabin with six bedrooms, a hot tub, and theater room. Dad and I would ski through the Christmas tree fields until we found the perfect one; Mom and I would cook Christmas dinner in the chef's kitchen, and we'd end the holiday with a pile of presents and lots of eggnog. That house, along with our Bahamas condo, was now the property of the government. I hoped someone was using it, the thought of our furniture under sheets, the hot tub frozen over, too depressing to consider. I didn't even know where my parents were this year. They hadn't called on Christmas Day, and we'd spoken once since my eviction, long enough for Mom to give me Nicole's number, no apology or explanation given for their actions, their voices bubbly, lives busy, glamorous plans apparently still in effect.

"Ms. Madison?"

"Yes," I said, stepping carefully toward the car, trying not to turn an ankle in my four-inch Brian Atwoods. "Are you the Brantleys' driver?"

"I am." He didn't offer a name, just opened the Escalade's back door with a polite smile, supporting my hand until the moment when I released it to grip the door frame. "I've already taken the Brantleys to the event. I have instructions to bring you to the house, pick up Chanel, and arrive at the party by eight."

The same instructions Nicole had given me three times already, her over-enunciated words making it clear that she assumed I was an idiot. I nodded at the man, tucking my bag in the floorboard and bringing my feet in. He shut the door gently, then walked around to the driver's side.

The large SUV felt small with just the two of us inside. I opened my compact and checked my lipstick, glancing up front to the driver. "How was your Christmas?"

"It was quiet."

Well, *that* was a conversation starter. I had expected for him to politely return the question, giving me an opportunity to share my own story. Cammie, Benta, and I had failed in our attempt to play house. Our turkey had burned to a crisp on the outside, but was rare on the inside, my soufflé fell, and Benta's try at haricots verts produced water-logged beans as limp as drunk dick. We'd ditched the food, and settled on the couch with a box of Ferrero Rocher chocolates and two bottles of champagne. Adding Netflix to the mix, my first NYC Christmas had ended up being pretty damn awesome, my thoughts only flitting to my parents a handful of times. It had been nice, spending it with the girls. It felt so grownup, like we were finally adults, even if we had failed horribly in our cooking.

I fiddled with my necklace and tried another tactic. "How long have you worked for the Brantleys?"

"Three years."

Talkative guy. Any more chattering and I'd need to put in earplugs. It was too bad. His voice had a layer of accent that made it absolutely delicious.

"Are they nice to work for?"

His eyes moved to the review mirror, our gaze connecting. He had a very direct stare, one that—once established—was hard to break. And his eyes … damn. A dark blue that picked up the lights from passing cars, causing a shimmer across their depths. "They're fine."

It was quiet. Three years. They're fine. Hell, I'd worked for the Brantleys for six days, and I could fill up a thirty-minute drive with stories. This guy was really committed to the strong, silent vibe he was rocking. Or he had taken to heart the lengthy confidentiality agreement that Nicole had made me sign.

I gave up on conversation and leaned back against the seat, watching the city go by, Christmas tree lights out, a sea of white and rainbow at every turn. It was my favorite time of the year, the New York streets turned into festive art, all of the dirt and grime of the city hidden by a layer of snow. Nicole was celebrating New Year's Eve at an animal charity event, one where she would parade Chanel around for the cocktail hour before passing her back to me. At 10 PM, a holiday fashion show was scheduled, and Chanel would make two appearances: first in a red gown, then in a diamond-studded collar and a dusting of silver glitter. How PETA was encouraging the ethical treatment of animals by subjecting poor Chanel to this, I didn't know. But then again, I wasn't getting paid to think.

The car stopped outside the Brantleys' home, and I waited a few long seconds, expecting the Driver-Without-A-Name to get my door. When he stayed buckled in place, the vehicle settled into park, I sighed, opening the door myself and stepping out into the cold night air.

The wealthy of the city lived in a different bubble than the rest of us. One where there were no worries of minor problems, the majority of which were easily solved by money. One comprised of beautiful women, powerful men, the drug of success heavy in the air, punctuated with diamonds, caviar, and ego. For the first time, I was an outsider, the Brantleys' car driving down the back alley of the hotel, a gorgeous old building recently remodeled, its stop short at the loading dock, a flurry of white-coated cooks unloading a catering truck.

"Here?" I asked, looking out the window, my heart sinking.

"Mrs. Brantley said to drop you off here. Use your service provider pass to get in." The driver casually tossed the barbs out, unaware of how they stuck in my thin skin. *Your service provider pass.* My visions of elegantly mingling, a champagne flute in hand, counting down the seconds as the ball dropped, a handsome stranger dipping me backward for a kiss, disappeared. A honk sounded behind us, and the driver looked back at me, his eyebrows raised. "You gonna get out?"

I grabbed Chanel's bag and shouldered it, holding her close to my chest, and opened the door, a second honk blaring, more aggressive than the first. "Jeez," I muttered, shooting an irritated look toward the vehicle, the driver raising his hands from the steering wheel in the universal gesture of asshole drivers everywhere. I elbowed the door shut and gingerly made my way around the back of the SUV, my heels uneven on the potholed street, one step slipping slightly, my recovery step putting me into a snowy spot. My heel sank, all the way to my ankle, and I gasped, half from the cold, half from the damage it would cause to my suede heels. Beside me, the Brantley's driver pulled off, seemingly unconcerned over any plight to my Atwoods or me.

"Need a hand?"

I was frozen in place when the man spoke, my left hand stretched out for balance, my right still clutching Chanel, my legs spread, one on firm ground, the other still submerged in slush. I lifted my eyes from my wet ankle and then, staring into his face, lost all train of thought.

He was beautiful. Chiseled masculinity wrapped in a tux, a small smile turned up the corners of his lips, a phone held to his ear as he extended a hand. Carefully, my body balancing as my free hand moved, I reached out, sliding my palm into his and tried to keep upright as his hand firmly closed over mine, dominance in the grip, the heat of his skin shocking, the moment of our connection one that felt a full minute long. He squeezed my hand, pulling me forward as I freed myself, both heels hitting the sidewalk, then released it, the moment lengthening as his eyes continued the contact, his stare holding me in place before he stepped back. He spoke into the phone. "I'm here now." He moved the phone away from his mouth. "Are you okay?"

"Yes. Thank you." I nodded, and he turned away, his voice low and urgent, my eyes trying to peek at his event nametag, a yellow-edged one, before he stepped away, my gaze following him as he jogged up the back steps and toward the event. The tux fit perfectly on his strong build. Dark, tousled hair, as if he had recently run his hands through it, the scruff of a five o'clock shadow barely visible as he opened the door, the most deadly things hidden. Those hazel eyes. Deliciously playful mouth. Strong features and knowing smile.

Chanel whined, and I glanced down at her, a line of drool dripping off her muzzle, its drop to the ground barely missing her velvet dress. "Right there with you," I whispered, taking a deep breath before heading in, my right foot squishing with every cold and miserable step.

7. Canines, Couture & Conversation

I leaned against a wall in the service hall, at the back of the fashion show, a long line of pets before me. Nicole was about four evening gowns back, holding Chanel and laughing loudly at whatever the woman next to her was saying. They'd already made one sweep of the stage, Chanel's costume change done without incident. I shifted, my feet aching from the tile floor, my arms crossed over my chest, the room drafty compared to the ballroom, where four huge fireplaces burned. I'd gotten only a peek at the room, having to run inside to find Nicole, a glorious five minutes spent on the Persian rugs, gigantic chandeliers overhead, a string orchestra playing discreetly in the background.

My stomach growled, loud and unladylike, and the girl beside me gave me a look, like I had any control over my organs. I should have eaten, but I'd assumed there'd be food at the event. It was a correct assumption, my naïveté being that I would be allowed to *eat* the food. Earlier, I'd tried to reach for a spring roll and was practically tackled by an older woman, who pointed to my yellow nametag like it was a scarlet letter. That was, apparently, how they sort the Important from the Unimportant, via cheap stickers, mine hurriedly stuck on a custom sequined mini from Italy, back when I flew two thousand miles just to shop. My couture didn't matter to her, just my yellow nametag. Yellow, like the sexy stranger's from outside. Turned out he was a service provider just like me, both of us playing visitor in a gilded world. My fantasies of a Cinderella ending with him dried up faster than my wet pump, which continued to squish with every step, even *after* I visited the ladies room and held it under the hand dryer.

The service provider tag shouldn't have made him less attractive, but it had. I needed a man who had his shit together, who could help me figure out what *I* was doing. Whose next work commitment wasn't unclogging a toilet, no matter how well he filled out a rented tux.

Nicole stepped off the runway and stopped, thrusting Chanel in my direction. "Take her home," she said, her eyes looking past me, scanning the rest of the line before eyeing the ballroom door. "And put her to bed. Then you can go home."

So … no midnight celebration for me. I was too cold and tired to care. Plus, the thought of standing in a dingy hallway while the ballroom chanted the countdown was depressing. I nodded, reaching out for Chanel. "Happy New Year," I managed.

"Oh. Yes." She looked surprised, her eyes dropping to my outfit as if realizing, for the first time, that I was at the party. "Happy New Year."

I pulled out the card that I'd been given for the driver, his name in silver font above his number. *Dante Radicci.* I called the number, tapping the card against my leg as I huddled against an unused corner of the hall, waitstaff passing frequently on their way to and from the kitchen, my hunger growing with each pass of their trays.

After speaking to Dante and arranging pick-up, I hung up and glanced out the back door, the loading dock empty, the alley free of cars.

"Thinking of running?"

I turned at the question, seeing the stranger from earlier, his hands in his pockets, strolling toward me. He'd lost the jacket, it draped over one arm, and his bowtie hung loose, the top button of his shirt undone. I glanced away. "Waiting on a driver."

"Leaving before midnight?"

I looked back. "My boss wants her baby taken home." I lifted Chanel with a small smile.

"You look tired." He raised a brow, and I wanted to launch across the hall, despite my tired state, and tackle his sexy ass.

I swallowed. "Just disillusioned. It's a new job. A little different than I thought." Wasn't that the truth? It turned out *actually* working wasn't fun. Another life lesson not learned from my parents.

"You're … what? A pet nanny?" He glanced at Chanel and stepped closer. I tensed. Service provider or not, I wasn't entirely sure I could resist myself if he came any closer. I could use some servicing myself.

"Personal assistant." The reply came out wrong, dripping with self-importance. "What are you doing here?" I nodded to his nametag and prayed that he was at least management.

"Maintenance." He glanced up at the ceiling. "It's an old building. This is its first big event. I'm here in case it falls apart."

I followed his eyes, suddenly nervous. "Is that a possibility?"

He laughed. "No. But there are a lot of little problems that could arise. Small fires." He ran a hand through his hair and I noticed grime across his knuckles.

A *maintenance* worker. Great material for porn. Not so much for Chloe Madison's Life Plan. I leaned down and picked up Chanel's bag, edging closer to the door. I needed to leave before I lost all common sense. "Well." I pushed open the door, a cold breeze sweeping through the opening. "Happy New Year," I chirped in parting, shivering despite myself.

He didn't move, just smiled, as if he could see right through me. "Happy New Year," he said softly.

I shifted Chanel higher in my arms and walked out, into the dark and empty alley.

Better to risk my safety on a dim New York street than my heart to a blue-collar stranger.

January

They say the job makes the person. It needed to work faster. I was a disorganized mess, one that lived on fast food and my best friends' scraps. I beat on the glass of my old world and desperately wanted back in, each day in my new life more discouraging, the varnish of my prior life rubbing off, a new Chloe emerging.

I didn't want her—I only wanted the past.

8. New Year's Resolutions & Regrets

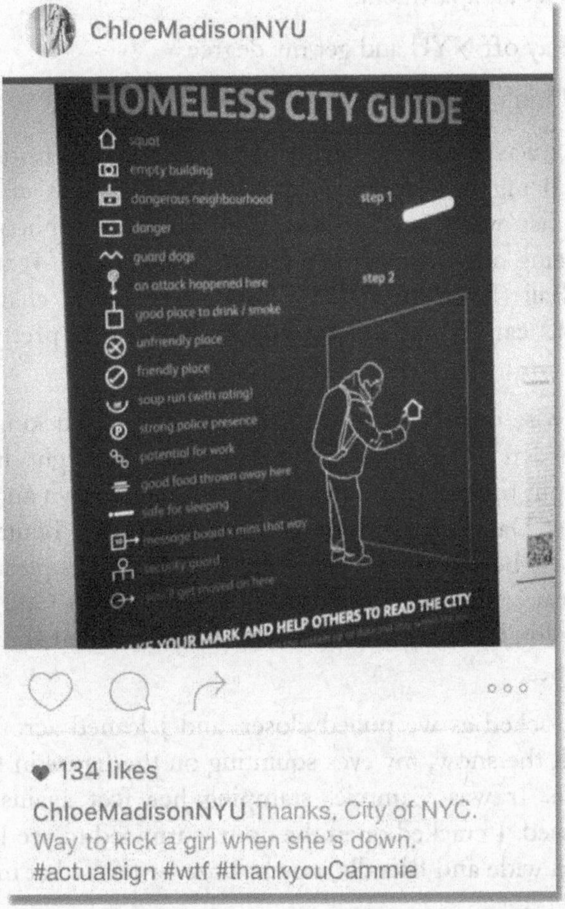

New Year's resolutions suck. When I'd packed up my condo, I'd found mine from last year. The list was on the back of a Nordstrom receipt and was filled with crap like *lose fifteen pounds* and *start meditating* and *pin more*. There were ten things on the list, and I had only successfully completed one: *switch to diet soda*. Whoopee.

Knowing my track record, I still sat down and made a list. I did it in the backseat of the Brantleys' Escalade, Dante taking me home after work, the constant stop and go of the traffic giving the writing a slightly jagged appearance, as if the words were haunted. I kept it short, wanting to actually accomplish the list, each item pretty damn important.

1. Get an apartment.
2. Pay off NYU and get my degree.
3. Don't sleep with Vic.

Granted, it was more of a to-do list than proper resolutions, but whatever. Being new to the grown-up table, I was allowed some slack. My list was also *way* less glamorous than Nicole's, whose included being nominated for an Oscar (Resolution #4) and buying a house in Bali (Resolution #18). But I figured the chances of her getting an Oscar and me not sleeping with Vic were pretty neck-and-neck.

I carefully tore out the page and folded it in half, sticking it into my wallet, the action reverent, as if the location might increase my chances. I put the wallet into my purse, reaching down and pulling on my heels as Dante turned down Cammie's street. Benta lived in a luxury tower, but Cammie loved her brownstone duplex. I wasn't a fan. The heat came out through a steam radiator, for God's sake. The woman couldn't stand germs but bathed in water that shot from 200-year-old pipes.

The SUV rocked as we pulled closer, and I leaned across, trying to see through the snow, my eyes squinting on the figure in front of the brownstone. It was Cammie, stamping her feet against the cold, looking pissed. I cracked open the door, surprised to see Dante jump out, his grin wide and friendly, one he'd never flashed at me.

Hmmm. So the ice king *did* melt. Maybe I just wasn't his brand of heat.

His grin instantly softened Cammie's scowl. I stumbled out, slipping on the icy sidewalk, Dante completely unaware as he shook Cammie's gloved hands, her giggle floating my way. I tried to sneak by and their lovefest came to an end, Cammie's hand reaching out and grabbing my coat. "Can't go up there."

"Why?"

"Something clogged up the plumbing on our floor. The whole place is flooded. I'm waiting for a ride."

"Boyfriend coming to pick you up?" Dante spoke from behind me and I turned at the question, raising my eyebrows.

"No, just a cab." Cammie said, smiling. She glanced at me. "I thought we could go to Benta's."

"Let me drive you."

Wow. Definitely not the Dante I knew. He and Cammie were suddenly in movement, one of his hands on her elbow, helping her across the curb, the other opening her door, apparently no need to consult little Chloe in the decision-making process. I slogged alone through the snow, and managed to climb, unescorted, into the passenger side.

We pulled away, and Cammie beamed at me, any irritation over the plumbing gone. "He's *hot,*" she mouthed, nodding toward the front.

I shrugged as if I hadn't noticed, more than a little irritated at Dante's 180 toward friendliness. Then again, Cammie and I had always appealed to different types—a good thing for a friendship. "Go for it," I mouthed back. I settled into the seat, turning up the heater, and watched her do just that.

9. *My old friend: Tiffany*

I woke up Saturday morning on Benta's loveseat, a spare comforter wrapped around me, a puddle of drool underneath my cheek, to the distinct sounds of a hookup. Not skin-slapping, breath-gasping actual humping, but something solidly in the second-base vicinity.

My spot in the living room gave me a front-row view of the action, happening on Benta's kitchen counter. Cammie's dark bare legs were wrapped around one hell of a jean-covered ass, her pale pink nails digging into the guy's white T-shirt.

"Ahem." My subtle throat clear got me nothing, the frantic kissing—if anything—heating up.

"Cam." I reached for my cell, ready to throw it at her, my eyes instead catching on the time display. And *that was* when my irritation grew tenfold. Not even eight. On a *Saturday* morning. I rolled over on the loveseat, throwing the blanket over my head, not at all interested in meeting her date. I had a pretty good idea of who it was, especially when I heard the smooth scrape of an accent whisper her name. I hid under the covers, eavesdropping despite my best attempt to go back to sleep. At some point among their whispered goodbyes, I fell back asleep and was spared anything more 'til noon, when Cammie and Benta pushed me awake and into clothes, promising sushi and sake.

An hour later, and I would scream if I heard Dante's name one more time. Cammie wouldn't shut up about him. Granted, I might have been a *teensy* bit jealous, my own romp envisioned with the strong and silent Italian.

Plus, to be honest, how awkward would it be if this turned into anything—my co-worker and my best friend? Chances were it wouldn't. In the five years I'd known Cammie, she'd never had a relationship last more than a few months. Her eye … *wandered.* That was the nicest way to say it. Tell her she couldn't touch something, and she'd trample your ass in her haste to dig her fingers in. Benta, on the other hand … well, Benta was weird. I could spend an entire week talking about her crazy love life, one that included some of the freakiest sex on the planet.

After two sake bombs, courtesy of my friends, I forgot any irritation about being woken up early. Cammie was freaking *beaming* at us as she dissected every last moment with Dante, so I couldn't help but be happy for her on that front too. Not that I could really stay mad at the person keeping me from sleeping on the streets.

We left lunch slightly buzzed, stumbling our way into her apartment, no evidence of flooding present, where she wandered to bed. I found cleaning supplies, determined to be the Best Houseguest Ever and clean the kitchen. I had Spotify playing, a Lysol wipe in hand, and was on a stool, emptying out the cabinet above the fridge, when I moved aside Cammie's cereal and felt it. My fingers closed on it without thought, pulling it out, the box instantly recognizable, a powder blue one with a tag that made my stomach curl into a tight fist. I stepped off the stool and wondered why, in the jumble of healthy crap that had been in that cabinet—there was a jewelry box with my name on it.

I didn't have to wonder *too* much. The box was trademark Vic, my name scrawled in his rough handwriting on a crisp white tag. My denied engagement ring had been Harry Winston, but every birthday, Valentine's, and "just-because" present was from Tiffany's.

I sat down on a stool, smoothing the label's white ribbon with a trembling finger. Half of me wanted to rip off its lid in my haste to see the gift. The other half wanted to drive to the closest dumpster and fling the box inside. *Vic had picked this out.* Thought of me. Still wanted to spoil me. For a girl who'd spent Christmas ignored by everyone but my two friends, it hit hard. I gently tugged on the ribbon and lifted the lid, seeing a folded note on top.

When I opened the note, the spicy scent of him floated up from the linen stock.

My love,

I will think of you every Christmas for the rest of my life. I hope, whatever you do this year, you are happy.

Always yours,

Vic

I set it down, my heart seizing, the words painful to read. I picked up the box and looked at the pendant earrings, delicate clusters of diamonds that circled a larger stone. Perfect. Not that I had expected anything less. I closed the box and pushed it back, lowering my head 'til it rested on the counter and allowed myself a moment of tears.

I *missed* him. I loved him as strongly as I did when we were together. Yes, he'd broken my heart. But it had taken every bit of my willpower not to relent when he'd begged for forgiveness, when he'd drunkenly professed his devotion to me from a busy street while I stayed cozy in my old apartment, pretending not to hear. When he'd cried. The man, despite everything else, knew how to get me. Knew how to seduce and how to wrap my heart up so tight that I was scared I'd never rip it free.

I hated him.

I loved him.

I wanted him.

I missed him.

And I really should call and thank him for the gift.

10. Prawns & Porn

ChloeMadisonNYU
119 likes
ChloeMadisonNYU My favorite library ever.
#newyork #beauty #architecture

I didn't call him. Instead, I did the right thing, putting on my big girl pants and writing him a letter. A polite letter in which I thanked him for the gift, but firmly refused it. I stated that we were no longer together, and I didn't feel such gifts were appropriate. I wrapped it and the Tiffany's box together and put them in a bag for his driver to pick up.

My high road was a short one. Less than ten minutes later, I threw the letter in the trash and put the earrings in their proper place: my earlobes. I glanced at my watch, realized I had less than twenty minutes to escape before Cammie got home, and called Benta.

"Want to treat your poor best friend to dinner?"

The girl didn't hesitate, and forty-five minutes later we were sitting at a rooftop bar and ordering drinks.

"Cute earrings," she noted, gesturing with her straw toward my ears.

"Thanks." I waved to the bartender, trying to divert this conversation to appetizers.

"They look like something I saw a few weeks ago. In a box. From Viiiiicc." She stretched his name into three syllables.

Shit. I stopped trying to get the bartender's attention and turned to her. "You *knew*?"

Of course she knew. Cammie couldn't get her eyebrows waxed without a sidekick so Benta had been the first call made when Vic dropped off the gift. They'd decided I was better off not knowing and hid it.

"I *told* her it was too risky keeping them at her house, especially with you staying there." She rolled her eyes, as if to say, *Rookie mistake…*

My irritation mounted. "I can handle Vic. It wasn't up to either of you to keep that from me."

"Oh please!" Benta's cheeks flushed with heat. "Do you *remember* what you were like after that breakup? How you lived on your couch, binging on reality TV and subjecting every poor food delivery guy to your sob story?" It was true. I still couldn't order from my favorite pizza place. "I *know* you. Right now, you're thinking that you should call Vic and thank him for the earrings. Let me tell you, Vic bought that present with the change rattling around in his cupholder. It's not like he *thought* out the gift and is sitting by the phone, anxiously waiting on your call."

I shut my mouth, my witty comeback dampened, the picture she drew of Vic exactly what I had been envisioning.

Benta leaned forward. "Forget Vic. Let me set you up with this guy we've hired. He's *gorgeous*, Chloe, and he's hilarious."

"Yeah?" I looked at her. "Then why aren't you dating him?"

"He's too passive for me. I need a man who'll fight back when I kick."

Too passive. Wow, she knew how to sell 'em. "Pass. I could use some singledom."

"You've been single eight months. It's been long enough."

Food came, saving me from a response, and I pulled out my phone. Checked my email and saw a few from Nicole. Skimmed their contents and murmured support while Benta checked out the bartender's ass.

The last email caused me to look up, catching her stealing a sip of my drink. I snagged it back. "Nicole just emailed me, saying she'll be in Vegas in March."

"For what?"

"The …" I scrolled down the email. "Adult Entertainment Expo. Not sure what that is. Sounds boring."

At Benta's snort—mid-crunch of a shrimp—I jerked my head up, just in time to see her eyes water as she pounded her chest. She waved off my help, grabbing her ice water and holding up a finger as she drank.

When she finally came up for air, her voice wheezed. "The Adult Entertainment Expo? I forgot you were working for the condom supplier of the world."

"Why? What is it?" My phone wouldn't cooperate, a Google search taking as long as Benta to put me out of my misery. I looked at her impatiently.

"It's a *porn* convention. In *Vegas*. Too bad she isn't taking you."

A porn convention? I would have doubted the intel, but Benta would know, her family created an online dating website that makes Tinder look like a kiddie ride. The woman reviewed sex statistics and dating trends over breakfast. She laughed at my look and grabbed my drink, toasting me while finally getting the last of her shrimp—and my daiquiri—down.

A *porn* convention. Working for Nicole got stranger every day.

11. Parenting 101

I rolled the ball across the floor, Chanel scampering after it, her nails clicking across the floor. My phone rang and I pushed to my feet, grabbing it off the desk, the name on the display making my heart jump.

"Mom?" I shut the door and leaned against it.

"Hey darling. We were just calling to check in."

"I've left you a bunch of messages."

"Oh, I know. We've just been busy."

"For two months?" My voice was hard, a tone I had never used with her before.

"Don't be a pill, Chloe. We're dealing with a lot right now."

So was I. I swallowed the response. As tough as my new life might be, it didn't compare to what they must have been dealing with. They were facing jail time, possibly for the rest of their lives.

"Anyway, I've got to run. I called because I'm trying to find the name of that masseuse—the one you used to help with your lower back."

"The masseuse?" Chanel stopped by my feet and looked up at me, her tail wagging.

"Yes. I can't remember her name. Tom said you would know it."

Tom. My father. I pictured him standing there, his eyebrow raised, waiting on the masseuse's name. A name I couldn't remember. "Is he there?"

"He's busy, love. Do you remember the girl's name?"

"No. I'm sorry." I thought of all of the questions I had for her, my knowledge of their new life based mostly on an *American Greed* episode that had aired last week. "Did you get my email about my new job? I'm—"

"I'll have to catch up with you later, sweetie."

"But—" There was a beep, the call ending, and I looked at my cell, our conversation lasting less than two minutes.

Two minutes. Not long enough yet it told me all I needed to know.

They didn't miss me, and certainly weren't stressing over my well-being. How was that possible? Were they *that* confident of my ability to survive? What if Cammie kicked me out? Or I lost my job? What if one of my calls that they had ignored had been from the hospital?

I didn't know anything about having a child. And we may have never been very close. But surely, written somewhere in Parenting 101, they were supposed to give a fuck.

February

Cammie, Benta, and I first bonded over gladiator sandals in NYU's spring orientation. This was back when *everyone* was wearing them and we thought we were *so* above that. I didn't pick them because they were kind and compassionate. I didn't pick them for their fierce loyalty. I picked them because they wore the same things I did, carried the same purse, and had the same lifestyle. They preferred fashion shows to poetry readings, and shopping to working out. They were spoiled, as was I, and we melded together in a blend of entitlement.

I was always the worst in our bunch. The least reliable. The most self-centered. It was the general expectation that I would flake in any time of need.

And I really expected, in the dark parts of my soul, for them to leave me over this. For our friendship to wither away into nothing, our common ground lost. Instead, they rallied—feeding me, housing me, and distracting me in times of struggle.

They had been better friends than I deserved, our friendship turning a corner, becoming deeper through all this. I hoped, one day, I would be able to return the favor. At the very least, to become a better friend.

12. Finding a New Pad

ChloeMadisonNYU
102 likes
ChloeMadisonNYU My personal dominatrix. She keeps me in line.
#BentaBaby

Benta's new boots clipped across scratched wooden floors, her new Givenchy bag slouching on the tiny table before me. I pulled my jealous eyes away and studied my phone, calling the next realtor, my gaze lifting to Benta as she returned. I left a message, taking the coffee from her. "Thanks. We've got one place left."

"Good. These boots are killing me." She sipped her coffee and leaned forward, looking at my notepad. "What's your top choice so far?"

I shrugged. "Probably that last one."

"In *that* neighborhood?" The corner of her mouth lifted in what could only be described as a sneer. I let out a controlled sigh, swallowing a hundred snide thoughts. There were moments, in between my unending gratitude for their help, that I really hated her and Cammie's wealth. Hated even more my jealousy of that wealth.

"Sorry," she mumbled. "But really."

I let out a pitiful groan, leaning back in my seat. "You think *I* want to live there? I'm desperate. And I'm wearing a hole in Cammie's couch."

"I'd offer to let you stay with me, but I value our friendship too much." She smiled sweetly over her cup, and I couldn't help but laugh.

"Thanks." My cell rang, and I scooted back in my seat. "That's the next realtor. Let's go."

It was our last showing of the day, and the one with the most promise, mainly because it was in Manhattan. Anything within walking distance of the Brantleys' was gold to me. Granted… this one was twelve blocks away. A hike, especially for someone with my limited experience with cardio. But that was all secondary because it had *just* hit the market, was in my price range, and Benta was about out of patience. I would have taken Cammie; she could handle low-rent experiences better than Benta, but Benta had a driver *and* carried chocolate on her person, so she won the Who Helps Chloe Pick an Apartment competition, hands-down. Lucky girl.

All we had to do was walk in, and I was in love. First off, it had a closet. TWO, if you counted the coat closet. It was the type of thing I wouldn't have thought twice about in Miami. Or, hell, three months earlier. But standing there in last season's jacket and my working-girl mentality, I swooned a little. Benta reached out and gripped my elbow, so yeah. I think there was some sexy knee buckling.

The only thing was, I had to complete what the broker described as a "rigorous" application process. It was family owned, and they were picky about their tenants, yada yada yada, so I needed their approval. I stopped listening on the second sentence and (politely) snatched the application out of the realtor's hand so fast she blinked.

Later that night, with my feet tucked under me on the couch, I read over the application, attempting to polish off my rough edges before I scanned it over to her. My name, birthday, and address were all easy. Cammie's address was highly respectable, and she had cheerfully volunteered to play pretend landlord, should they make a reference call.

Marital status? None.

Relationship status? My pen hesitated over that one. If I put *Single*, would they worry that strange men would visit at all hours of the night? *Ha. I would never be so lucky.* If I put that I was in a relationship, would they want my imaginary boyfriend's information? Or worry about two of us living in the place? I wrote *Single* in clear, dignified letters, hoping my neat handwriting would win them over.

Occupation? I tapped my pen on the counter and tried to think of the most glamorous description of my job. *Closet Organizer? Pomeranian Companion?* I settled on the boring title of *Administrative Assistant.*

I read over the application a final time and wondered if I would be good enough.

13. The Italian Stallion

Cammie and Dante were having sex. Ridiculously loud sex. I sat on the couch, one thin door away from grunts, screams and a repetitive knock of her bedframe, and tried to watch *Pretty Little Liars* on DVR. Chewed really loudly on popcorn in an attempt to drown out the sounds.

Cammie, apparently, was a shrieker. How I hadn't discovered that in four years of BFF bliss, I didn't know. And Dante was making this breathy, grunty noise, which sounded unappealing when I described it, but was oh-my-god hot. I gave up on *PLL* and lay down, Adele playing through my headphones and *still* not drowning them out.

I rolled over on the couch and added a pillow to the mix.

Another fifteen minutes passed, and I glanced at the wall clock, impressed. Irritated, mind you, but impressed. The bedpost hit the wall, followed by a wail that lasted so long our neighbor pounded on the walls and screamed something along the lines of *shut the hell up*. I smiled despite myself. Closed my eyes and tried to go through tomorrow's work itinerary. My job description had finally graduated from dogsitting, Nicole unleashing enough information to fill three pages in my notebook. This week was her trip to Vegas, strict instructions left to "keep Chanel entertained." Whatever that meant. I listened to Cammie moan and brainstormed dog-friendly activities. Maybe we could hit a dog park. Make homemade dog biscuits? I watched the second hand move on Cammie's clock and ran out of dogsitting ideas.

Vic and I had wanted a dog. We were going to get a Goldendoodle. I thought of the last time I saw him, when he'd used his key and let himself into my old apartment, crawling into my bed in the middle of the night, all apologies and tender touches and kisses. I had rolled over into his arms, and pretended for a few hours, that everything between us was okay. And it had been—in the hours before I tearfully kicked him out—wonderful. I felt a pang of something sharp and fresh and wondered, with Adele crooning in my ear, when the pain would go away. I wondered how much of my pain was heartbreak and how much was hurt over his betrayal.

The song ended, and I realized that Cammie's shrieks had stopped. I pulled the earphones off and waited a beat. The bathroom sink began to run and I let out a sigh of relief, stopping my playlist and unplugging the headphones, setting them on the coffee table.

I closed my eyes and pushed thoughts of Vic aside. My interview for the apartment was in one week. I prayed, for the sake of my innocent ears, that it went perfectly.

14. Pop Quiz

Being late to an interview was never good. I knew that, which is why I walked into the tiny office, stuck on the ground floor of my *fingers crossed* new apartment building, three minutes early. The couple who owned the building, ancient New Yorkers, were already there, stuffed behind a little desk. The woman checked the time, the resulting glare causing me to steal a glance at my own watch. *Still* three minutes early.

"Nice of you to join us," the woman said dryly. "I take it you are…" she peered at a clipboard in her hand, "Chloe Madison?"

"Yes." I stepped fully into the office and extended my hand, the man considering it before reluctantly shaking it. When I offered my hand to the woman, she simply sniffed.

"I have a bit of a cold," she explained. "Please sit."

"We have some questions to ask you," the man grumbled, glancing at me with eyes that probably lifted a ton of poodle skirts at one time.

I perched on the edge of the chair and gave my best smile, my suit a little tight in the thighs. "Certainly." I'd spent the night before reading over every question on the application, prepping for all of the topics they might bring up. I'd carefully rehearsed how to answer any questions about my parents' occupations, why I'd left my other apartment, and how long I'd been at Cammie's.

"Who is the mayor of New York?"

The presses in my brain stopped. In my four years in New York, I had barely picked my head up from my books, or my drink, or Hulu, long enough to notice current politics in this giant city. I swear, the first name that almost spilled from my lips was Giuliani. Thank God I stopped *that* brain fart in time.

I swallowed, sweat dampening the back of my shirt. "I-I … I just graduated from NYU. I'm afraid that my studies have taken up the majority of my time."

My answer passed, no contempt blazing in their eyes. Burying oneself in studies was, apparently, a point in my favor. "What major?" the woman asked.

"Real Estate with a minor in Psychology." I breathed a little easier at a question I knew. I just hoped she wouldn't ask me to produce a diploma.

"You aren't up to date on New York politics? Or any politics at all?" The man wasn't letting this go.

To lie or not to lie, that was the question. I smiled and tried not to fidget. "Politics in general. I just haven't had time to stay properly informed."

"What political party are your parents?"

"Republican." I crossed my fingers and hoped it was the right answer. The man actually *smiled,* and I relaxed a little.

"And what do your parents do?" The woman flipped a page of my application.

Oh God. It was so hot in there. I felt a bead of sweat run down my back. "Investment banking." Be short and sweet, Cammie had coached.

The woman smiled. A miracle. I guess she liked that answer. She glanced at the man, who cleared his throat and leaned forward, resting the tops of his fingers on the desk as if he was playing the piano. "It's very important to us, Ms. Madison, that this building maintains a certain level of decorum. We won't tolerate parties or loud music or a lot of young people coming in and out at late hours."

"I understand. I'm very focused on my career right now. I won't be a problem." I forced a smile and hoped it was convincing. I knew what they were worried about. And that girl, just a few months ago, was me. But ever since losing my money, ever since moving in with Cammie, ever since working for Nicole… I'd gotten pretty boring. I had, fortunately or unfortunately, grown up. Was staying in more than going out. I was what they wanted. And I was desperate for the apartment.

They asked a few more invasive questions. Did I eat meat? What was my opinion on the United States' involvement in the Middle East? Was I involved in any charitable organizations? Did I have a 401(k)? Did I understand that there would be absolutely no pets of any kind allowed in the apartment? The last question—the only appropriate question out of the whole bunch—gave me the first hint that I was passing the ridiculous interview. The deal was sealed five minutes later, when they passed me the keys, along with a three-page list of rules for tenants.

I would move in on the fifteenth. And even though it was my third apartment since moving from Miami, it felt like the first time I'd really be living here. Maybe it was my name on the lease. Or the hours of work behind my deposit. But I knew one thing: it felt good. Scratch that. It felt *great.*

New York City better get used to my face. I was here to stay.

March

I didn't understand why they wouldn't call. At the very least, parents should call on a girl's birthday. She shouldn't spend it huddled in a corner of a crowded bar, pretending to be happy. She should be able to have one real conversation with someone who understood the pain of losing everything. She shouldn't have to smile over cashmere gloves from her best friends when all she really wanted was her cell phone bill to be paid.

15. I Blame it on the Ah-ah-ah-ah-Alcohol

ChloeMadisonNYU
97 likes
ChloeMadisonNYU Giving Uber a run for their money. #vintage #nyc #taxi

The man bent over, a loop in hand, and peered down at the earrings. He nodded, pushing them aside, and reached for my watch, a sixteenth birthday present from my father. I chewed on the edge of my pinky, my nails nude for the first time in years. I'd tried to paint them myself, the result a disaster—dark purple polish that looked like it'd been applied by a child, as much off my nails as on.

"You have a receipt for any of this stuff?" The man peered at me, suspicion in the worn lines of his face, the contents of my jewelry box dotting the velvet surface before him.

"No." I raised an eyebrow, my look daring the man to accuse me of theft. The man was selling Casio watches, for God's sake. He should be tripping over himself for my pieces.

I hadn't brought everything. I'd keep a pair of diamond studs that my parents had given me for my high school graduation. Kept an emerald pendant that had been my grandmother's, along with a handful of other sentimentals. But everything else, sadly, was here. In this dimly lit pawnshop in Midtown, one with a huge sign screaming their inventory of jewelry. An upscale jeweler had been my first stop. But they only sold on consignment, wanting a hefty sixty percent cut, and I had needed cash now. So there I was, in my first visit to a pawnshop, and hopefully, my last.

"I'll give you four thousand." The man rested his hands on the glass display case, leaning over my things.

"What?" I stared down at my pieces, several of them worth that alone. "That's ridiculous." Panic welled in my chest and I swallowed hard, vowing not to lose my cool. I pointed to Vic's earrings. "Those earrings were easily ten grand, and I just got them last month."

"This is a pawn shop." He looked at me as if I were mental. "This ain't Tiffany's. I got to make a profit, and price things low enough to sell." He lifted up my watch, a diamond-studded Tag. "Not many of my clients are looking for pieces like this."

Glancing at his other inventory, I believed the man. I held out my hand, asking for the watch, and he handed it back. I studied the face of it, thinking of the day I received it, then glanced back up at him. "Five thousand," I said, sliding the watch on my wrist and fastening it. "Without the watch. That's more than fair."

"Forty-five hundred. Cash."

"Okay." I nodded without looking at him, thinking of the apartment I so desperately wanted. I didn't have to sell these to make the deposit, but doing so would mean the difference between bare bones living and some security.

With a price agreed upon, the rest was quick. He inventoried my items, wrote out a receipt, and counted out a stack of hundreds. I pulled my wallet out and passed over my license, then returned it to my jacket pocket. Watching him count out the bills, my chest loosened. He put it all neatly in an envelope, one too thick to fit in my other jacket pocket. I stuffed it in my purse, carefully zipped it shut, and was out the front door, steps quick and happy, feeling rich for the first time in months.

The wind howled through the early night and I stopped in the middle of the crowded sidewalk, ready to splurge, pulling out my phone to find an Uber.

The shove was brutal, square in the middle of my back, my phone flying from my hand as I fell forward, my knee hitting the sidewalk hard, a gasp of pain all I could manage as my palms scraped the concrete. My bag, an Alexander McQueen, was jerked away, wrenching my shoulder in the process, my shout of protest taken by the wind.

The asshole wore a brown jacket and had dark hair. That was the only thing I saw as I hobbled to my feet, my knee screaming in pain, the bright green edge of my purse disappearing as he ran through the crowd, then rounded a corner and was gone.

I yelled, I pointed, and was ignored, the crowd moving around me, one girl meeting my eyes with a regretful frown as she stepped past. I stared after him, thinking of my money, all of that cash, *gone*. Just like that. One more New York mugging, like the hundreds that happened every day. It wasn't worth a call to the police; I hadn't even gotten a glimpse at the mugger. Stupid me, skipping out of the pawnshop with a giant smile on my face. I should have had Dante drive me. I should have worn sweat pants and a fanny pack. I should have just sold the stuff on eBay like Cammie had suggested.

"Is this yours?"

I looked over, to the short man, a stranger, who held out my phone, his eyes worried as he gave me a onceover. I took it from him, smiling as tears pricked my eyes. "Thanks," I whispered.

"Are you okay?"

I nodded. "I'm fine." I stepped away from him, limping slightly, and looked down to see the knee of my jeans ripped. Waving away his concern, I headed for the warmth: just two doors down, a neon Bud Light sign called my name.

I never used to drink beer. I preferred wine or champagne, my fancy mouth above something so barbaric as a two-dollar beer. Now, in a booth stuck along the back wall of a burger joint, a bucket of peanuts before me, I tipped back an ice cold Pabst Blue Ribbon. They were the special, I was told by an enthusiastic redhead—a bucket of six for seven dollars. I felt my pocket, reassured by the feel of my wallet, and ordered the bucket, resting my foot on the opposite bench and rubbing my knee while I contemplated the depressing turn my life had taken.

I could have called Benta or Cammie. Gotten a drinking partner or, at least, a safe ride home. But there was something satisfying about a pity party for one. Something entirely blissful in finishing one, then two beers, while feeling sorry for myself. I understood my problems. They didn't. They had no idea what any of this was like. And it wasn't from not asking me. But they didn't know the questions to ask. We'd never talked about money before, so they didn't think to ask if I was okay. They bought my food and offered loans and moved on with their lives. They didn't ask if it hurt that my parents didn't call me. They didn't ask if I was lonely.

The stress over money.

The worry over my parents.

How much I missed them.

How I felt so lonely.

The fight to keep positive when everything seemed to be falling apart.

They. Didn't. Understand.

I opened a third bottle. The taste really wasn't that bad. With the salty peanuts, it was almost good.

He always smelled good. I leaned against his shirt and inhaled the familiar scent, an expensive one that was custom mixed for him. My feet were dragging along the floor. I frowned, confused, and lifted one, catching it on something and Vic grunted. "Stop kicking me."

I giggled. "I'm not kicking you." The wind hit my face and I burrowed into him, my feet off the floor, someone carrying my legs and I saw a familiar face open the door—Jake, Vic's driver. Vic ducked into the car and I was helped inside, my body falling back into the hard warmth of his chest.

Words spoken, a blur of them between people, *so* many people, and Vic shook me gently. "Chloe. Chloe. Where's your purse?"

Purse? Through the blur, I remembered my money. *Losing it all.* I shook my head. "Don't have it." I wondered how he was there. How many beers I had had from that bucket. Had I called him? I must have. I reached for my jacket pocket, feeling the hard outline of my phone.

The door shut, the cold air gone, and I gripped at the front of his shirt, pulling myself tighter to him, his arms wrapping around me. "What happened?" he asked, looking down at me, our eyes meeting.

"Nothing," I whispered, closing my eyes. I might have been drunk, but I knew one thing—if I told Vic about the money, he'd give it to me. I'd already sold the man's earrings. I didn't need another IOU hanging out there.

"Did someone hurt you?" His voice was louder and I winced, my head shaking.

"No. I fell. On the street."

He pressed a soft kiss on my forehead, his eyes searching mine. "Come home with me tonight."

The seat beneath me was heated, the Rolls silent and smooth as we moved through the city. In his arms, in that spot, I could have stayed forever. I shook my head. "I can't."

I expected him to fight me on it. To take me to his home, damn any of my opinions to the contrary. But he didn't. For once in our relationship, he listened to me. Maybe it was because he had another girl waiting on him, a date or fuck interrupted. Maybe he felt sorry for me in my pitiful state. Whatever the reason, he and Jake carried me up to Cammie's, her yanking open the door, the worry on her face clearing as she gathered me in her arms. She lectured me for not answering my phone, drowned me in bottled water, and then put me to bed, her touch as comforting as my mom's had once been.

I shouldn't have called Vic. I shouldn't have been that weak. But in that moment of vulnerability, I'd needed to be taken care of. And Vic … he'd always done that for me. He did it better than anyone.

16. Well. This is Awkward.

Chanel must be constipated. That was the only thing I could figure, because she'd been trying to poop for three blocks now. The major issue was that I thought her first squat was *the* poop of the walk, and I'd bagged and trashed that niblet of poo, so now, anything that was squeezed out, I had nothing to pick it up with. Which left me standing there, as she went through the poop squat, looking like a Fifth Avenue asshole.

We finally made it back inside the house, my knee aching, a constant reminder of last week's mugging. I still couldn't believe I'd been mugged. Four years in the city and it chose the worst possible moment to occur. And since that night, nothing from Vic. I didn't know whether I was glad he wasn't pushing the mistake of my weak moment, or if I was hurt that his *I'll love you forever* had such little weight. I undid Chanel's collar, her butt hitting the thick carpet as soon as she reached it, dragging herself by her front paws, a long smear of brown leaving a crooked trail behind her. I groaned, setting her leash on the foyer table, and about jumped out of my boots when there was a deep chuckle from behind me.

"Sorry." Clarke's hands came up in surrender, and I held a hand to my chest, embarrassed.

"I thought you were in Vegas," I said.

He grimaced, his head shaking a little. "No. When at all possible, I try to avoid the condom business."

I had to smile at that. I'd been surprised that Nicole, as high-handed as she was about everything, had gone.

"Nicki loves it," he followed up, as if in answer to my thoughts. "She's a god there. They do a better job of kissing her ass than I do."

"Yeah?" I said faintly, not wild about the thought of sharing the space with him for three days. I'd had big plans for that stretch of time, my Netflix queue already packed and ready for watching. I'd envisioned locking my office door and having a movie marathon with Chanel, broken up with naps and runs downstairs to use the cappuccino machine.

"Don't worry about that," Clarke nodded to the carpet stain. "One of the girls will get it."

"Okay." He rested his hands on his hips and I noticed his hands. Long fingers. Thick thumbs. I'd read, on *Cosmo* somewhere, about thumbs. Thumbs and their correlation to *other* body parts.

I picked up Chanel, needing to escape before my thoughts about Nicole's husband turned completely inappropriate. "I think Chanel is constipated," I blurted out, and any imagined sexual tension dried up with the words.

"Oh." He didn't seem worried. "Look in her medicine cabinet. There's some medicine there. Nicole gives it to her when she's stopped up."

"Great." There was an awkward moment of silence between us, then he stepped back.

"Well," he said. "I'll be in my office if you need me."

I nodded, watching him leave, one hand fishing in his pocket for his phone. I looked down, into Chanel's face, and wondered where in the world a Pomeranian's medicine cabinet would be.

17. My Super-Sexy Super

ChloeMadisonNYU
155 likes
ChloeMadisonNYU 60% unpacked, 100% happy. #home

I was on my bed. *Mine*, pulled out of storage, and deposited in my new apartment. Freshly washed Serena & Lily sheets underneath me, Tegan and Sara playing on my iPhone, a candle lit. There were cardboard boxes everywhere, and I couldn't find my hair dryer if my life depended on it, but I had privacy and a real bed and *no* chance of listening to Cammie's orgasms, and that was all that really mattered.

The girls and Dante helped me move, the four of us squeezing into a U-Haul and making the trek up to the Bronx to my storage unit. I paid the past due balance, rolled up the door, and rediscovered all of my stuff. The Louboutin sandals I was wearing the night I first met Benta. The leather loveseat Vic and I got to third base on for the first time. It was strange being surrounded by my old things. I felt out of place in them. I wasn't sure if it was because I no longer needed them to feel complete … or if it was being surrounded by pieces of a life I'd most likely never have again.

The sun came through the window, the room warming and I reached for my phone, checking the time. I groaned when I saw it, sitting up in bed and putting on my heels. I downed vitamins and snagged a banana from the counter, pausing when a knock sounded on the door. Grabbing my purse and keys, I flipped the light switch on the wall and yanked open the door.

I was late to work, a piece of banana in my cheek, unprepared to meet perfection. But there he stood, one hand on my doorframe, his head lifting when I opened the door. Pure beauty, dripping with masculinity. Real dirt on the work boots that shifted on the carpet, real wear on the jeans that hugged his thighs and hips, tan skin and biceps that bulged when he pushed off the doorframe and put his hands on his hips. I stood in place, my jaw hanging, and stared.

"Miss Madison?" His voice was gruff and sexual, the drawl you wanted to hear right before he bit your earlobe, the rasp that, should he moan your name, would combust your panties.

I swallowed. "Yes?"

He stuck out a hand, and my eyes dropped. Strong fingers. Calluses. I couldn't think of the last time I shook a callused hand. "I'm Carter. I'm the building's super. You've got a leaky shower head?"

I reached out and slid my hand into his. Swallowing the bite of banana, I managed speech. "I know you. The… umm…" I wracked my brain for the name of the hotel.

"New Year's Eve Party," he supplied, smiling, and I couldn't take my eyes off his mouth, his lips with just a tint of pink. Our hands were still held, his palm hot and smooth despite the calluses.

I blinked, pulling my hand back. "Yes." My eyes drifted over him, this look so different from his tux, hotter in a completely different way. "You work here too?"

"Yep." He dipped to pick up a toolbox and I remembered the reason he was there.

I stepped back and held the door open. "The bathroom's the second door—"

"I know where it is."

Of course he did. He walked through the door, his broad shoulders barely fitting, and I watched him pass by the kitchen, toward the bathroom. "Do you need me to wait?" I called out, glancing at my watch.

"Not unless you want to," he called back. "I got a key, so I can lock up when I'm done."

Not unless you want to. Oh, I wanted to. I wanted to do a hundred different things with that man, the least of which was watch him use his hands on my showerhead. But work beckoned.

"I'm gonna head out then," I called out. "Nice to see you again." *The understatement of the month.*

"You too."

I hesitated another moment, then I pulled the door shut behind me.

And I'd thought this apartment was perfect before. I stepped on the elevator and pressed the button, leaning back against the wall and picturing his face. Blue-collar had never been my thing, too many millionaires in this city to bother with anything else. Then again, my tastes seemed to be changing. I might have to dip my toe into that pool once or twice. Just to taste that poison. Just to have it on my skin.

18. Hunger Fried My Brain

I could feel him in the house. When Clarke moved from his study to the living room, a phone to his ear, his laptop settling on the coffee table, his build hunched forward, I watched. When he stepped out on the balcony, his hand running through his hair, the door left open, the breeze brought in his scent.

My new favorite distraction: trying to understand the man. Three months of working for Nicole had proved that she was cray cray and *not* in a good way. She must be amazing in bed. Or he needed her condom money. Or maybe Raging Bitch was his flavor of aphrodisiac.

I sat at the dining room table and stared at Nicole's list, one she had emailed that morning, including things like *schedule wax* and *find replacement knob for our dresser in bedroom.* I was so glad I gave the extra effort and made NYU's dean's list. So glad I learned Mandarin. When it came time to screw in that replacement knob I'd be sure to curse my situation using it.

"You busy?" Clarke's question startled me, my jump causing my pen to fly across the table, a long ink mark left on one of Nicole's linen napkins. I grimaced.

"Sorry." He wiped his hands on a paper towel, balling it in his fist.

"It's fine. I'm sorry." I reached out, across the table, half up in my seat, and grabbed the pen. I felt air on my back, my sweater rising too high and I flushed, sitting back in my seat. "No. I'm not busy." Or should I be busy? My mind warred over the correct answer, seeing as I was on the clock.

"I'm getting hungry. There's a Cuban place down a few blocks…"

I nodded. "La Nina's. I know it." Vic and I had eaten there, the restaurant small, lighting low, atmosphere romantic. My cheeks flushed at the invitation, then my brain kicked into overdrive. Dinner with Nicole's husband? Probably a bad idea.

"Great. Got something to write with? I'll tell you what I want." He eyed the pen in my hand and seemed to be waiting for something.

Oh. He wanted me to pick him up food. Duh. Of course he did. I was suddenly mortified, hoping that my idiotic thought process hadn't shown, my hands fumbling at my notepad, pulling out a fresh page of paper, my mouth curving into a professional smile as I looked up at him. Thank God I hadn't told him off, given him a lecture on boundaries.

He looked at me oddly. I swallowed hard and tried to speak casually, my voice coming out a little raspy. "What would you like?"

"Arroz con pollo. Extra plantains. And some pineapple soda." He reached in his pocket and brought out a wad of cash, pulling some twenties and holding them out. "And whatever you'd like."

"Oh, I have a date," I babbled. "We're going to eat. Dinner, I mean. We have reservations." My mouth wouldn't stop moving, my brain feeding it information too slowly, my panicked attempt to shut up only causing more words. "We're very happy."

Yes. Me and my imaginary boyfriend are positively ecstatic.

His eyebrows half-hitched, and his odd look deepened. "That's great to hear, Chloe." He said the words slowly, the way you might speak to a small child. I didn't blame him. I sounded ridiculous. My attempt to cover up my confusion at his non-invitation had only pushed me further into the pathetic pool, my risk of drowning imminent. And turning down free food? I immediately regretted every part of the slip.

I took the cash and stood, my hand grabbing at his order, desperate to get away.

Funny that after four months of working, I still hadn't processed my role as The Help. I still saw myself on some sort of equal platitude with Clarke, where my mind would jump to a dinner invite rather than an order of food. I was out the door and four blocks down the street, wheezing against a streetlamp, before I realized I should have had Dante drive me.

April

I was so focused on my own life, my own issues, that I forgot everything else. I wasn't thinking that Nicole Brantley, with her gilded world of perfection, would have her own struggles and a pile of secrets. And I certainly wasn't planning on those secrets changing everything for me.

19. The Calm Before the Storm

ChloeMadisonNYU
204 likes
ChloeMadisonNYU This is Lucy. I sneak her apples and she listens to my problems. #ilovethiscity #lucyisamazing #centralparkfriends

The city was a seductress. It dragged you through slushy, freezing hell, and then gave you a brief window of sunshine and made you fall in love with it all over again. It was one of those days, rays of sun warming the huge windows of the Brantley home, my eyes continually pulled back, moment after moment, bits of the outside beckoning. Finally, after organizing Nicole's scarf drawer and syncing her Spotify playlist with her iTunes account, I decided to take Chanel on a walk. We didn't go on a lot of walks. She had a pee pad on an upstairs balcony and did her miniscule bathroom breaks out there. Her exercise was taken care of by running around five stories and six thousand square feet.

I dressed her in a leopard print jacket, one with a fur-lined hood and put her booties on. The booties she hated, but Nicole had a tantrum if she stepped on the "dirty street" without foot protection, so I made Chanel suffer the indignity, whispering apologies to her the entire time. Last week, I had wasted a good fifteen minutes counting her shoes. The dog has seventy-three pairs. Too bad I can't wear her size.

Chanel didn't really want to go out. She lay down when I put on her harness, the diamond-studded piece making her transition to hooker dog complete. I laughed and pulled on the leash, causing her bejeweled body to slide along the wood floor. She ignored my tough voice, only jumping to her feet when I reached for the treats.

I glanced at my watch as I stepped off the last step, the house behind me too quiet. When Nicole was home, you heard it. Her television, her phone, her music, her voice. She lived in a constant state of interaction, fed on it. I checked the time, wondering where she'd gone and, more importantly, when she'd be back. The prior week, I'd been out getting creamer for her coffee, and walked into a full-blown hissy fit, her fury at my absence *way* overdone. This stroll outside was the first time I'd left the house since, my fear of her too great to risk. But on a rare sunny day in winter, I felt bold, certain that she'd want Chanel taken out.

I stepped down the sidewalk, Chanel skittering ahead, her enthusiasm mounting now that she was out in the fresh air. "Easy," I said, holding her leash tightly. On the street, a black hearse passed, the rumble of its engine catching her attention for a brief moment.

Looking back, there were so many signs, so many omens. I should have known that something bad was coming.

20. Stepping in Shit

One block over and back from the Brantleys, I dodged a puddle and tugged at Chanel's leash. She was distracted by a discarded Starbucks cup, growling fiercely at it when I glanced down the street and came to a stop.

There was a stranger, leaning against a streetlight. Not an odd sight in this city, but it was the woman in his arms that held me in place. Nicole. He said something to her and his voice floated innocently through the air, like he had no worries, certainly not little ol' me fifteen feet away. I was close enough to see Nicole's breath frost in the air as she leaned in and smiled up at him. Close enough that, when his hand reached down and palmed her ass, I could see the crease in her leather pants. Close enough that I noticed her grip on the top of his jeans, the top of her fingers slipping in between material and skin. Close enough that I worried, when I gagged a little in my mouth, that they heard me.

I'd known Nicole wasn't perfect. The sweet bubble of kindness that I met the first day had popped. I'd seen her tempers. Her high maintenance ways. The insecurity that she tried desperately to hide. The woman had *everything* but wanted more. I knew that, but still … she was MARRIED. Not that I knew anything about being a wife, but monogamy seemed to be the number one rule of the union. And yet his mouth was coming down on hers, her hand digging into his hair. It wasn't a first kiss; it was natural, like they'd done it a hundred times before. I wanted to pluck off one of Chanel's booties and throw it at her, followed by that dirty Starbucks cup. She was married to *Clarke*, the beautiful man who worked nonstop and *still* got up an extra hour early to cook her breakfast. The man who massaged her shoulders when she bitched, brought her flowers, opened her car door, and looked gorgeous doing it all. She had all *that*—yet was in this stranger's arms.

The guy wasn't even drool-worthy. He wore a plaid cardigan (yuck) and had a beard, one of those flimsy ones that signified a late attempt to jump on the trend. He looked mid-thirties, with a thin build, his legs spread in black jeans, the hint of a light gray T-shirt peeking out from beneath the cardigan when he shifted toward me. He glanced in my direction, and I got a good look at his face. It wasn't ugly. It wasn't beautiful. It was normal. *Nothing* when you compared it to Clarke.

Our gazes met and I knew the judgment must have shown on my face. I knew I should turn away but didn't. I'd forgotten how to function. In the world of fight or flight, I froze in place and got eaten.

Chanel stopped her interrogation of the empty Starbucks cup, the leash going slack, her leopard print body trotting forward. I pulled on the leash, tried to turn but she saw Nicole and lunged forward, yipping loudly.

Oh shit. I pulled harder, my eyes flitting to Nicole and watched, in almost slow motion, as her head snapped my way. She raised a hand to her mouth, stepping back from the man. I scooped up Chanel's rigid body, fighting her strain toward the pair, her yaps loud and harsh in the quiet cold. Shushing her, I turned away and blocked her view with my body, my flats quick on the street. I was running by the time I climbed the steps to their house, out of breath, Chanel's body wiggling to be free, our fall through the front doors done with a fair amount of drama, despite my best attempt to be quiet. Nancy, one of the maids, rushed in, her hurry ceasing when she saw it was just me.

"You're tracking snow in. Get those stupid shoes off the dog before she ruins the floors." She snapped out the words, oblivious to my situation.

I wanted to tell her that I also thought the doggie shoes were stupid. I wanted to tell her that I just saw Nicole kissing a stranger and—Chanel darted out of my hands, her booties tip-tapping across the floor, leaving dots of water. I scrambled to my feet, going after her, apologizing to Nancy. She shouted at me to remove my shoes and I chucked them off, the action too enthusiastic, one flying up and hitting a large crystal dancer that sat on the entrance table, everyone but Chanel freezing as we watched it fall to the floor.

At any other time, it would have been a beautiful sound, a thousand tiny splinters of glass on marble. We stared at the damage, Nancy letting out a sharp gasp.

"Fuck," I whispered. Between catching Nicole in the act and destroying this, I was most likely staring at unemployment in that pile of crystal.

What could I have done? What could I have said? I still didn't know what the right action was to take on that Manhattan side street.

Should I have confronted her? Pointed a judgmental finger at Nicole and asked what in the hell she was doing?

Should I have looked away, pretended I didn't see anything?

Waved cheerily as if cheating was an everyday activity?

I stared at the broken crystal and drew a complete blank.

21. What Had Happened Was...

"You broke this?" Clarke looked up at me, a question on his face.

"Yes. It was an accident. I was trying to catch Chanel … my shoe…" My voice faltered; my explanation weak as hell.

He looked down at the dustpan, the crystal remains inside, Nancy keeping the evidence and pointing it out the *minute* he'd walked in the door, as if I had planned to keep it a secret. He straightened and picked up his drink, taking a hefty swallow before glancing at his watch. "Where's Nicki?"

"I … ahh … I don't know." My voice shook, no alibi created for Nicole, his eyebrows raised when he looked at me. "She left a few hours ago," I managed.

"She's gonna loose her shit over this, excuse my French." He tipped back the heavy tumbler again, small cubes of ice falling against his mouth, and I watched the move of his throat when he swallowed the last of it.

"I'm sorry." The words were rusty, the feeling of panic foreign, my hat not used to being in hand. I swallowed the last bit of my pride. "I really need this job, Mr. Brantley. Please don't fire me."

He raised a brow and said nothing. The silence pushed at my composure and I struggled to maintain it. "I can't afford to replace it but I'll work extra hours until it's paid for." A commitment that'd take five years to honor. I held my breath, hoping he wouldn't accept it.

He shook his head. "No. Just…" he let out an aggravated huff. "Don't break anything else. Take your shoes off before you come in if you have to. I'll deal with Nicole … tell her I did it."

An honorable woman would have stood firm and pushed for a payback schedule. I took the low road, gushing my thanks, his hand lifting to stop my babble. "Go and find Nancy. I want to talk to her, make sure our stories are on the same page. Just don't talk to Nicki about it." *No danger of that.* I did some sort of grateful bow thing and then fled the room, in search of Nancy, my heart still beating hard in my chest.

I didn't deserve for him to cover for me but couldn't afford anything else. The man saved my ass *and* kissed Nicole's, yet he was the one getting screwed over. How could she cheat on him? Why?

I wanted to walk back in his office and tell him what I'd seen. Let him handle it however he saw fit. It was what I would have wanted someone to do for me.

But then I thought of my new apartment—of the next rent payment, due in just two weeks. If I lost my job right now, I wouldn't be able to pay it. And I couldn't imagine Nicole keeping me on if I blabbed about her affair.

I continued upstairs and went inside Chanel's room where I hid, like the chicken I was, until it was time for me to go home.

22. Have Morals, Will Sell

I stood in the doorway of the west guest room in shock. The bedroom furniture gone, there was a couch, doggie bed, and basket of toys to the left. To the right, against the window, a large desk, fresh roses, and a new MacBook. It was an office.

"This is for me?" I asked, confused. I had walked into the Brantley house a bundle of nerves over Nicole's cheating and the broken crystal. I'd been terrified to see Nicole and worried over how she'd act. I certainly didn't expect an enthusiastic welcome, her arm looping in mine and tugging me up the stairs. I half expected, when she dragged me toward the bedroom, that it would hold shackles and an ultimatum. Not this.

"Well." Nicole clasped her hands together and turned slightly, surveying the room. "You certainly deserve a work space." Then she beamed at me, this horrible fake smile with stretched cheeks, thin lips, and gleaming teeth. For a smile, it held no friendship, no kindness, no goodwill.

I said nothing, walking over to the desk, my hand drifting over the items.

"Plus," she continued, "Filming will start soon on that new movie … the uh … you know…"

"*Boston Love Letters.*"

"Yes!" She snapped her fingers. I thought of her kiss with the stranger and looked away, focusing on the stapler. It was hot pink with sparkles, appropriate for a preteen girl. *How could she forget the name of the movie?* She wasn't Angelina Jolie, juggling six projects at a time. It was the only thing on her plate. Then again, I couldn't remember my middle name when I'd stared at the two of them. Maybe being in his presence killed brain cells.

"Also…" she started slowly, "I'll need you more. On set, you know. The hours are long. Sometimes ten-hour days and I'll need you to run errands, get me food, that sort of thing."

I nodded and braced myself for whatever bullshit was about to come.

"Would thirteen hundred dollars work?"

I looked up from the stapler. "What?"

"A raise. Thirteen hundred a week. Would that work?"

She called it a raise, but I understood what it was. A bribe. I'd keep her secret and get paid. And she—she'd keep her affair.

The path to take was clear; I should gather up my dignity and leave. Ride the subway home and feel all self-righteous while doing it. Only … I *needed* this job. Needed the raise. An extra twelve hundred bucks a month? I'd be able to pay my new rent without holding my breath that the check cleared. I could take taxis and order more than soup when I went out with my friends. I could breathe a little more and stress a little less.

I could sell my morals.

Two months ago, I would have grabbed that raise with a squeal of pleasure and hit Nordstrom on my way home. Now, I hesitated. I did.

Her eyes were arrogant; they watched me as if she already knew my answer, her confidence in my ability to be bought depressing. I wanted to refuse, to hold my head up and march right out of there. Instead, I nodded. "Okay."

23. Please. Yell at Me More.

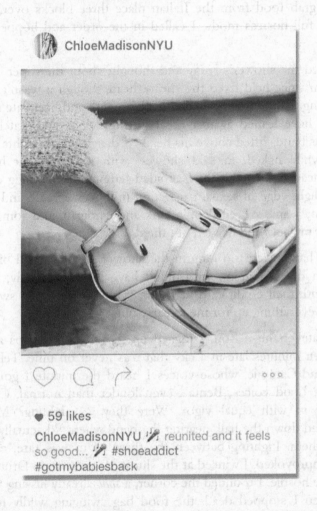

ChloeMadisonNYU 🎤 reunited and it feels so good... 🎤 #shoeaddict #gotmybabiesback

It took a full month, but I finally unpacked the last of my boxes. Finally, no more digging through suitcases and boxes looking for a flat iron. No more wearing the same heels three days in a row because all the other options were "in a box somewhere."

I plopped down on my couch, picking up my phone. A celebration felt due, and since neither of my friends had surprised me with a housewarming party, I'd throw my own.

Twenty minutes later, after listening to Benta bitch about her boss, and Cammie swear on Jesus that she missed my face, we had a plan in motion. A plan that gave me about an hour to change out of my sweats, grab food from the Italian place three blocks over, and be back in full hostess mode. I called in the order and hopped in the shower.

I adjusted the shower's spray and thought about the super. I hadn't seen him since he'd fixed the showerhead, though it wasn't for lack of looking. I should have taken Nicole's wrath and been late that day. I could have leaned against the bathroom door and watched him work, his hands lifted above his head … dangerous thoughts to think about while naked, in said shower, with a convenient handheld showerhead *right* there. But I avoided temptation, jumping out with only a slight edge of sexual frustration (it'd been a year!) and yanking on skinny jeans, a Free People tank and cardigan, and some flats. I grabbed my keys and headed out the door.

I might have taken too long in the shower. Or we could blame my delay on the restaurant, who didn't have my order ready, *then* had issues with their credit card machine, *then* took their dear sweet time packing everything up for me to carry out.

But whatever the reason, I jogged up the building's steps at 10:17, seventeen minutes late in a city that was never on time. Tell that to Benta and Cammie, whose voices I heard the minute I got off the elevator. Loud voices, Benta's even louder than normal, Cammie's chiming in with equal vigor. Were they … fighting? My steps quickened down the hall, nearing the bend where I'd actually be able to see them. Fighting between the three of us was rare, especially when unprovoked. I winced at the slur in Benta's voice. Drunk Benta could be hostile. I rounded the corner, a *shhh* already hissing from my lips when I stopped dead, the food bag swinging wildly from the abrupt stop, my eyes fixed on the two girls who were camped out in my hall, legs sprawled on the hardwood, a wine bottle on the floor between them, a second one open between Cammie's thighs, their hands aggressively waving, scowling up at the man who stood over them.

Standing between my two best friends, his hands on his hips, a T-shirt stretched tight across his chest, worn jeans snug on his hips, was the super. Who, if you missed my earlier swoonfest, was *gorgeous*. But right then, in the middle of my hall, with both girls screaming, he looked pissed. And pissed was an even hotter look on his face. If I were his girlfriend, I'd make it my mission in life to piss him off every day of the week.

Apparently, the best way to do that was to get drunk in the hallway of his building.

"Hey." I stepped closer and was completely ignored, no one's head turning my way. "Hey!" I whisper-yelled the word, setting the food down and righting the tipped bottle. Then I stepped into the fight, waving my hands in the air. "Shut up!" I hissed.

That worked. The girls stopped, Cammie blinking up at me as if wondering who I was and what I was doing there. I looked at her warily and wondered how much of the bottle between her legs she'd had.

"You're late," accused Benta, pushing off the wall and dragging to her feet. "And this asshole is trying to kick us out." She glared at him. "You know my dad could buy this whole building."

"I'm impressed," he scoffed, and I wanted to smack her myself.

"I'm sorry, the restaurant was backed up." I dug in my pocket and pulled out my keys.

"I don't need drunk girls waking everyone up. I thought this was explained to you during the interview process."

"Waking everyone up?" Cammie yelled and I winced, her voice five decibels higher than necessary. "It's ten o'clock."

"Shut up, Cammie," I chided. "Please, both of you, go inside." I held out my keys and Benta snatched them. I listened to her struggle with the door and stepped around her, approaching the guy, who glared in my direction.

And just let me say *again*, this guy needed to walk around pissed 24/7. I could scoop sex appeal off his cheekbones and bottle it in lube and be happy for the rest of my life. "I'm sorry," I whispered. "I thought I'd be back before they got here." Behind me, I heard them get the door open, their move inside, and the angry slam of it shut.

His jaw clenched. "Are you guys going out or…" His eyes dropped to the bag of food.

"Staying in," I said regretfully. "But we'll be quiet, I promise. Seriously."

"I don't think the brunette has it in her to be quiet."

He was absolutely correct; Benta would probably scream lullabies to her future babies, but I wasn't about to admit that. I tried a smile. Some inspirational poster somewhere once said that a smile could cross all barriers.

The poster was wrong. He didn't smile back. He scowled. I almost dropped my panties in response.

"You are the only one-bedroom on this floor. Everyone here pays a lot of money for this space and expects a certain level of peace. Please don't make me evict you."

At the word *evict*, any hope I had for an impromptu hallway sex session dried up. I couldn't get evicted, couldn't land back on Cammie's couch, couldn't pack up all of my things and send them back to storage. I wouldn't.

I swallowed. "You're not going to have to." I stepped closer, clasping my hands together. "I swear." From inside the apartment, Benta yelled my name, stretching the short word into about five syllables. I winced and tilted my head toward the closed door.

"Yeah," he interrupted. "You should get to that." He stepped back, and I missed the minty smell of his soap. Then he turned and walked away. And I swear I only stared at his ass for the first five steps.

I squared my shoulders, grabbed the bag of food, and turned the handle, prepared to give Benta and Cammie the reprimand of their lives.

24. Mo Money, Mo Problems

Day ten of being a sellout. Being the girl who took a pay raise instead of the high road. The girl who felt guilty when she wasn't throwing dollar bills in the air, making it rain.

Three hundred extra dollars a week. I felt rich. Rich … and completely sleazy. It didn't help that the man Nicole was cheating on, the one I was keeping in the dark by taking her bribe, had covered my ass on the broken crystal.

I almost wished he hadn't done it, his kind act making it even harder for me to swallow Nicole's affair. Did knowing about it and not saying anything to him make me as guilty as her? I groaned, plopping my head on the desk, and winced when the tip of the holepuncher caught me in the temple.

Next to me, upright against the desk were three Vuitton trunks. I'd spent the morning packing them with every possible thing that Nicole would need to outfit her trailer. Nicole had left the packing list, written in metallic pink ink, taped to my office door, a smiley face in its upper right hand corner like we were best bitches now. It was *ninety-seven* items long. Ninety-seven. I actually counted them, losing a personal bet with myself that it was over a hundred. The list included things like Q-Tips and Spanx, but also Valium and condoms. Three weeks ago, I would have admired her ability to bring her condom promotion to the movie, but ever since I saw her making out with a hipster in broad daylight, I was rethinking her condom motives. I almost didn't pack them in a passive-aggressive attempt to thwart her adulterous plans.

"Chloe?" Nicole's voice came from behind me and I straightened, peeling a Post-It off of my cheek.

"Yes?" I turned.

"Ready to head to set?"

"Yes." I scooted my chair, grabbing at my bag. Turning to her, I gave my best attempt at a smile, while scanning her for signs of infidelity. Nothing. There should be a sign, the words TRAITOR blazoned across her forehead. Then again, if cheating were that obvious, I'd have caught Vic before I did.

Today was the first day that Nicole would be on set and—let's not be coy—I was excited. Clueless, but excited. My knowledge of the film industry was limited to watching film geeks run around the NYU campus with lighting kits and cameras. This would be different; this was *real*. Well, as real as a straight-to-TV movie could be. And I was pretty sure that was what it was. I couldn't find anything out about it online. Plus, Nicole was the queen of the TV movie circuit, her résumé boasting one episode in a soap and seven movies no one had ever heard of.

If I hadn't IMDB'd her ass, I probably would have been more excited. Especially because Nicole had been walking around like *Boston Love Letters* was A BIG DEAL. And her agent and publicist had been frequent visitors to the Brantley household in the last few weeks. So who knew? Maybe this would be a feature film. I was just excited to be getting out of the house, my new office feeling more like a jail cell. On the set I could make some contacts, maybe find another job that wasn't laced with deception. Seeing Clarke's innocent face on a daily basis was seriously increasing my wrinkle count. I could *feel* crow's feet forming, caught a glimpse of them in the mirror just that week. Granted, it was a dingy mirror in a dark bar bathroom, but I'm almost positive they were there. Hiding. Lurking. Waiting.

I watched Nicole leave and studied the trunks. Hitched my bag higher on my shoulder and grabbed the first handle with both hands. Grunted a little when I lifted it.

"Don't do that." The world's hottest husband spoke from behind me. I turned to face him. "You'll kill that back of yours. Dante and I can get those."

"Thanks." I glanced around for anything I might be leaving, grabbing my Swell off the desk and sticking it in my bag.

"A raise, huh?"

"Excuse me?" Maybe he'd want money for the vase, after all.

"Nicole says she gave you a raise." Clarke stepped forward and bent over, grabbing one trunk in each hand and lifting them easily.

"Yes." I looked down, examining the fascinating hem of my shirt.

From the hall behind us, Nicole barked into her phone, voice loud, her hands gesturing wildly. No wonder she was so skinny. The woman worked off a thousand calories a day by sheer expression alone. Clarke glanced at her and lowered his voice. "So, you'll be on set with Nicole?"

"Yes—" I stopped myself just in time, swallowing the word *sir.* "I will."

"Keep an eye on her." He said the words shortly, with a bit of an edge. "For me."

"Keep an eye on her?" I asked hesitantly.

"You'll understand what I mean." He held my eyes for a heartbeat, then nodded and turned, the trunks in hand, and headed for the hall.

I followed numbly, almost bumping into Dante, and I pointed out the last trunk, whispering my thanks to him. I watched Clarke and Nicole move down the stairs and wondered, his last directives echoing in my mind, what he was talking about.

May

I hated her more with each passing day. I hated her for what she was doing to Clarke, and I hated her for bringing me in it, for tainting my journey of self-improvement.

Most of all, I hated all of the things I saw in her that reminded me of myself. It was like she was the Ghost of Christmas Freakin' Future. A ghost I despised.

Maybe it wasn't too late for me. Maybe all this was just my wakeup call.

25. The Benefits of Grape Bubble Gum

My movie set salvation had a full tattoo sleeve, hot pink hair, and matching nails. Any question I had about her inappropriate appearance was forgotten within five minutes of her walking through the door. She was the assistant I hoped to one day become, one who knew everyone, anticipated everything, and was utterly calm despite it all.

"Yo."

That was her introduction. She propped open the door to Nicole's trailer and popped a bright purple bubble of gum. I was alone, surrounded by trunks, and in the midst of a panic attack. The girl saw my face, stepped inside and shut the door.

"What's wrong?"

I didn't think, just held out my list of Nicole's demands, all screamed at me with morning breath fifteen minutes earlier, when she walked into the trailer and had an absolute conniption. I had scribbled down the items while Nicole stalked around the tiny space, waving her arms and opening and slamming things shut.

"Ha." Another pop of purple gum by the tattooed stranger, the grape scent hitting my senses. *Grape.* When was the last time I'd had grape bubble gum? Elementary school?

She passed the list back. "Her contract outlined what would be in her trailer. She knows that."

"So … I tell her no?"

She laughed. "Nicole Brantley? No. You call an outfitter and get her what she wants. But *she's* paying for it, not the studio."

I took the list from her outstretched hand. "And she'll be okay with that?"

She shrugged. "She doesn't belong in this movie anyway. Trust me, she won't do *anything* to jeopardize her role. If she told you to get these perks, she expects to pay for it."

I blindly followed the woman's lead, listening as she made a call and rattled off Nicole's list without pause. I dumbly handed over Nicole's AmEx and verbally approved the ridiculous price the guy quoted. When she locked my phone and tossed it back, I finally found the manners to introduce myself.

"I'm Chloe. I'm new. Nicole hired me a couple of months ago."

"Hannah." She reached out and shook my hand. "I'm Joey Plazen's assistant."

My hand stalled halfway through the shake. "Really?"

She grinned, detangling from my grip. "Really."

"Joey Plazen? *The* Joey Plazen?" my voice squeaked.

"That's the one." She headed for the door.

"He's in *this* movie?" I couldn't figure it out. Why would an A-list movie star be in something like this?

She paused in the doorway. "Yeah. It's a big budget film."

"But…" I couldn't think of a nice way to ask my question.

"You wanna know why Condom Queen's in it?" she asked.

I nodded.

"Great question." She raised her eyebrows at me and, with another pop of gum, left.

26. Saved by the Super

ChloeMadisonNYU
23 likes
ChloeMadisonNYU Rain rain go away.
#nyc #iforgotanumbrella

I finally discovered the meaning of a hard day's work. It had rained all day, the bottom half of my pants soaked. Running from vehicle to trailer, lugging all of Nicole's things over every inch of the film grounds, had covered my skin in a film of sweat, rain, and dirt. And my *hair*. I'd been hoping for beachy waves, but with all the moisture, it'd become a teased out cotton ball. My feet were too tired to properly pick up and down and I dragged the soles of my flats across the nasty sidewalks until I finally reached the stairs to my building's front door, my hand heavy as I reached for the handle.

When the front door of our building swung out, my hand wasn't yet on it, and the swift motion caused me to stumble back, my foot missing the step below, the dark New York City sky tilting forward as I fell back.

I almost died. A backward tumble, down six concrete stairs, onto the sidewalk. For sure, my head would have cracked, brains spilling out, blood gushing, heartbeat flatlining.

But I didn't die. I didn't because a hand reached out, a body rushed forward, and my wrist was grabbed, my back supported under the warm cover of an umbrella. I inhaled the rich scent of oranges and leather on a dress shirt and looked up, my body carefully righted on wobbly feet.

"Carter?" I found my footing and stood. My super-sexy super was there in a dark blue dress shirt, charcoal pants, a thick watch glinting, hair neat, sex appeal kicking.

"Are you okay?" He looked at me with worry. "Are you crying?"

Crying? I reached up and ran my hand underneath my eyes. My fingers came away black. Oh. Guess that cheap mascara I'd grabbed wasn't waterproof. *Great.* I probably looked like a drowned raccoon. "Rain," I mumbled.

"Sorry about the door." He stepped right and opened the door, holding it for me.

"It's fine." I stepped inside. "Fixing something in a suit?" I nodded to his outfit, the hour late.

He glanced down, then shook his head, a wry smile crossing his lips. "Ah—no. I live here. C9. Perks of the job."

Oh. Of *course.* "Lucky me. I guess I can find you whenever I need you." As soon as the response came out, I felt the blush creep along my cheeks. I rushed to cover my words. "Going out?"

He smiled. "Just down the block. Whiskey Tango. It's my friend's place."

I nodded. Whiskey Tango. Fancy shmancy. God, he looked hot. And he lived in the building; that was a fun fact. C9. Not that I'd ever need his room number.

"You gonna make it upstairs okay?" He looked at me carefully, probably wondering why I was still standing, staring at him.

I nodded, trying for a casual smile. "Yeah. Of course. Have a good night."

"You too."

He waited until I got on the elevator, the gesture sweet, and I waved a goodbye as I stepped on. In the moments before the door closed, I heard the front door settle and wondered, the elevator starting its ascent, if he would return home alone.

C9.

C9.

C9.

Interesting.

Not that I'd ever need it.

27. Meeting a Movie Star

Week two of being on *Boston Love Letters'* set and I already felt so much smarter. Most of my education came from Hannah who took me under her bubble-gum-smacking wing. The rest of my education came from watching, leaning my butt against any spare surface and collecting as much information as I could.

The movie was about Jenna (played by Nicole) a middle-aged waitress who started getting love letters from a stranger. The stranger ended up being Mark (played by the talented and gorgeous Joey Plazen), a younger guy who lived across the street and watched her every day through his window. Which, in normal life, would be totally creepy, but it was *Joey Plazen*, so of course it'd come across romantic and sexy.

And it really *was* big budget. Like, an actual gonna-be-in-theaters movie. While Nicole strutted around like she was big shit, I kept my mouth shut and tried to not mess up. I hadn't yet found out what Clarke wanted me to watch out for, but I spent all my time stuck to Nicole's side. Taking notes when she barked. Texting Hannah when I was lost.

I was mid-text, doing exactly that, when I first met Joey Plazen.

"Hey."

I didn't lift my head. I couldn't. I really, really needed to know where Set 14 was, and what the hell a stinger was, because Nicole needed one on Set 14 "ASAP." I finished typing out the questions, adding extra question marks for urgency, then pressed SEND, looking up in agitation once it went through.

Any chance I had of responding was stuck in my throat. Joey Plazen was the actor who kicked Brad Pitt's career to the curb. The guy who raced cars on the weekends when he wasn't sunning himself on his two hundred foot yacht. The guy who bed costars without apology, got in street fights (and won), and who went full-frontal in his last role, an action movie that had no need for penis-flashing but whose ticket sales absolutely exploded as a result. I'd gone with Vic to the theater. Squirmed in my seat when Joey had pulled off his shirt, revealing a rippling set of perfect abs. Audibly gasped when he pulled at the drawstring of his pants and ditched the sweatpants, revealing pure freaking perfection between his muscular thighs. It was never a good idea to audibly gasp with Vic. Talk about passing a blowtorch to an arsonist.

He'd reached over. Slid his hand up my thigh, underneath my skirt, tracing his fingers lightly over the lace line of my panties. I'd pushed his hand away and he'd resisted, exploring further, the pads of his fingers persistent as they nudged past my underwear and pushed inside. I felt his breath, warm against my neck, the bite of his teeth as he nipped my neck. "You like him?" he'd whispered, his voice gruff, too loud in the silent theater, and I'd shushed him, digging my nails into his arm as I squirmed in my seat, his fingers knowing exactly how I liked it. I'd cursed his name as he pushed me further and further along the edge of oblivion, watching the movie through half-closed eyes as Joey Plazen had fucked his costar. I'd watched until the absolute last moment, when my head hit the back of the seat, and I'd fully succumbed to Vic's touch.

I blinked the memory away and tried to focus on Joey Plazen's face without thinking of what lay beneath his jeans.

"Hey," I finally managed.

"You're Nicole's assistant, right?"

I nodded, not trusting my voice.

"Cute." He peered down at me. I said nothing, not crazy about his tone. "You mute?"

"No." I pushed myself to my feet. "Can I help you?"

"Do me a favor," he said. "Keep your boss out of my way."

"Out of your way?" That'd be difficult to do, seeing as they were co-stars.

"Yeah."

I laughed. "Okay," I intoned, in a manner that left zero doubt as to my sincerity.

"I'm serious. She doesn't belong here." Joey Plazen's sexiness was taking a serious nosedive. "And I need lunch."

I raised my eyebrows. "I think you have an assistant." My phone lit up, Nicole's ringtone playing, and when he glared at me I almost laughed. God, I'd seen that glare so many times. Threatening bad guys. Scowling at love interests. I'd seen it enough that there, on the set, surrounded by fake backdrops, it had no impact whatsoever. "Got to go," I sang, answering the phone and stepping away, any response from him lost in the bark of Nicole's greeting.

Right before she ended our call, I glanced back over my shoulder, but he was gone.

"Joey's *pissed*." Hannah popped her gum and wrapped a hand around my arm, pulling me into a dark spot between two trailers.

"Why?" I didn't look up from my phone, time short. In fifteen minutes, we needed to be at an all-cast meeting where our great director, Paulo Romansky, would finally make his first appearance. I didn't want to be late, not with the thin ice that Nicole seemed to be on. The more I found out on set, the more I discovered exactly how disliked Nicole was by cast and crew. We were talking serious hatred being spewed, and it wasn't for lack of her trying. She'd been bending over backward to try and win over hearts. We'd brought in sushi and afternoon cupcake deliveries, hired on-set masseuses, and she paid for everyone's drinks at the bar around the corner on Friday night. Nothing helped. No one wanted her here. The general consensus, whispered over scripts and coffee, was that she had bought her way onto the project. Poured some condom dollars in, saved the movie's financing, and got herself a starring role.

But regardless of their snide comments and her crappy résumé, I knew that the woman could act. I'd watched her beam at Clarke. Giggle and wrap her arms around his neck. Lie so smoothly that if I didn't know the truth, I'd have believed every word. I hadn't seen her boyfriend since that day on the street, but I'd been paying attention, noticing the lies about her whereabouts and the extra cell phone she carried in her purse. She couldn't play the part of the devoted wife so well without acting chops of some kind. Maybe *Boston Love Letters* was her chance to really show them off. Maybe now, with all of the pieces in place, she'd actually move into the limelight she seemed to so desperately crave.

"I can't talk Hannah, we've got that meeting—" She kept tugging me aside, like she had something urgent to say.

"You can't do that—just blow him off."

It took me a minute to remember who she was talking about. Oh, right. Joey Plazen. I dismissed her concerns with a laugh. "Whatever. He needs to get over himself. No offense, but your boss is an asshole."

Hannah's eyes widened and she sucked in a deep breath of air, her dark purple nails biting into my forearm. I noticed, a moment too late, that she wasn't looking at me, but *behind* me.

And then I heard the devil himself speak.

"You girls done with your chat?"

I grimaced, watching Hannah mutter an apology and dart out into the light. I stood, cornered and chilly in the shade, and crossed my arms. Screw his Oscar, screw his looks. I was sick of entitled assholes. "I'm sorry. Is chatting not allowed?"

"Not when you're on the clock." His frown enhanced his dimple, a dimple I once had stuck to the inside of my locker. "The meeting's about to start." I fought the urge to roll my eyes at him.

"Then I guess we should get to work." I smiled brightly and turned sideways to squeeze past him. He stepped back and stalked toward the meeting.

Diva. I killed a few minutes fishing for a pretend something in my purse. Once enough distance was present, I followed suit, glancing at my watch as I moved.

I arrived to the meeting late. I tried to slip into the back of the room, but no one budged to accommodate my scrawny ass. The room was packed—stuffy and hot despite the freezing temperatures outside. I ended up in the doorway, my hand gripping the frame just so I could crane my neck over a crew of teamsters.

Someone in front was talking, an unfamiliar voice droning on about call times. I found Hannah a few heads over, and raised my eyebrows in greeting. She gave me a small smile. "Who's that?" I mouthed, pointing a finger forward, over the crowd, to the guy talking. They should have given the guy a box to stand on or something.

"Romansky" she mouthed.

Duh. I should have figured. But, with all the hushed drama around this guy, I expected his arrival to come paired with glittery spotlights and a marching band. Last week, he'd been in Japan, the set a clusterfuck of activity without its director, everyone prepping for the filming that would start tomorrow. Hannah turned back to the front, her clipboard up, pen moving, and I bit my bottom lip. *Crap.* Clipboard. Paper. Pen. All items that were sitting back in Nicole's trailer. All items a good assistant would have, especially for a meeting like this. I heard the director rattle off a list of meetings and times, and I whipped out my phone and tried to type, tried to save at least one appointment. There was a low chuckle from my left and I turned to find Joey Plazen shaking his head at me. I felt the itchy crawl of embarrassment heat my cheeks. He tapped on a shoulder and the crowd parted, crewmembers crawling over themselves to clear a path, his steps moving easily toward an empty chair that looked like it was reserved for him.

Through the parted bodies, the hole beginning to close, I got my first glimpse at the man at the front of the room, our director, the famed Paulo Romansky. A man I had seen before, one fateful afternoon back on the Upper East Side: Nicole's hipster boyfriend.

28. Oh. I Totally Get It.

Everything suddenly made sense.

Nicole's secret fling.

Clarke's stern directive to watch her on set.

Her role in a big budget film where she didn't belong.

The pieces fell into a big arrow that pointed directly to the man at the front of the room. Nicole was sleeping with the director. It was so obvious I was almost insulted.

How stereotypical could she be? Everyone was walking around snidely suggesting that she'd bought her way onto the film, but *oh NO*. It was so much worse. Especially since Romansky was also married, to one of those Victoria Secret models with insured legs. I had a moment of pity for his wife but I'd seen plenty of photos of her. She'd bounce back. Literally. Her return to glory would be the perky boobs-in-a-million-dollar-bra type of bounce back.

I lost sight of him and tried to spot Nicole over the scores of heads, over a hundred people crowding the room. So many people and Hannah said there'd be even more once filming started. I gave up on my search for Nicole and slumped against the doorframe.

I needed a drink. I couldn't imagine this meeting ending and having to face Nicole. Not when my face was getting all flushed and itchy and it felt like I was going to—of all things—cry. Cry! Where in the hell did *that* weakness come from? It wasn't like I was emotionally invested in Nicole's marriage, wasn't like I'd just discovered the affair. But now that I knew who he was, it seemed even worse. Did Nicole even *like* this guy? Or was he just a stepping-stone she took to get this role? I could handle an affair for love, but cheating on Clarke for a role—that was where my brain stopped working.

My mind flashed to Clarke, the intensity on his face when he'd cornered me in the house. "Keep an eye on her." He'd said the words shortly, with a bit of an edge. "For me."

What good would keeping my eye on her do? What would I do with more information? And wasn't that why Nicole had given me a raise? To keep her dirty secrets?

I groaned and dropped my head to my chest, too confused to know what to do. In my back pocket, my cell buzzed, and I fished it out of my pocket. It was a text, from a name I'd rather not see right then.

Clarke.

The text was short and deadly. *Seen anything?*

I stared at it, no idea how to respond. The meeting ended, bodies bumped against me in their exit, and I still stared down at those letters.

Seen anything?

June

C9. C9. C9

Carter lived in C9. Not that I'd been thinking about it. But I couldn't stop imagining the *what ifs*. Especially when I was alone in bed, my body lonely, my hands wandering, my cool sheets sensual in their brush against my skin. *What if* he knocked on my door? *What if* I was in bed, like this, just waiting? *What if . . .* I rolled over in bed and pulled my blanket over my head.

C9. It was one floor and three doors away. I didn't know how long I could fight against it. I swore his damn apartment was calling my name.

29. How to Lie Without Lying

I zipped up the front of Chanel's coat, buttoning the top button and adjusting the hood, her tiny tongue darting out and catching my wrist. I smiled at her, picking up her tiny body and heard his voice. "Chloe."

I set down Chloe in her travel bag, taking my time before I turned to face him, trying to smile. "Mr. Brantley. Good morning."

The words came out well. Smooth and casual. Like my heart wasn't pounding. Like my mind wasn't racing over what to say when he asked the question that I knew was coming. I'd never responded to his text. I couldn't think of how to. Finally, after four or five hours had passed, I decided to just ignore it. Because, you know, that always made problems go away.

Clarke stepped into the kitchen, the click of his shoes painful on the polished floor. I held the edge of the counter tighter and leaned against it, trying to think of something to say. The air suddenly felt thick. Hot.

Clarke stopped three feet from me. Close enough I could see the worry in his eyes, the pinch of his forehead, the bits of silver in his dark hair. Silver. He seemed too young for silver, yet too masculine for anything else. I looked at him and couldn't understand why Nicole would want anything else. How could she kiss Paulo when she had Clarke?

I looked away, reaching for my coffee cup and took a sip, hoping caffeine would help.

"Was I right? Is she…" he paused as if the words caused him pain. Closed his eyes and folded his arms across his chest. Dropped his chin for a moment and when he raised it, every feature was hard, his next words dark and low. "Is she … sleeping with Joey Plazen?"

The small bit of coffee in my mouth threatened to spew forward in a *Pitch Perfect* stream of embarrassment. I clamped my lips shut, swallowed hard to force the coffee down, and it went down the wrong pipe. I coughed, wheezing as I gripped the counter and leaned forward. Clarke moved closer, a concerned look in his eyes, and I waved him off. His sexy hands rubbing my back might be the only thing that could have made my condition worse.

When I finally regained my breath, tears at the corners of my eyes, I tried for composure. "You think she's sleeping with *Joey Plazen*? Seriously?"

His eyes darkened. "Don't protect her."

"Listen to me." I squared my shoulders and met his stern gaze head on. "Joey Plazen *hates* her. I'd never tell Nicole this, but he complains about her to every cast member who will listen. There is absolutely *no* chance they're having an affair."

He yanked out his tie, letting out a heavy sigh. "Are you sure? I thought…" He ran a rough hand through his hair and scratched at the back of his neck, tilting his gaze back to mine. "It's just…" he continued, "something's *off*. And it's been off before." He lifted his chin. "In Paris."

I knew what he was referring to. Five years ago. There'd been rumors, then photos, then footage from the hotel elevator. Nicole had been filming a tiny made-for-TV movie that no one knew about, until her affair with her co-star had made all the gossip sites. Her co-star had been married to a pop music superstar and had publicly begged forgiveness, but Nicole had always vehemently denied the evidence. The story had fizzled out, but the Internet never forgot, the story still popping up in my Google search.

"I swear, nothing's going on between Joey and Nicole. *Nothing*." I emphasized the last word, and his frame relaxed a little.

"Okay." He wiped a hand over his face and straightened. "Thanks. I'm sorry to even ask."

"It's okay." I smiled, like a good little honest assistant. Didn't even check out his ass as he turned and left the kitchen. Returned to packing Nicole's bag and avoided Chanel's critical gaze.

For a good little honest assistant who hadn't lied, I felt filthy.

30. Evidence & Betrayal

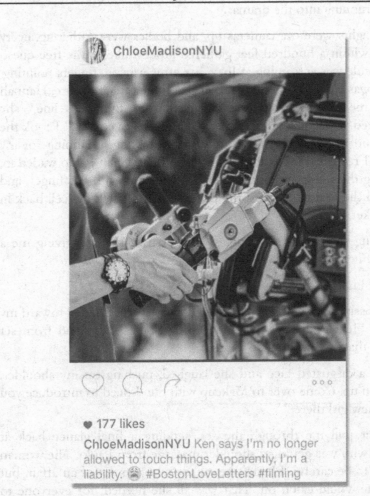

ChloeMadisonNYU
177 likes
ChloeMadisonNYU Ken says I'm no longer allowed to touch things. Apparently, I'm a liability. 😩 #BostonLoveLetters #filming

I was in Nicole's trailer when I heard her scream. The sound faint, it came from outside and I locked my phone, almost grateful for the interruption. I had just started playing Vic's voicemail, one left the night before, his words slurring but intentions clear. He loved me, he wanted me, would I please forgive him … the same message I had heard ten times before. The same message, just like the others, that I saved, too weak to hit the *delete* button. I'd already listened to it four times, my behavior bordering on pathetic. I stuffed the phone in my pocket and swung open the door. Jogging down the steps, I followed the sounds of a Nicole Brantley hissy fit, rounding a set stage and almost running into the drama.

Set 5. Lights were on, cameras up, and bodies were gathering, every person within a hundred feet gathered around like it was free queso day. Nicole was screaming at Joey, her arms waving, fingers pointing, and he was laughing, a combination that lit her anger on fire. Hannah passed me a bottled water and giggled. "She flubbed a line," she whispered. "Joey made fun of her. It didn't go over well." I took the water and realized the opportunity I was missing. Grabbing for my phone, I recorded the second half of the fight. Then Paulo waded in, avoiding the stabby motions Nicole was making with her finger, and stopped the drama. I ended the recording, and stuck my cell back in my pocket.

"Planning to sell that?" Hannah whispered in my ear, giving me a whiff of her granola breath.

"No!" I hissed.

"The gossip mags will pay bank for that shit." She nodded toward my pocket. "Just don't let anyone see you. You'll be banned from set quicker than it takes Joey to jack off."

I made a disgusted face and she laughed, pushing on my shoulder. "Lighten up. Come over to Makeup with me. I need to introduce you to the new girl there."

I let her pull me through the set, sending a final glance back at Nicole, who was getting a shoulder massage from Paulo. The woman needed to be careful. I hadn't heard any whispers yet of an affair, but someone would catch on. That was all she needed, for everyone to realize it wasn't Nicole's bank account that landed her this role but something else.

In my pocket, my phone burned hot against my butt. Hannah had a good point, one I hadn't thought of. Once I used the video, I needed to delete it.

I texted the video to Clarke. It seemed like a good idea. The video protected Nicole while putting to rest any of Clarke's concerns about an affair between her and Joey. A brilliant move on my part, if I could say so myself.

Clarke texted right back.

Thx. Sorry I was paranoid.

A harmless text, one he'd probably sent during a meeting, his attention half on the words as he nodded in response to something an associate said. I opened the text in a corner of Makeup, sitting Indian-style against a wall as I listened to Hannah barter Joey memorabilia for free makeup.

It's okay. I understand. I typed the reply, then locked my phone and stuck it in my pocket. I understood, all right. More than he knew, not that he cared about my baggage. I closed my eyes and leaned against the wall. Wondered how late today's schedule would go. The prior night, we'd been on set until eleven, my feet physically aching by the time Dante dropped me off at home. And our mornings had been starting at 6 a.m. There weren't enough lattes in the city to make me a morning person. I started to doze against the wall when my phone buzzed again.

You just made my day. This has been haunting me.

I typed back. *No problem. I thought of u when they started yelling. It's not really her fault. Joey's been an ass.*

Well … she can be a diva. Thanks for putting up w/ her. How's ur week going?

I smiled. Wondered how much to share. *It's good. Exciting. I like being on set. Are u going to come by?*

I stared at my words, the dots indicating his response pending. Why had I asked that? It was a horrible idea to put in his head. Then again, it *would* be helpful to know if he was going to come on set. Make sure that Nicole and Paulo weren't humping in the bushes when he strolled in. I smiled at the image, a bit of wicked glee at the idea of her getting caught.

The dots stopped. Then restarted. I imagined him biting his lip, thinking over the response. When it finally came I sighed in relief.

Probably not. I'll let my girl work in peace.

A good response. One that a trusting and loving husband would make. My girl. So freaking sweet. I locked my phone and tucked it underneath my legs.

My girl.

It bothered me, a pang of sadness hitting hard at the endearment. I must be lonelier than I realized. Single didn't sit well with me, not in this big city, not in my empty apartment.

I scrolled through the texts and deleted them all, including the video I had sent to him. There hadn't been anything wrong with the communication … but still. Something about the whole thing felt tainted. The video. The lies. *My girl.*

I confirmed the deletion and wondered how this would all implode, and when.

31. Am I a Terrible Kisser?

Shit. One of the lids was coming off. The lid was on one of the two cups of coffee between my elbow and my body, one decaf and one regular because I couldn't, for the life of me, remember which one Nicole had requested. I also carried two plates, one of fruit and one of sushi, the queen's breakfast of choice, a banana jostling close to one edge. Eyeing it, I rounded the corner of the props warehouse, hugging the edge in case anyone was coming in the opposite direction.

Someone was. Someone in a white oxford and slacks, his head down, phone out. I tried to dart left, tried to call out a warning, and didn't manage either before BLAM. *Impact* with the beautiful Joey Plazen.

I'd never heard such a sexy curse in my life. He spoke Italian in some part of it, a rough accent coming into his voice as he stepped back, coffee going EVERYWHERE, a California roll sticking on his shoulder. I gasped, covering my mouth, which was convenient, because the next sound that spilled out of me was a laugh. A *laugh.* I had no earthly idea where it came from. Or why it came out. It was a disaster, coming out around my hand, and his head snapped up when he heard it, his eyes locking on mine with murderous intent. I shouldn't have laughed. It wasn't funny, and he was probably due on set, but coffee was dripping from his chin, and a piece of mango was sliding down his arm, and I was so horrified by the entire thing that a laugh was the only thing my body knew to produce. So I laughed. And then, to make matters worse, I couldn't stop. I didn't stop when he shook out his hands. When he flicked the California roll and the mango off his previously crisp shirt. I didn't even stop when he stepped closer and pushed me back against the wall, his warm hand covering my mouth.

"Stop laughing," he gritted.

I couldn't. My body was shaking I was laughing so hard.

I finally did stop. I stopped when he moved his hand and silenced me with his lips.

My last kiss had been outside a club, in the snow, with an asshole. This kiss was with a different asshole, against a wall, on a movie set. Unlike the other asshole, this asshole … God, he knew how to kiss.

I was laughing when his lips pressed into mine, a hard and insistent *shut the hell up* move that instantly worked, my laughter halting, his body pushing against mine. His coffee-soaked shirt was cold and wet against my Vince sweater, but I didn't care. The hard press of his lips lifted then immediately came back down, this time softer and sweeter, my mouth opening, our kiss deepening. I gripped at the wall behind me, fought the urge to reach for his head, dig through that hair, and I almost moaned when I felt his hand wrap around my waist and pull me away from the wall and into his body. He tasted like coffee and sugar, and his fingers bit into my waist in the moment before his mouth ripped from mine. He let go and stepped back, leaving me panting against the wall, my glazed vision fighting to find its focus.

"Huh." He let out a puff of air and twisted his mouth. "I thought that would be better."

His expression was almost wistful in its confusion, his words without any sarcasm. My ego took a nosedive, and he shrugged, glancing down at his outfit.

"Shit. Get me a change of clothes." His words were dismissive, an order handed out with absolute certainty of being obeyed. He gave me a parting wink then strode off. God, he was an ass. An ass that made Vic look positively gentlemanly. I pushed off the wall and looked down at my cream sweater, now ruined. The coffee was a lost cause, and Nicole's sushi … I looked at the few pieces still stuck to the plate and wondered if they were salvageable.

Get me a change of clothes. I was, apparently, the only one with shaky legs and a raging libido. *I thought that would be better.* I wiped my hands on my jeans and pulled out my cell. Sent Hannah a text that the asshole she called a boss needed new clothes. I ignored the colorfully grouchy emoticons she sent back in response, too busy trying to clean up the mess. *I thought that would be better.* Ouch.

First kisses could tell you a lot. Ours told me that his sex appeal wasn't limited to his looks. Ours told me that any attraction I felt for Joey Plazen wasn't returned.

First kisses were often last kisses also.

July

I used to think that I was hot. Nabbing one of New York's most eligible bachelors did that to a girl's ego. But then Vic cheated on me. And my track record ever since had sucked. Between the thousand-dollar asshole and Joey's reaction to our kiss—paired with zero date invites in the last year—I was failing terribly as a single in New York.

Nothing was going right.

32. We're all Sluts for Cash

ChloeMadisonNYU
88 likes
ChloeMadisonNYU Our city smells like tourists and sunscreen. Summer is officially here.

"Hey, Nicole's girl."

The first time he'd spoken to me since our disastrous kiss, and *that* was how Joey Plazen summoned me. By command, one step above him slapping his knee and whistling at me like I was a dog.

I ignored him and kept walking, a juice in one hand, new shooting schedule in the other. Two weeks wasn't long enough to heal the sting of *that* snub.

"Hey!" I zagged right and heard him curse as he jumped over a mass of cords and tried to catch up. I swallowed a smirk, speeding up a little. "Chloe."

I stopped, spinning around and raising my eyebrows, his arms coming out as he reached me. I took a casual sip of the juice and winced, too much ginger in the blend.

"Where are you going?" He tucked both hands in the front pockets of his jeans.

An unexpected question. I stared, taking me a minute to remember where I had been going. Oh, right. To pick up Nicole's cardigan. "Wardrobe." I managed the word and took another sip. Waited for him to say something—anything—and when he stayed silent, his eyes roaming over the concrete between us, I turned to leave.

"Chloe." My name was a puff on his lips, and I heard the scrape of his shoes when he lunged after me, his hand closing on my shoulder, a gentle pull that I ignored.

"What do you want, Joey?" Because that's what it was. He wanted something. If I'd learned anything from two months of being on set with Joey, it was that every smile was a bribe, every flirt was a favor, and our kiss against the wall … that was just entertainment. Benta had more properly defined it as him trying to put me in my place. It had certainly, if anything, put my ego in check and killed any fantasies of a future between us.

"You know, for an assistant, you sure do walk around with a stick up your ass."

WOW. Whatever he was chasing me down for just moved a *lot* further out of his reach. I kept walking.

"Chloe…" When he closed his hand on my shoulder a second time, it was harder, his fingers biting in and holding on, his pull forcing me to stop. I looked down at his hand.

"Move your hand or I'm pouring this juice all over it."

He lifted his hand and held it up in surrender. "Chloe, please. Let's grab lunch. I don't have a scene 'til two."

"Why?"

"I can't ask you to lunch?" He scowled, and I liked that. I understood grouchy Joey. It was the random spurts of friendliness and sexuality that unsettled me.

"I can't know your motives?" I smiled as sweetly as I could and he looked irritated. I guess he hated Fake Chloe as much as I hated Fake Joey. Ugh. Our names *rhymed.* How had I never noticed *that* before?

"I just want to talk. That's it."

I examined his face warily. The conversation was getting weirder by the minute. I glanced at my watch. "Chat now. I've got stuff to do."

He glanced over his shoulder. "Here?"

I bit back a sarcastic comment about him needing privacy and eyed the crowded path. I nodded to our left, cut between two trailers and walked to a quiet spot behind a rack of lights. "Better?" I asked, my voice quieter.

"Yeah." He rubbed the back of his neck, suddenly hesitant, then leaned closer in to me. "We need Nicole to cough up more cash."

It was so unexpected I laughed. I'd heard that rumor since the day I walked on set, snide comments following Nicole wherever she went. The general consensus among the crew was that she'd bought her spot on the cast, a rumor I hadn't debunked. It distracted them from the truth: that Paulo was more interested in what was between her legs than what was filling her pockets.

Joey glared. "I'm serious, Chloe. The film is way over budget. The studio is balking."

"So? Don't most movies go over budget?"

"Yeah, but the studio is already skittish, especially with Condom Barbie's name attached. Paulo approached me about needing a cash infusion."

That surprised me. I didn't know crap about movies but it seemed odd to ask the star to fund it after filming had begun. "Is that normal? A director approaching you to help fund the film?"

"No. But Paulo and I are the ones who found this script and pitched it to the production company. I offered to step in with cash then but it wasn't needed."

"So put in the cash now."

His eyes darkened. "I'm not paying for Nicole's mistakes. The only reason we're over budget is her. She's taking three takes longer than anyone else, and has Paulo's ear, requesting script changes every other day."

Something was off. I watched his toe stub at the ground, saw the flex of his jaw as he looked to the side. I'd lay down odds that Joey *couldn't* step up with the funding, and it had nothing to do with Nicole and everything to do with a lack of cash. Maybe he wasn't as successful as he wanted everyone to believe. Or as responsible with his success.

I didn't call him out. Instead, I asked how much was needed, flinching at the twenty million number he threw out. An amount he seemed intent on Nicole covering.

"Will she do it?"

I shrugged. "Why are you asking me? You see her nine hours a day, ask her."

He reached out and grabbed my hand, a move right out of his Endearing Gestures Toolbox. "You know her. What's their financial situation like? Is that kind of additional investment feasible?"

I studied him. Joey was actually *worried*, the tension in his grip indicating exactly how interested he was in my response. For all his bitching about Nicole tanking the film, he wanted to see it through. He wanted to see it funded. But not only that … he wanted to see it *succeed.* Maybe Big Bad Joey Plazen wasn't the confident ass he portrayed. Maybe when cut, he bled insecurity just like the rest of us. He raised his eyebrows and stared at me, waiting.

"I don't know," I finally said, tugging my hand back. There'd been a few hints here and there that money wasn't as free-flowing as it might have once been. Which wasn't to say the Brantleys were downsizing anytime soon. But Nicole was yacht-shopping last week and Clarke shut down that idea down *really* quick. "I don't think it's a given. A possibility, maybe." I glanced at my watch. "I have to go."

He nodded and stepped back. "Thanks."

"Sorry I couldn't help out more."

He flashed a smile, one almost convincing enough to look carefree. "No biggie. Someone will come forward, if she won't." He waved, turning away, and I watched him walk off, not buying his sudden ease.

Twenty million. I smiled, heading to Wardrobe, the sum unthinkable to a girl who had just stocked her fridge with stolen McDonald's condiment packets.

33. Knock. Knock.

C9. I stared at the number, innocently set into the door, and chewed on my nail. Glanced at my watch, which hadn't changed. Still fifteen minutes past midnight.

If only I hadn't stopped by the bookstore and furiously scanned the tabloids…

If only I hadn't swung by Benta's, who'd had boy drama to discuss…

If only I hadn't watched three freaking episodes of *PLL* with her…

If only I had taken the subway instead of a cab…

If only I hadn't made the ultimate tourist mistake and left my keys in the cab…

I was up the stairs to my building, reaching for the key before I realized what happened. I sprinted down the steps, waving my arms and screaming at the cab, which continued its merry path a block away. I muttered a line of obscenities, stomping my feet in the middle of the street, my keys still lying on the seat of the cab, my Fendi fluffy keychain lost forever.

I trudged back up the steps and leaned on the front door, doing a half-hearted search on the taxi commission's website. It took five minutes to find out that the only chance I had of getting my keys back was by filing a lost item report *in person.* Talk about archaic practices. As I closed the browser, one of my neighbors opened the lobby door, and I gratefully slipped in, one step closer to home.

The elevator was halfway up before I realized I didn't have a way to get *into* my apartment. The spare key I'd left for Benta and Cammie—stuck under my mat after the night they'd nearly gotten me evicted for being drunk and loud on my doorstep—I'd used it a week earlier when I couldn't manage to find my house key in the depths of my purse. It was still sitting on my kitchen counter, patiently waiting to be returned to its rightful place under my mat.

I'd run out of options. I stared at the door of C9. Carter's apartment. At least I'd remembered the unit number, all of that obsessing coming in handy. I glanced at my watch one last time before reluctantly lifting my hand and knocking on his door.

I woke him up. When he opened the door, I could see it in the rough mess of his hair, the scratch of his voice, but more noteworthy: his lack of clothing. Bare-chested, he braced muscular arms against the doorframe, his biceps popping, shoulders strong and wide, a six-pack screaming attention to the gorgeous cuts on either side of his hips. Bright yellow pajama pants hung low on his hips, the ties undone and I forgot about my lost keys, forgot all about my Netflix plans, forgot everything but a raw desire to drop to my knees and yank down those pants.

I swallowed. "Hey Carter."

"It's late."

"I left my keys in a cab." I gestured toward the street for some unknown reason, my eyes continually tripping back to his abs. *Damn.*

"You need a place to crash?" There was a smile in his tone and I pulled my eyes up to his face. God, he was pretty. Had some dark stubble going that made his eyes pop. And he was actually smiling. Maybe Benta and Cammie's party in the hall had been forgiven.

"Ah… no." *Maybe*? I struggled to explain. " I can't get into my apartment. Do you have a spare?"

He pushed off the doorframe and stepped back, running a rough hand over the back of his head and I could get a freaking foot massage by running my soles over the hard ripple of those abs. "I should. Come on in."

"Thank you," I murmured, meekly stepping inside and sneaking a look around. It was sparsely furnished, a leather sectional laid out before a large flat screen, a farmhouse-style table the only other piece of furniture in the room. "Your apartment is bigger than mine."

He laughed, walking over to the kitchen counter and digging around in a drawer. "You sound so surprised."

"Well." I didn't finish the sentence, standing awkwardly in the entranceway. My second glance saw the art on the walls. "Wow." I stepped closer, the piece in the foyer area *gorgeous*, a hundred swirls of color centered around a woman's face. "Is this…?" I touched it to test my eyes, my hands brushing over the raised oil brush strokes. "Holy shit. This is a Presa Little."

He looked up from the drawer and met my eyes with a look of wary surprise. "Yeah. You know her stuff?"

"Umm … yeah," I said softly, turning back to the piece. "I've followed her for a while." My parents had had a Presa Little in our Colorado home, purchased on one of our shopping trips to Paris. Mom used to spend the day shopping, and Dad and I would hit galleries, art something that we both loved. "How did … her stuff is wicked expensive." I glanced at him and saw his face darken.

"She was a friend of mine. It was a gift."

He stepped closer, coming to stand beside me, my hand still outstretched toward the bare canvas. A Presa Little original. A six-figure piece, easy. And from behind him, in the hall that probably led to his bedroom, another one, midnight blue swirls of ocean—

I stopped thinking about the painting or my keys, because right then he pulled me around, closing the gap between us and pressing me gently to the wall, my hair against a painting that could buy me a future. "Are you sure you lost your keys," he grumbled, "or did you wake me up for something else?"

I put my hands where I'd wanted to for the last ten minutes, sliding them down the bumps of his abs and over the line of his hips, hooking my fingers underneath the waist of his pajama pants. "Both?" I whispered.

There was a moment of silence, his eyes on mine. They were wary, as if he didn't trust me. And hungry, as if he was fighting just to keep away. I stared up at him, my breath catching in my throat, and begged him for more with my gaze. He sighed, his eyes falling to my mouth, and I felt the moment he gave in, his head lowering, his lips pressing to mine.

Instantly, I could taste his need, his want. It was in every stroke of his tongue, the growl in his throat, his hot hands rough on my skin. My hands went further, underneath his pajama pants, and slid around, gripping his hard ass. His hands wrapped around my waist, picking me up and he carried me to the wooden table, setting me on its surface, his hands busy as they yanked my shirtdress out from underneath my butt and pulled the fabric up and over my head. Then he laid me back, our kiss continuing, a deep feast of starved souls. And I was. In the last year, every kiss I'd received had been a taunt, a tease, or a mind fuck. I hadn't been *really* kissed, or touched, or desired in so long. And there, in his apartment, his hands hot on my skin, his mouth feverish against mine … it was as if I were experiencing everything for the first time.

His fingers slid under my bra strap and pulled it down.

His lips moved off my mouth and trailed down my neck, sucking on a spot on my collarbone, his fingers sliding gently down, over my panties, my knees lifting up, feet hooking around his back and pulling him closer.

I felt every single one of his fingers as they brushed in between my legs, and I shuddered, his mouth pausing, head lifting to look at me. "You okay?" he asked. I reached down and pushed his hand back. "Don't stop," I gasped. His fingers moved, gently circling, teasing, getting closer and closer until one brushed over my clit, the silk of my panties providing the perfect barrier, my hips all but exploding off the table. "Oh my God," I gasped. "Carter."

His mouth, a hot, wet place of perfection, left my neck and moved up, his eyes careful and concerned, watching my face as his touch moved, his eyes darkening when he saw me reach the edge. "Don't stop," I begged.

"Don't worry," he said, lowering his head and biting gently on my neck. "Take your time," he whispered, and I whimpered as his mouth trailed lower, skipping along my skin, a quick scrape of his teeth across my stomach, the intensity building, every sensor in my body tuned to and focused on his fingers. God, this was *with* my panties on. What would it be like when I was naked? When it was his cock and not his fingers? When he was inside me and pushing deeper, his hands holding me close, his…

"Oh my God, I'm—"

"Not yet," he growled, and his hand ripped at my panties, pulling them down, and his hot mouth was suddenly where his fingers had been, his hands on me, holding me down as he explored me with his mouth, his tongue light and constant as it played across my clit then dipped lower and deeper. The man had no fear, no hesitation, and I dug my hands in his hair as I tried to stay in control, tried to stay coherent. The sensation … it was building, spreading outward from his mouth, every muscle tensing, my body clenching in preparation for what was coming, and he groaned my name in worship and

in that sound, raw and primal…

in the clench of his hands on my skin…

in the wet, perfect flick of his tongue…

in the dark look of ownership and confidence in his eyes…

in the buildup, a hundred pieces of arousal climbing together…

I lost words, I lost thought, I lost every single piece of myself. My shoulders came off the table and I whispered his name, my eyes closing, hands grabbing at him, his mouth staying on me as the intensity grew and stretched and inhaled my world.

I fell down to earth lazy and broken. My legs rolled off his shoulders, and I lay there on his table, his fingers soft as they trailed away, his mouth sweet as it slowly kissed its way off my skin, his arms strong as they lifted me off the table and carried me away, down a dark hall with another stunning Presa Little painting, and onto a bed that was big and soft.

There, he drew me into his arms. *Take your time*, he had said. Quite possibly the best three words I'd ever heard during sex. I ran my hand along his forearm and shifted against him, closing my eyes and listening to the beat in his chest.

There, lulled by the metronome of his heart, I slept.

34. The Walk of Shame

I opened my eyes and felt the weight of an arm across my stomach.

I didn't move. Didn't breathe. I let my eyes adjust to the morning light and caught as many details as I could from my place in the bed.

Light gray walls. No furniture sitting on the charcoal floors. No curtains framing the windows. His room had *nothing* in it. No dirty clothes, no dresser, no desk, no phone charger hanging off the wall. I eyed the closet door and wondered if it was packed full or OCD organized. I bet on organized. The sun was shining through a clean window, his baseboards were dust-free, and his freakin' fan blades sparkled from above me.

So. One upside to my fall into a handyman's bed: it was clean. I straightened my right leg, realized my lack of panties, and remembered a second upside: a long-awaited orgasm. An orgasm that had been great for me but had left him with nothing. I smiled despite myself. A sexual gentleman. Vic wouldn't have let me sleep until the scales were even.

My experience with random hookups was fairly limited, and I wondered at the next step. Should I roll out from under his arm and sneak out? Would we pass each other in the hall and smile and pretend nothing happened? Would he want to have a relationship talk? I stared up at his sparkly clean ceiling fan and felt the first tinge of panic.

Nicole's ringtone suddenly blared, scaring the hell out of me. I bolted upright, throwing off his arm and crawled over his hard body, headed for his bedside table, my fingers stretching to grab my cell. I answered it while turning around his clock. Saw the time and panicked, throwing some bullshit Nicole's way while I looked around for my shorts.

"They're in the living room." Carter was sitting half up, his bare torso on glorious display, watching me with an amused half-grin stretched across his face.

"Thanks," I whispered, hopping off the bed. His hand reached out and grabbed my wrists, pulling me back and I was suddenly right *there*, inches from his face, his other hand at the back of my neck, his mouth soft as he gently pulled me in for a kiss. I closed my eyes and enjoyed the moment. Nicole barked a fresh set of orders through the phone and I quickly came back down to earth. "I have to go," I whispered and pulled away. I waved at him and mouthed an apology, jogging down the hall. "I'm literally right here, Nicole. I'm walking in the door now."

I found my underwear and my shorts, pulling them on. A spare key for my apartment lay right next to my shoes, my apartment number neatly printed on the tag. I stared at it for a moment, something about the way it was laid out, felt like a giant *Get Out of Here* sign. I shrugged off the feeling, pocketing the key, my feet shoved into my shoes, and ran out.

I waited on the street, my eyes scanning for a cab, and tried to understand the roll of feelings. I felt like a thirteen-year-old girl. One who had just *cough* kissed a guy and had no idea how to handle it. I wasn't even sure, catching sight of a cab, why I was analyzing this. We hadn't even had sex. It was a one-night thing, nothing more. I had nothing in common with the man, wasn't even sure he *liked* me. I had caught him in a weak moment and gotten a mind-numbing orgasm from it. End of story.

Probably.

Hopefully.

Not.

35. Becoming Famous

ChloeMadisonNYU
114 likes
ChloeMadisonNYU Reading magazines for work. No really, I swear.
#sometimesIlovemyjob #fashion #gossip

The stack of publications before me grew. *People, In Touch, Variety,* the *Times,* the *Hollywood Reporter*—I added *Star* to the pile and picked up the next, flipping through the newspaper, my eyes skimming for any mention of Nicole. My stomach flipped when I stuck the blue flag on page 7A, right by a story naming *Boston Love Letters* an expensive vanity project, one set to tank.

I shifted on my stool, in the Brantley's kitchen, and eyed Nicole, who thumbed through a stack of mail. She wandered over, tossing the mail on the counter and reached for the newspaper, pulling it from my hands, her eyes darting over the article. "Is everything—?" I didn't get the rest of the sentences out, barely having time to duck when she picked her phone off the counter and threw it.

"CLAARRRKKKE!" She screamed the man's name like she was on the battlefield, and I heard his feet, heavy down the stairs. Then he was in the kitchen, T-shirt damp with sweat, ear buds hanging from around his neck. He stopped in the doorway, his hands braced on the frame, and looked at Nicole, his eyebrows rising in question.

"I *told* you this would happen!" Nicole screamed the threat as if it were the plague, and thrust out the newspaper, stretched tightly so we could read the headline: *BOSTON LOVE LETTERS ALREADY IN TROUBLE.* I slowly eased to my feet and picked up the laptop, ready to escape the carnage. "Chloe!" Nicole barked, pointing a finger in my direction. "Don't go anywhere!" I slunk back down on the stool. Chanel deserted my feet and ran for cover, her nails clicking down the marble hall and out of sight. Lucky bitch.

"Nicole, calm down." Clarke let go of the doorframe and stepped closer. Brave man. I shifted slightly, hunching behind my laptop in case things started flying in my direction. As quickly as possible, I navigated over to TMZ to see if there was any news about *BLL* there. This shit was about to get nuclear if they'd grabbed the story too.

"Calm *down*? Do you know what this says? It says *I'm* the reason we're behind schedule and over budget. It calls me a C-list actress!"

"Well, this *is* your first big—" His stupid statement was cut off by another scream, this one punctuated by Nicole's toss of the newspaper onto the floor, her fists waving in the air as she physically jumped up and down on it. *Jumped* up and down. In four-inch slingbacks. I watched in fascination.

"Fix *TTHHHIIISSS*!" she screamed, continuing her jumping fest, her breasts bouncing with each hop.

"I'll call the publicist. We'll get the papers to issue a retraction," he started.

"It needs to be done NOW. Or so help me God…"

"It'll be fixed." He made a shushing sound and stepped closer, his hands reaching out and rubbing her arms, pulling her protesting body into his chest. Her stance relaxed for a moment, folding into his arms and pushing away only when she realized he was sweaty.

"By tomorrow," she pouted, stepping out of the ruined newspaper bits.

"Okay." Clarke shot a relieved look my way, and I smiled weakly, wanting nothing more than to be out of their kitchen, their house, their lives. Nicole snapped her fingers at me.

"Chloe, order beignets from that place around the corner." Her tone was mild, like nothing had happened, and I nodded, looking down at my laptop.

And that was when I saw it. The top story on TMZ. *Joey Plazen dating a new Mystery Blonde?* Right below the headline was a grainy photo of Joey, his lips pressed hard to his latest conquest.

Me.

36. A Big Dick

It'd been less than four hours since the TMZ story hit and the entire world of entertainment had gone nuts. I locked my phone and resisted the urge to chuck it in the trash, my social media exploding as every friend I'd ever had felt the need to tag me on every news outlet that picked up the story. Thank GOD I wasn't on Facebook anymore. One less gallon of blood in the shark-infested waters.

My phone rang and I glanced down, Nicole's name lighting up my screen for the third time in the forty-five minutes I'd sat on these steps. Ignoring Nicole was dangerous, but I had to talk to Joey and whatever she needed would draw me from that task. I silenced the call and wondered, for the tenth time in the two weeks since my hookup with Carter, why he hadn't called. Granted, we hadn't exchanged numbers. But he was a resourceful guy, with full access to my rental application. From behind me, Joey's trailer door swung open, and I pushed my butt off the steps and stood, wiping off my Hudsons, ready to give Joey a serious piece of my mind.

Instead, Hannah stared down at me. "You waiting on me?" She dug her phone from her back pocket as if to check for calls.

I shook my head. "Him. I have to talk to him about the … you know." I glanced around nervously. Nicole was still clueless. One benefit of me cutting out her tabloid articles, I could hide all mine with one visit to the shredder.

"The what?" Hannah raised her eyebrows, showing off impressively applied purple shadow and matching lashes. Apparently, the Joey Plazen camp didn't stalk the tabloids. I suddenly felt pathetic, my attention-hungry boss and me.

"Pictures of me and him." Her eyebrows rose even higher. "No, not *those* kind of pictures," I rushed to explain. "Tabloid—is he in there?"

"He's all yours," she said airily, jogging down the steps. "But I'm just gonna warn you, he's in a bitch of a mood."

That was fine. I was in a bitch of a mood too.

I pushed open the door and stepped into Joey's trailer, him sitting directly before me, on a worn leather couch, a notepad in hand, empty coffee cup on the table before him. "What do you want?" he growled.

I shut the door. "Have you seen the articles about us?"

"I don't read the tabloids. First thing I learned."

"They're calling me your new *fling*. They have a picture of us *kissing*." I spit out the words, and he lifted his eyes from the notepad, looking into my face for a long moment before tossing the pad down.

"So? Your street cred just went way up. You should do some interviews. Tell them I have a big dick and made you come ten different ways." He laughed and reached for the cup, raising it to his lips before scowling into it. "Get me some coffee, will you?"

"No." I glared at him.

"You're seriously going to make me get my own coffee? I stopped doing that like eight years ago." He gave me a wounded expression that was so blatantly adorable that I almost laughed. No wonder his ego was so big. He was impossible to hate.

"Yes." I glared despite my urge to smile. "This is serious."

"Don't worry about the pics; they'll move on to something else in a few days." He waved his hand at me and stood, lifting the cup.

"Can't you do something? Tell them we're not dating?"

He turned around, away from the coffee pot. "I don't date. They know that. And besides," he shrugged, "you're not my type."

My self-esteem sank further, passing right through the floor. "Do *they* know I'm not your type?"

He turned away and lifted the pot, tossing words over his shoulder at me while he poured. "They should. I like brunettes. More specifically, ones with curves and exotic accents." He shrugged. "You're … you know."

My fragile ego was almost glad he didn't finish that sentence. "You know, you did kiss me." I grumbled the accusation and was glad his back was to me, unable to see the embarrassed burn on my face.

He turned around, watching me over the top of his cup. "I kissed you because I was irritated and you were being a pain in the ass." He shrugged again, lifting his cup up for a sip. "Things go smoother for me if everyone's a little starry-eyed." He tilted his head at me. "I mean—you didn't think—?"

"No!" I hotly responded. "It's just… you've got to work on your insults. I *do* have feelings, you know."

"Sorry." He smiled. "If it makes you feel better, I like your spunk. You keep me on my toes."

I scrunched up my face in response. "You like me for my personality? Another insult to my ravishing beauty."

"But a complement to our friendship."

"You're not my type either, you know," I grumbled out the lie, turning to leave.

He laughed. "So I'm forgiven for the tabloid's heinous behavior?" he called out.

I didn't respond, pushing open his trailer door and letting it slam behind me.

His parting shout came faintly through the door. "Just remember to brag about me! Big dick, Chloe! Remember—big dick!"

A big dick? Yeah. I'd say that was appropriate.

37. My Boss Is A Bitch

"You are a genius." Nicole beamed at me, her whitening trays stretching her smile in a terrible way. "Genius." The word was muffled through the plastic, and I bit my cheek in an attempt not to laugh. "Throwing off the press like that?" She clapped her hands together with unrestrained glee.

"Glad it worked." I smiled sweetly, as if the smearing of my personal reputation was something I did intentionally, just to distract the tabloids from *BLL*'s financial woes.

"Here." She pulled out the top drawer of her trailer's vanity and rummaged through it, pulling out a piece of paper. "You deserve this."

I looked down at the paper, which was a card from the Waldorf's spa, announcing their grand reopening, along with an offer of fifteen percent off. A *coupon.* Nicole was offering me a coupon as gratitude. A coupon for spa services that I couldn't afford. I held it out to her. "I can't afford…" I swallowed hard. "Thank you for the offer, but I'm trying to save money right now."

She looked at me with confusion, her eyes darting from me to the card. "Oh," she finally said, reaching out and plucking the card from my fingers. She hesitated, then held it back out. "Then book me a facial and massage. For Saturday, if they have availability. These long days are killing me." She turned back to the mirror and bared her teeth, examining the color before checking her watch. "How much longer do I need to keep these on?"

"Another five minutes," I said quietly, rubbing the back of my neck in a futile attempt to relieve some of my own tension.

She let out a huff of irritation and I decided, right then, her nails drumming against her counter, that I hated the woman.

38. Knight in Shining Joey

"*There's* the love of my life!" The shout was loud enough to stall productivity, and I glanced over my shoulder to Joey, who held out his arms and walked toward me as if he expected an embrace. I stopped him three paces out with the dirtiest look I had.

"Ouch." He stopped in his tracks and clutched at his heart. "Don't tell me. A divorce already? Perez will be so devastated. He drew hearts around us and everything."

I fought a smile and he threw an arm over my shoulder, ignoring my attempt to push him off.

"Don't worry about it," he said quietly, steering me around a set stand and toward the catering truck. "All of your problems are solved."

The chances of Joey solving all of my problems in six hours was highly unlikely. I let him pull me along, my feet weighing twenty pounds, and it had nothing to do with my supercute boots. "I'm not like you Joey. My parents—"

"I know all about your parents," he interrupted. "My publicist gave me the scoop. And don't worry about it. Katie in Mixing has already agreed to sleep with me, just to throw the wolves off your scent."

"What?" I came to a stop, his arm dropping from my shoulder. "Are you serious?"

"Don't feel sorry for her." He winked at me. "I'll make sure she enjoys it."

Oh, I was *sure* she'd enjoy it. "And how will *that* help?"

"We'll leak some photos, I'll grope her in public, and our little kiss will be forgotten as quickly as your boss's embarrassing attempt at a career." He smiled that famous smile, and my mind stuttered, still stuck on Katie's involvement in all of this.

"Katie's going to *sleep* with you? Just to throw off the press?"

"Uh … yeah. Technically, we'll be fucking more than sleeping but…" He shrugged. "You get the point. In twenty-four hours, I'll have solved all your problems." He stepped toward the truck and urged me forward with his hand. "Come on. You owe me a drink."

I followed him to the catering truck, unsure if Katie in Mixing was stupid or lucky. Unsure if *I* was stupid for believing in this plan. Was he right? Would it all go away that easily?

August

Vic the Dick
Is such a Prick
He took my heart
And stopped its Tick

And to think I got a C in Modern Poetry.

39. Sinking Deeper

ChloeMadisonNYU
68 likes
ChloeMadisonNYU 3 pounds of perfection.
#puppiesofinstagram #letsleepingdogslie

It was hailing. The top of the SUV drummed with the pelts, a soothing beat except that soon Dante would stop and I would have to step out into its fury. I watched hail bounce off the hood of a taxi and hoped it would stop before we got to set.

We were a few hours behind Nicole, a grooming appointment for

Chanel taking up the morning. Dante laid on the horn, cursing out a passing car, and I glanced at him. He was being quiet. Extra quiet. I'd tried to chat with him, even poked a few jabs at him, but had gotten nothing. Not a sharp response, not a laugh, not even a smile.

"Everything okay?" A minor in psychology and that was the best I could manage. Pathetic.

"It's fine."

"You don't seem fine."

He glanced back at me. "*You* seem fine."

"What's your point?"

"With *Paulo.*" He sneered the name.

Oh. I swallowed the remaining bit of peppermint in my mouth. "When did you find out?"

"Nicole got out late last night. Mr. B told me to go pick her up. I guess she didn't get the message. I pulled up and saw them together."

I didn't know what to say. My first emotion was relief at finally having someone to talk about it with, to confide in. Except, Dante seemed *pissed.* At me? At Nicole? At both of us? I couldn't tell. I studied him, picking up on the tight grip of his hands on the wheel, the hunch of his back.

"So you're just gonna cover for her? That's your job now?" His voice was cold, almost mean—a tone I'd never heard him use.

I looked out the window, his words more accurate than he realized. My job *was* to cover up the affair—and that job was the only thing keeping me fed, keeping my cell phone on, keeping my health insurance active. He was loyal to Clarke … but necessity, right now, was keeping me loyal to my bank account.

I raised my voice to talk over the hail. "It's not my business. I stay out of it. She wants to have an affair, whatever." My words came out airy, showing nothing of the way it bothered me. And it *did* bother me. I had a pit in my stomach half the time I was on set. I worried whenever she disappeared. I felt guilty whenever I thought of Clarke. I wasn't heartless. I just had to act it, for long enough to get on my feet.

Then again, most downward spirals probably started that way. Small moral adjustments made and justified by income needs. Maybe that was how my parents' crimes had started. I sucked in a deep breath, startled by the thought.

It was a lot easier to be judgmental and morally sound, back when I didn't have to worry about money.

40. Codeword: SugarTits

I sat cross-legged on my couch, a bowl of cereal in my lap, and flipped through channels. My cell rang and I glanced at it, Vic's name on the display. I wavered, a second of indecision before I picked up the damn thing and answered it.

"Hello?"

His voice whipped in and out, bursts of static hitting the receiver. "Hey babe."

"Hey Vic." I gave a convincingly aggravated sigh and then mentally high-fived myself.

"You dating movie stars now?" Ah. There was the reason for his call. Jealousy had always been Vic's weakness, possessiveness his calling card.

I looked at my half-eaten bowl of Lucky Charms. "Seriously? I don't have time to talk about this."

"Joey Plazen is a piece of shit, Chloe. He's stuck his dick in half of LA."

There were so many immature comments I could make in response to that but I shut my mouth and managed, for once, to not sound like the jilted ex. "Shocker. You don't like him. I do."

I hung up quickly, before he could say something that stung. My chances of dating Joey were slimmer than Nicole Ritchie, but the chances of falling back into Vic? *That* was a real danger. I shouldn't have answered the phone, shouldn't have fanned his fire. I stared at the phone and wondered if he'd call back, then scooped out a handful of Lucky Charm marshmallows. I shouldn't have egged him on, especially since Joey's photos with the girl from Mixing had already hit the Internet, his quest to distract the press through sex completed. Using Joey to make Vic jealous was a lost cause.

I had a moment of weakness and pulled up Vic's Instagram, scrolling through his recent posts, all from Dubai where forty-six minutes ago he'd posted a pic of some brunette lying back on a bar with champagne in her belly button, hashtag *cheers*. I threw my phone back down and flipped channels for another twenty minutes. Called Benta, who sent me to voicemail. Called Cammie, who answered, mid-movie. I whispered an apology, then scrolled through numbers, my list of friends significantly reduced after graduation.

I stopped on Joey Plazen's name and considered it. Moved on. Made it all the way through the alphabet and back. Then, his sexual sacrifice still fresh on my mind, I texted him.

hey

It took him five minutes to respond—*hey*

what r u doing?

—bored?

YES

—I'm on a date. Want to join us?

WHY did you respond if you're on a date?! I inserted an angry face emoticon.

—shut up and come out with us. No paps in sight.

OK

The polite thing to do would have been to leave Joey and his date alone. My boredom, though, trumped social etiquette. Joey sent me the name of the pub and I threw a leather jacket on over my top, traded my Toms for heels, then grabbed my keys and headed out the door.

My spirits had almost lifted, my steps light, my push on the elevator button cheerful. The doors opened, and Carter stood there, our heads lifting and eyes meeting in awkward and perfect unison.

Almost three weeks since we'd hooked up. Two weeks since I resolved to forget that mistake and return to the world of Successful Men. That plan took a nosedive the moment Carter opened his gorgeous mouth. "Hey." He smiled and I was done for, my girl parts beginning to pant inside my La Perla panties.

"Hey."

"Going down?" His grin widened, and I laughed.

"Yeah." I stepped on, my eyes lingering over his dark jeans and worn black V-neck. "Where are you heading?"

"Grabbing something to eat." He leaned against the side of the elevator and crossed his arms. "You?"

"Just meeting up with some friends." I fiddled nervously with my phone. "They're at an oyster bar a few blocks over. If you want, you can join us." I shrugged, like I didn't care either way.

He scratched the back of his head. "I don't want to interrupt a girls' night or anything…"

I had to laugh at that, the elevator doors opening. "No. *Please.* You'll save me from being an awkward third wheel. I was bored, my friend Joey is out on a date, and now I'm about to crash it." I stepped off the elevator. "You'd be doing me a favor," I added.

He opened the door for me. "If you're sure. Is it Kumamoto?"

I nodded. "Yeah, you know it?"

"Yep." He steered me right and pointed ahead. "This way."

I followed his lead, stepping over the curb and crossing a side street. While we moved, I pulled out my phone and texted Joey.

I'm bringing someone. Behave.

—ooh, fun. Is she hot?

I rolled my eyes. *Yes, he's super hot.*

—I only misbehave with women.

I stuck my phone in my back pocket and smiled over at Carter. "Just wanted to give them the heads up."

"So we're good?"

I didn't know if "good" could ever describe this situation, but it was the only adjective I had. "Yeah. We're good." I stepped over a crack, and he moved closer, offering his arm. "Don't let me forget," I said. "I have your spare key."

He looked down. "You ever find your set?"

"No. But I had a copy made of yours, so I'm good." I smiled up at him. "I'll hide it so I don't have to bother you next time."

"I didn't exactly mind."

I blushed, glancing down at my heels. "I should warn you about Joey, my friend we're meeting." I rushed into the subject change before it went from slightly awkward to full-out weird. "He's an actor. Joey Plazen. That's … that's who he is. My friend." I looked up at him nervously, not sure of his reaction. I shouldn't have mentioned it in advance, should have just casually introduced them like Joey wasn't the Movie Star of the Century.

"Joey Plazen?" His steps slowed. "That's who we're meeting?"

"Yeah. We work together."

He shrugged. Chuckled a little and kept walking. "Okay."

I let go of his arm when we got to the place. "Joey says they're on the back deck," I murmured to him as we moved through the crowd, which seemed thick for a weekday. I understood why when we got to the deck's entrance, two security guards blocking the door. "Deck's closed," one said curtly.

I glanced down at Joey's text and inwardly groaned. *The password is Sugartits.* I rolled my eyes and held up the screen, showing it to the guard.

We were waved through, and wove around and through empty tables, spying Joey before he saw us, his hand on a redhead's ass, his mouth at her ear and I coughed loudly as we approached. He turned, raising a beer. "Chloe!" he cheered, stepping forward and hugging me. When he turned to Carter, his hand froze, his face tightening, first in recognition, then in anger. "Carter." He dropped his hand. "You fucking prick."

My introduction to the redhead stopped, my head turning, and I stared at Joey, then at Carter, in shock.

41. Phi Iota 4 Life

My eyes darted from Joey to Carter, whose mouth was a tight, straight line. A tight line that broke into a wide grin, and he held out his arms, walking into Joey's chest and clapping him on the back. Joey shoved him off with a scoff.

"Get off me, man. You move back to New York and drop off the grid. Can't return a phone call for shit."

"I had stuff to deal with. You had Hollywood."

"Wait," I interrupted their reunion. "*How* do you guys know each other?"

Carter slid a hand around my waist, his fingers sliding under the bottom hem of my sweater, each digit a sly reach further into my heart, and he pulled me against him. "Fraternity brothers, believe it or not."

"Phi Iota for life," Joey mocked, reaching out and slapping palms with Carter.

I watched the exchange, more confused than before. First off, I didn't even know Carter had *gone* to college. Second, what were the chances that, in this huge city, they knew each other? "Why didn't you tell me you knew Joey?" I turned to Carter with an accusatory stare.

The corner of his mouth crooked up and he leaned forward, putting his lips against my ear. "You mean … in our many conversations?" he murmured.

"Talking about me?" Joey drawled and I rolled my eyes.

"It's not all about you," I snapped, taking a beer from the counter and taking a sip.

"So … you two know each other." Joey's gaze dropped to Carter's arm around me, then back to my face. His eyes held mischief and he practically beamed at me, the way I looked at Chanel when she performed a new trick. I shifted uncomfortably.

"Yep." Carter drawled, his fingers running along my skin. "You okay with that, Plazen?"

A waitress appeared with a tray full of beers and Joey snagged two, holding them out to us. "Hey, I'm *all* about that. Though Chloe, you should know you can do better than this loser."

Carter didn't seem insulted, taking the beer with a laugh and I took mine and latched onto Joey's girl, effectively ending the awkward group conversation about Carter and me. The girl turned out to be really nice, and we perched at a table next to the guys, our conversations each taking their own directions, lines occasionally floating from table to table as the night passed. It was nice, seeing Joey with Carter. It was the first time I'd seen Joey relax with someone, and the most I'd seen of Carter outside of the bedroom. I sat back in my chair and drank in the opportunity to watch him, the way his dimple appeared when he laughed, the run of his hand through his hair, the way his mouth held the edge of the beer, the way his eyes would darken, just a hint, when he glanced at me. By the time we stood and said our goodbyes, I wanted him so badly it hurt.

When we left the restaurant, the streets were in fog, the city quiet.

"This is my favorite time in New York." I tilted back my head and looked at the sky, the moon illuminated the clouds, just a sliver of it all seen through the frame of skyscrapers.

"August?" He reached out, taking ahold of my hand, his fingers linking loosely through mine.

"No." I smiled. "This time of night. Anywhere else in the country, everyone would be asleep. And a lot of New Yorkers are." I gestured to the closed storefronts we passed, the dark apartment windows. "There's this hush over everything, but there's still the energy…" I tried to think of how to describe it, my words failing me.

"I know." He smiled. "It's like a secret world, hidden in the city. The night owls."

I glanced at him. "Yeah. I like that. A secret city of night owls."

He pulled gently on my hand and I stopped next to him, his head turning up to the sky next to me. "Hear it?"

I closed my eyes and tilted my face up, turning into all of the sounds that my city ears tuned out. The muted beat of someone's bass. The splash of a puddle as a taxi drove by. The rumble of the subway underneath our feet. The soft music of an open window, a dozen stories up. Somewhere, a dog barked. "Yeah."

"You know, you're different than I expected."

I stopped listening to the sounds of the city and turned to him, our hands still linked. "In what way?"

"I don't know." He looked away, back up at the sky. "I'm still figuring that out."

"Good luck." I let out a soft laugh. "I'm still figuring that out too."

That couldn't have made sense to him, it didn't make much sense to me, but he said nothing, just stepped forward, toward our building. I followed, us moving quietly through the fog, my face damp by the time we took the steps to our building.

The elevator stopped and I was surprised when he held open the door of the elevator and didn't get off on my floor.

"I had a great time tonight." He leaned against the elevator door, keeping it open.

"Me too. Thanks for coming."

"Thanks for inviting me." Great. We had manners down pat.

"Have a good night." He reached forward and pulled gently at my jeans. Dragged me close enough for one short kiss. Way too short of a kiss. I almost frowned when it ended but saved face, flashing him a parting smile and turning away. I walked toward my door and said a silent curse when I heard the elevator door close.

Damn the man. When I wanted him, he left me hanging. When I didn't want him, he wormed his way into my thoughts and stayed there. I stepped into my apartment and shut the door. I never remembered to bitch at him about his three weeks of silence after our hookup. I'd had plans, concocted during our walk to the bar, to politely tell him off. Let him know that three weeks of silence after going down on a girl could give her a complex. It wasn't *too* late. I could still go up and put him in his place. Straighten him out.

I sat on the couch and pulled my shoes off, pushing aside any excuses to go upstairs. One side effect of starting to find myself? I could decipher my own bullshit.

42. My Party Planning Skills Suck

ChloeMadisonNYU
129 likes
ChloeMadisonNYU All the best bitches.
Waiting on the birthday girl. #ChanelBrantley
#birthday #rufflife

New York City loved its parties. And the rich of the city loved to throw them, each soiree an excuse to flaunt their wealth while exhausting their staff. As an NYU student, I was all for a good party. As Nicole Brantley's personal bitch, I was learning to hate them. Chanel's birthday, I thought I'd be able to manage, had actually gotten excited by the thought, envisioning a party so perfectly executed that puppy attendees would leave with their minds permanently blown.

I forgot this was upper crust New York.

I forgot this was Nicole Brantley.

I forgot that I had absolutely no party experience in anything other than looking hot and slinging back expensive champagne.

But this was Chanel's birthday party, and I had confidence on my side. So surely it would be *fabulous.* It had to. All the best bitches would be there. No, literally. The Best Bitches. We're talking top-notch AKC pedigree.

I fell down the rabbit hole, into the world of canine couture and pup-arazzi and tenderloin-topped cakes. I spent two hours on the phone with a bitchy assistant, trying to get Triumph the Insult Comic Dog (he's a PUPPET in case you weren't aware) to give me a firm RSVP. I sweated over an Anthony Rubio original for Chanel that arrived two sizes too big and two days late. And Nicole wasn't helping.

"You know this is her big day," Nicole said to me impatiently, as if I wasn't putting Chanel's interests first. "Did the Shankmans confirm? They have a Labradoodle that Chanel really got along well with. She'll be crushed if he doesn't attend."

I looked up from my laptop and over at Chanel, who was licking her crotch with some serious focus, and tried to find a response that didn't involve me tossing my laptop aside and screaming at the top of my lungs.

Now, with the party over, I'd come to grips with reality. I was not going to be the poster mother that I always planned on being. You know the type, moms who carried everything anyone needed, all fitting neatly in a designer purse. The ones who hosted sleepover parties with fifteen kids and whipped up a beautiful meal for unexpected guests without missing a beat. No, my future seemed more along the lines of throwing a TV dinner in the general direction of my kids before sulking off to my bedroom with a remote and Nutella for some "quiet time."

The first party disaster came with our celebrity guest: Mavero.

Mavero, the Australian terrier who appeared in all of the *Dog Whisperer* movies. Mavero, who performed in Kanye's latest music video. Mavero, who Nicole saw on a morning show and decided *must* attend. Mavero, who charged eight thousand dollars for a public appearance. I mean, WTF? Eight *thousand* dollars for a dog's two-hour appearance? His ridiculous fee aside, I also had to fax over proof of liability coverage. *FAX*. It took me fifteen minutes to figure out how to use the fax machine.

Mavero, it turned out, was an asshole.

First, he peed on Chanel's custom doghouse. Lifted his leg up right during Nicole's lengthy introduction of him and pissed all over the brownstone, designed to be a mini-replica of the Brantleys'. Nicole's face went ashen; I went for Mavero's contract. Turned out he was allowed to piss on anything he pleased.

Then, he bit the photographer. That got him put in his cage where he barked at the top of his doggie lungs until Nicole finally broke down and had his handler take him away. Nicole was *still* dismayed that Mavero didn't get to stay and watch Chanel open her presents.

At the end of the party, Nicole stomped into my office and read me a long list of complaints. The fact that I didn't roll my eyes once during her rant was a testament to my self-control.

She finally stopped, leaving in a blur of shimmer and highlights, my eyes glancing at the clock. Eleven PM. Just enough time to get to SoHo before it got too late. Benta's company was having a party of their own, one that wouldn't involve slobber and leg humping. At least, not from any dogs, though I couldn't promise anything from the men who would be there. The matchmaking industry was a frisky one.

I grabbed my purse and keys, kissed an exhausted Chanel, and turned out the lights, slowly trudging down the stairs, my desire to escape not enough to counteract weak calves and blistered heels. If I ever won the lottery, my mansion would be one story or have one hell of an elevator system. Nicole had turned off their elevator for reasons of pure insanity, something about claustrophobia and maintenance costs. The woman dropped a small mortgage on her bottled water delivery but choked on things like valet fees.

I rounded the second floor landing and saw the front door open, Nicole standing in the doorway, her back to me, her voice quiet as she spoke to whomever stood before her. Something made me pause, one foot a step higher than the other, and I leaned on the bannister and tried to see more.

It was *Paulo*, his stance hard and unmoving, Nicole's soft murmurs of the soothing variety. I watched as she reached out and stroked his face. This was *bad*; he shouldn't be here, not when Clarke was home. Nicole was getting reckless. Though, from the glimpse I got of Paulo's face, maybe he was the one getting reckless.

I didn't hear the footsteps behind me, but I knew that smell, a mix of leather and spice, when it floated by me. He paused next to me on the step, a worried look on his face when he spoke my name.

"Chloe? Chloe, are you okay?"

I tried to move, tried to think, tried to do something, but I could only watch as Clarke's gaze moved past me and down to the front door.

"Nicole?" he called, his steps easy and fluid as he jogged closer to his wife.

I watched Nicole's hand push at Paulo's chest, but it was too late.

43. Loving Him With Lies

I stood in place on the stairs and watched Clarke step toward Nicole and Paulo. Nicole swallowed, and I saw the moment when she decided to lie. I'd said it before and I'd say it again: Nicole could act. And she was about to pull off an Oscar-worthy performance.

"Clarke, thank God. A voice of reason." I watched her claws reach out, wrapping around Clarke's arm and pulling him closer, as if she wanted him there. "Paulo wants to pay for Chanel's doghouse. Since he hooked us up with Mavero."

"It's late." There was a layer of suspicion in Clarke's voice, and I mentally cheered him on from my frozen spot on the stairs. Surely he wouldn't buy that crap. Surely he would see what was really going on.

"Oh God, don't be such a New Yorker." She slapped a casual hand on his chest. "It's, like, seven on the West Coast."

"This isn't the West Coast." I'd never heard that tone in Clarke's voice before. It was still and dark, with a sharp edge. I silently moved down a few steps, closer to the train wreck that was finally unfolding, my heart beating faster. This was finally it.

"Clarke," Nicole said dismissively, the words *shut up* clearly in the name.

"You should leave." Clarke gripped the door's edge and, from my perch, I saw the white clench of his knuckles as he spoke to Paulo.

"It's so kind of you to offer to pay for the doghouse," Nicole blabbed on, her voice bright.

Clarke said nothing.

Paulo said nothing.

I stared at the action and wished I had popcorn.

"Chloe." Nicole's voice pierced through the room and I blinked, suddenly aware that I just stood there, like a creepy ogler on the subway.

"Yes?"

"Go home."

I nodded quickly, galloping down the remaining steps, my eyes down, my squeeze through the front door done without anyone shifting to give me room.

Someone shut the door behind me, the heavy wood slamming into place and snuffing out any sound, my eavesdrop dying a quick death in the cool night air.

It took a moment for me to move, stepping down the sidewalk to the next cross street, my arm raising out of habit and flagging a cab. I needed, wanted, to go home. Forget the party Benta was throwing that night. I wanted my bed.

An affair was a dirty virus, taking in innocents as it spread and grew. I could feel it diving under my skin, my corruptibility growing simply out of proxy. Maybe this was the end. Maybe, come tomorrow, I would walk into a different household.

44. Does Sex Solve Everything?

The next day, I carefully opened the door, pausing for a moment and listening for sounds of carnage, looked for splatters of blood, crime scene tape, or dead bodies. I saw nothing and eased inside. Whispered my hellos to the Brantley staff and trotted upstairs to my office as quietly as I could in my super-cute new sandals. I shut the door and didn't hear a peep from anyone until Chanel scratched on the door around nine.

Any concerns I had over Nicole and Clarke's marital woes were addressed an hour later, when—from the ceiling of my office—a loud thumping started. I stopped typing the letter to Mavero's management, demanding a full refund of his performance fee, and listened. Chanel let out a low growl and I picked her up, moving to the door and sticking my head out, on high alert.

Then, Nicole shrieked. Loud and long enough for me to instantly understand what was causing the thumping. Her hyena call was followed by a scream of Clarke's name, and I closed my eyes in thanks. If I had to listen to my boss have sex, at least it was with her husband, one indignity I could handle. I ducked back into my office, pulling the door shut and put on Spotify, blaring Gwen Stefani loud enough to drown out any more sounds of sex. My door swung open forty-five minutes later, a perfectly put together Nicole glaring at me from the doorway. I paused the music. "Good morning," I said.

"I'm shooting in Brooklyn today."

"Yes." I lifted her set bag that, sometime around her fourth orgasm, I packed with her snacks, clothes and makeup. "Dante is out front."

"Make sure everything I'll need for today is in there; I don't need you to hang around with me today." She pointed at the bag with one long finger, as if I might get confused.

"Okay." I nodded and noticed the humongous diamond still on her ring finger. Between the orgasms and her ring, it appeared to be business as normal for the Brantley marriage. Maybe she was done with Paulo. Or maybe she lied it all away and Clarke bought it. Or maybe I needed to stop speculating and get my butt moving. I stood. "I'm ready whenever you are."

Ten minutes later, I slid into the backseat and pulled out my phone, checking my texts as Dante headed to Brooklyn. One from Joey, two from the sound production girl, one from wardrobe. Nothing from Carter. Almost a week since our quasi-double-date with Joey. The double date where he'd left me panting for more with barely a goodnight kiss.

My fingers itched to text him. But weren't men supposed to pursue? Vic certainly never needed chasing. And I was the one who invited Carter out. I was the one who knocked on his door in the middle of the night when I got locked out. I was the one who'd done ALL of the pursuing. If the damn man was interested, he needed to make a freakin' effort. Was it possible … *cue Justin Long* that he was just not that into me? I sat on my hands to keep them from misbehaving and looked out the window, Dante slowing as we approached the temporary set.

When he pulled over, I hopped out, grabbing the set bag and running around to help Nicole. I rounded the back end of the car and saw the couple, running across the road in between moving traffic, their hands linked. My feet froze in place, Nicole huffing out an irritated sigh as she snatched the bag away. I stuttered out an apology, pulling my gaze away from the couple and busied myself getting Nicole on her way inside.

When I looked back, my hand on the car handle, they were gone.

45. The Myth of Sex Without Feelings

ChloeMadisonNYU
68 likes
ChloeMadisonNYU Seriously, I'm so sick of people right now. #citylife #overit

"Why didn't you tell me Carter had a girlfriend?" I flung open the door to Joey's trailer and glared, my hands braced on the open doorframe. Next time I rushed across town to confront someone; I was going to pack flats. I pushed that thought aside and was stuck with the mental image that had been playing on repeat: Carter and a brunette, running hand in hand across the street like they were on a freakin' Hallmark card.

Joey glanced up from the sofa, a half-eaten donut in hand, mouth full. Setting it on a napkin, he reclined against the leather and wiped at his mouth. "Hi, Chloe. It's great to see you too."

"Uh … do you guys need privacy?" Hannah piped from the recliner, her feet tucked under her butt, a clipboard on her lap.

"I hope so." Joey smirked.

"No," I barked, pulling the door shut and stepping closer, my hands settling on my hips, my feet burning. "Well?"

Joey finished off the donut, taking his time, my fingers itching to yank open his mouth and pull out a response. "Carter doesn't have a girlfriend," he finally said, sucking the end of a powder-coated finger.

"I'm gonna head out," Hannah interjected with a loud whisper, her exit barely noticed in my irritation.

"Stop covering for him. I *saw* them. The brunette with the long legs? Giant boobs?"

"Oh," he grinned. "You mean Brit." He laughed. "God, Chloe, you should see your face right now."

I wondered, in that moment, if I could kill the movie's lead and not get kicked off set. If Hannah would help me hide his beautiful body or if she'd turn me in. I wasn't paranoid. In their cross of that street, I'd had seen the grin on her face, the way their fingers were linked, the affectionate pull of her hand. Not that I had a claim on Carter but WTF. "Who's Brit?" I gritted out the name.

"Brit. She's … ah…" He grinned at me in the naughty way that made moviegoers everywhere swoon. "She's a fuckbuddy."

"A fuckbuddy." I repeated the crass term, not sure how I felt about it. Should I be happy that it wasn't a real relationship? Then again … I frowned. Was I just two or three nights away from being a fuckbuddy myself?

"You look stressed," Joey remarked, reaching forward and grabbing another donut from the bag. "I can see your wrinkles from here."

"Bite me." I stumbled right and collapsed into the recliner that

Hannah had so conveniently vacated.

"You like him, huh?" He passed me the bag of donuts, and I took one, careful not to get powdered sugar all over myself.

"I don't know," I grumbled, picking one. "Where'd you get these?"

"Hannah."

"I need a Hannah." I sighed, sinking deeper into the chair, and he laughed.

There was a long pause while we chewed, and I took a sip of coffee from his offered cup. "Don't worry about Brit," Joey said, glancing over at me. "They're just friends."

Friends … *who have sex.* The words hung in my mind even if they didn't leave his lips. Men didn't understand. They thought there could be sex without emotion but that didn't work. You couldn't get along, enjoy each other's company, *and* have smoking hot sex without someone's feelings getting involved. At least I couldn't.

"Besides," he drawled, leaning forward and patting my leg. "She's got nothing on you."

Oh yeah. What man liked giant breasts and a supermodel smile? I was dusting powdered sugar off my shirt, a smartass response on the tip of my tongue, when the trailer door opened, and the last person I expected to see stepped in.

And I'd thought my day was bad before.

46. The Worst Time to See Your Ex

There were times when you wanted to see an ex. When you were looking fabulous and hanging on the arm of a billionaire. When you were out with your girls and having the time of your single life.

You didn't want to see him in Joey Plazen's trailer with powdered sugar smeared on your skirt, your ego recently trampled by a *maintenance* guy. I jerked to my feet, a chunk of donut dropping to Joey's floor. "Vic?"

He stood in the doorway of the trailer, the sun streaming in behind him in a halo effect. The man always did know how to make an entrance. He stepped inside and closed the door, Joey moving forward, his hand outstretched. "Mr. Worth. I wasn't expecting you until this afternoon."

Mr. Worth? I grimaced and crossed my arms.

"Plans changed," Vic said smoothly, shaking Joey's hand, his Rolex glinting from under the sleeve of his suit. *I* gave him that watch, back when I spent weekends with Daddy's AmEx in my wallet and eight inches of Vic in my hand. He'd never wore the watch much then; go figure he'd wear it now. "They're giving me a tour in twenty minutes, then we're going over the budgets. I wasn't sure if I'd have another chance to come by. Sorry if I interrupted anything." He turned to me and smiled. "Hey beautiful." He stepped forward, his hands outstretched as if he was going to hug me, and I stopped that shit right there—moving away, my hand held up.

"What are you doing here?" I sounded accusatory and bitchy, and Joey stiffened, but I didn't care how it came out because this was *my* world and *Mr.* Worth didn't have a place in it. He didn't belong here, in Joey's trailer, his arms reaching for me.

"Mr. Worth is our newest investor," Joey supplied, stepping forward with a smile, his glare sending a dozen messages, the main ones: *be nice* and *this guy is important.*

"The newest investor?" I repeated slowly. "On *Boston Love Letters*?"

"Joey, could we have a minute?" Vic asked smoothly, moving aside to clear the exit.

"Absolutely, Mr. Worth," Joey said, and I swore on my life, if he kept calling Vic that, I'd chop off his balls myself. The trailer door opened, then shut, the trailer infinitely smaller even though there was one less person.

"Chloe," Vic said softly, and I knew, right then, in that one word, I was in trouble.

That'd always been the problem with us. I just couldn't resist the man.

47. The Hardest Kind of Drug

I was not a strong woman. I was weak, and still, over a year after our parting, deeply in love with this man. This man who was not good for me. This man who had a hundred faithful and dedicated bones in his body, but four or five wildly promiscuous ones, bones that jumped out of order occasionally and had their fun. Bones that shattered promises, ruined happily-ever-afters, and broke apart soulmates.

The sound of my name on his lips … it was a drug. A narcotic high heightened by Joey Plazen shutting the trailer door and leaving the two of us alone in this small, dim space. Vic stepped closer, and a light hint of his cologne flooded me with a hundred memories. For a thousand mornings, noons, and nights, this man was my future. I had picked out apartments, post-graduation plans and browsed engagement rings, all with his hand in mine. And despite his lies and my broken heart, hearing him whisper my name was all it took. I crumbled.

"Don't, Vic." The words were a plea, my feet stepping back and hitting the wall, his eyes darkening as he stepped forward, his hand reaching out, brushing up my bare arm before his palm settled on the wall by my head. A breath eased out of me as I closed my eyes and pressed against the wall, feeling the familiar warmth of him, the press of his body as his legs brushed across mine. I waited for the touch of his lips even as I stiffened, searching for a word, a protest, something to keep from falling. And through it all, my skin yearned, inches of exposure pulled between desire and distrust, the rough slide of his sigh letting me know exactly how close his mouth was to mine.

"Chloe." There was such torture in his voice, such unexpected pain, that I opened my eyes. I could see his whole face, the tight line of his jaw, the piercing stare that had pinned me from the first moment we'd met. "Chloe," he repeated, so soft it was almost air.

"Yes?" I should have said something else. *Vic, get off me. Vic, you're an ass. Vic, I watched you fuck her and our future, all in that minute in time.*

"I need you to want this."

I wanted it. I wanted it so badly that I was already wet. I wanted it so badly that my fingers twitched against my side, wanting to reach forward and grip his suit. I wanted it so badly that I looked at him and said nothing. Prayed he would turn and walk away because I wasn't strong enough to just say no. I closed my eyes, knowing he'd see desire in them. "Please, Vic. Don't." It was the best I could do, the best my weak voice could manage. And still … it sounded sexual. A plea for more instead of for less. *Please, Vic. Don't. Don't stop. Don't ever stop chasing me.*

My skin jumped when the soft skin of his lips trailed down the side of my neck, a light skim of pressure, hot breath floating out between his lips, his journey occasionally punctuated by a kiss. Then, he moved from my mouth and to the place that always weakened my resolve, a hand settling on my hip as he pushed a gentle kiss on my forehead.

"I need you to want this," he whispered through the kiss, his hips against me, showing me exactly how much he wanted it.

And that was the other problem. He didn't need me to just want hot passionate trailer-shaking sex. He needed me to want forever, too.

I lifted my fingers, running them up his arms, across his broad shoulders, and dug my hands into hair I had missed. His eyes met mine for one last moment of hesitation, and then his mouth crashed down onto mine. And there, in that frantic collision of tongues, I found my Vic. A man who took the lead, his fingers greedy as they ran down my body and up my legs, pushing my skirt up, my ears registering the sound of his belt as he yanked at its buckle.

"Wait," I gasped out the word in between kisses. "We can't, not here." It was a waste of words. This was the man who finger-banged me in a crowded theater, then threw enough cash at the manager to have the auditorium cleared so he could do a better job with his cock. This was the man who bent me over the kitchen sink at his parents' house during Thanksgiving dinner, the faint sounds of conversation floating down the hall as his hand covered my mouth and his hips pounded against my ass.

"Are you kidding? Joey Plazen would get down on his knees and suck me off right now if I told him to." He gritted out the words as he yanked down my panties, his mouth greedy on my neck when I turned my mouth away from him. "No one's coming in."

My response died when he got past my panties, his fingers pushed inside causing my knees to buckle. Two years of sexual history had taught the man exactly how, when, and where to touch me. In the last months of our relationship, that had felt like a problem. Too formulaic. But now? When his other hand got his belt loose and his pants unzipped? It didn't feel like a problem. It felt like Pompeii: no point in running, no point in fighting. I slid my hand under his jacket and gripped his shirt, spreading my feet slightly and tilting my pelvis, his mouth lifting off my neck, his eyes hard on me as he pulled his fingers out and pushed the full length of himself inside.

I cried out his name on the first thrust. Let him lift up one of my legs and wrap it around him on the twentieth. Ripped an expensive button on his shirt off when I came. Sank in his arms when he followed suit. He lifted me, our bodies still connected, and laid me down on Joey's couch. Pulled up my panties as he kissed my thighs, then my stomach, then my neck.

I didn't look at him. I couldn't. I couldn't bear to see myself reflected in those eyes. I curled onto my side, and wanted to take it back. I closed my eyes, my cheeks against the cool leather of Joey's couch, and prayed he would just leave.

Then, when he did, the door quietly shutting behind him, I wanted him back.

Life might be a bitch, but love? She kicked that bitch's ass.

"So when did you start banging the finance guy?" Joey's voice boomed out, and I rolled over on his couch and lifted my head, meeting his eyes, ones that twinkled in amusement. "He's not the finance guy. He's my ex." I said tartly, sitting up and pulling down my skirt, my panties still damp when I crossed my legs. Thank God I was on birth control. One thing that hadn't changed about Vic—he always did like to leave his mark. *Vic*. Oh my God. I closed my eyes in shame.

"Your ex is also the movie's newest investor," Joey remarked, leaning against the same wall where I had lost my common sense.

"Of course he is," I responded dully. "Was that the reason for your fawn session?" I smirked.

Joey raised his eyebrows at me, and I shut my mouth. It really wasn't the time for me to be throwing jabs. "I must say," he remarked, a grin taking over his handsome face, "you've got a hot fuck-me voice."

"A what?" I glared at him.

"You know … the moans, the screams, the way you called his name?" He winked. "It was hot."

I groaned, pushing to my feet. "Please tell me you're joking." I wasn't that loud. I *couldn't* have been that loud.

"Don't worry. Nobody else heard." He moved off the wall, scooping my purse off the floor and passing it to me.

I thought of the calls from Vic over the weekend. "When did he sign on to invest?"

"Friday. Twenty-five mill." He raised his eyebrows. "First, he drilled me over whether we were dating." He smirked. "Your ex must have some liquidity, Chloe. Investing in the movie just to keep tabs on you."

"My ex's *dad* has liquidity. Vic just has … access." When I had dated him, he hadn't yet turned twenty-five. But now, he had full access to his trust. The Vic I'd dated had thrown cash around like confetti. I couldn't even imagine a Vic with the coffers opened wide. This investment was probably interest on his bank balance. I stepped toward the door. "Sorry about the whole..." I waved my hand in the generic direction of our activity, not sure how to put it into appropriate words.

"This trailer has seen worse." He laughed, then grew serious. "Chloe, I really need this movie to work. We need his money to make it work. Nicole needs it too."

I laughed. "Nicole is the last person I care about, Joey."

"What about me?" he asked. "Do you care about me?"

"We've been friends for a month, Joey," I shot back. "I dated that asshole for two years. Do you know what he—"

"Oh please, Chloe," he cut me off. "There's obviously something between you two or you wouldn't have been howling his name within five minutes of me leaving."

I bit my lip and looked toward the door.

"Just ... please." His voice dropped. "Don't do anything to piss him off."

My hand was heavy when I pushed on the trailer door, my exit done without a response. I didn't know what to say, a hundred different emotions coming as I wove around cameras, stepped over cords, and slunk through the shadows of trailers. I climbed the steps to Nicole's trailer and said a silent prayer of thanks that she was shooting in Brooklyn. At least I'd have a place of privacy, a moment to recover.

I opened the door to her trailer and stepped inside, my eyes hitting the giant vase of flowers, a mountain of roses and orchids. My hand grabbed the card before my brain had a chance to stop it.

> *It'll always be us, Chloe. Our souls are connected for eternity.*
>
> *I love you.*

I sank onto the floor, leaning against the door, the card dropping from my hands, and cried. Wondered, through the tears, how early in the day Vic had ordered the arrangement. Wondered if he had known, placing the order, that I was going to let him touch me, let him inside of me.

Of course he had.

He was Vic. I was Chloe. It was done.

September

Confession of the guilty party brings a certain amount of trust to a situation. Being caught doesn't have the same effect. If Vic had come to me during our relationship, and told me that he had slept with his maid—I would have forgiven him, believed his regrets and trusted him not to do it again. It was the *deception* that killed me, that had carried me through so many weak moments. The affair had *only* stopped because I had caught him, and forced his hand. If he had stopped it on his own, un-coerced, and been honest … that would have made all the difference.

We would have never broken up. And I wouldn't be here, working for *her*, and struggling with this guilt.

I could tell Clarke. I could mail him a letter spelling out his wife's deceit.

Instead I watched, hoping that Nicole would do the right thing. And I prayed that when he did find out, that I wouldn't be there to see the moment. I couldn't stand the thought of looking into his face and seeing that pain.

48. Hunting Hotties

ChloeMadisonNYU
48 likes
ChloeMadisonNYU Makeup trailer. I think I'll just live here. #BLLmovie #glam #MAC

"This is stupid." That encouraging comment came from Benta, who was using her iPhone's camera as a mirror to apply mascara.

"It's not stupid. It's smart. If Carter's there, he'll see Chloe looking smoking hot." Cammie winked and handed me a lipstick. "If he's not, no harm no foul. Just another night out." Cammie reached over to rub Dante's arm. He nodded noncommittally.

"Dante?" I pressed from my spot behind him. "Is this stupid or smart?"

His eyes met mine in the rearview mirror. "His friend owns the place?"

"Yeah. I saw him headed that direction, dressed like he was going out." I repeated the same facts we'd already dissected ten times.

He shrugged. "Fifty-fifty chance he's there."

I sighed. "I know the odds. I want to know if I'm going to look pathetic showing up there."

He laughed. "Right now? Yes, you look pathetic. But he's not going to know all this underhanded plotting you guys got going on. He's only going to see you there, partying. He won't figure it out."

"Puh-lease." Benta had moved on to lip-gloss. "He'll figure it out."

"No," Dante said, stronger. "He won't. We don't think like you do. He will see you, want to fuck you, and that will be the end of that."

"Well that's just stupid," Benta grumbled, tossing her phone and her gloss into her bag.

"Men are stupid." Dante laughed, running his hand up Cammie's thigh as he made a right turn. "We focus on sex, food, and how to have more sex. That's all we are about."

"And love," Cammie said pointedly.

I drowned out whatever sappy response he gave, rolling down the window and tossing out my gum. Love was what got me into trouble in the first place. Love should be less stubborn. It should listen to red flags and reason. It should learn from past mistakes and guard itself from future ones.

I loved Vic. I thought I would always love Vic. But I *couldn't* be with him. Pure and simple, no matter what my libido said—I couldn't do it. It was stupid of me to fall into his traps, to let him buy his way into *BLL*, into my daily life, in hopes that he could win me back. Despite what happened last week, I was not winnable. I would not come back. I was single and happy, and tonight, I was moving on. Hopefully with ridiculously hot superintendent sex. Now that was four words I never expected to say.

The prior night, I'd stood at Carter's door like a total stalker and put my ear against it, listening for a hint as to what was going on inside. Silence. That was what was inside. I almost knocked. I was horny and trying to ignore thoughts of Vic and wanted something, anything. Even if it was just someone to talk to. But I didn't knock. I stood there for a full ten minutes debating, then I returned to my apartment. Pulled open my top drawer and reached for my vibrator. Wasted forty-five minutes on something Carter could have knocked out in five.

I didn't want another vibrator night.

Hopefully Dante was right, and boys were naïve, and if we did see Carter, it would seem random and fated—not like the devious plan of three girls and a lot of tequila shots.

Benta pushed at my hand and I glanced over, seeing the flask she offered. I took it with a smile, twisting off the top, quietly stealing a strong sip. Her arms wrapped around my neck and she hugged me. "It's a stupid plan," she whispered in my ear.

"I know," I whispered back.

"But we can be stupid together." She giggled, giving me a last squeeze and then let go, crawling over the center console to twist at the radio dial, blasting hip hop through the car.

The music was loud, their energy infectious, and neither distracted me when my phone rang. I fished it out of my pocket and looked at the display. Vic. I silenced the phone and considered, in a moment of tequila-fueled insanity, rolling down the window and chucking it out. It would have been deliciously dramatic. A clear sign to my subconscious that I was done with Vic. It also would have been as stupid as me chopping off my right arm. I tightened my grip on my cell and stuffed it back in my pocket. Pasted a smile on my face and looked away from the window.

Benta stared at me, her eyes narrowed.

"What?" I gave her an innocent face.

"Do I need to take your phone?"

My hand tightened on my cell for one weak moment. Then I pulled it out and handed it over. "Yes. Please."

I wouldn't have listened to his voicemail. Wouldn't have let, whatever he said, influence me or affect the night. I wouldn't have, a few drinks later, huddled in a corner of the bar and called him. Told him through tears and alcohol, that I still loved him. That I still missed him. That I wanted him and our old life back.

I was sure I wouldn't have done any of that. But, just in case, I let Benta hold on to the phone. Sometimes we all needed protection from ourselves.

I'd been to Whiskey Bravo before, knew the relative location of the ladies room and deck, but we got pulled in by the crowd and ended up upstairs, in a dark corner that I'd never seen. There was an open table there, and we pounced on it. My clutch stuck in between my knees, the stool cool against the back of my thighs, an air vent blew right down, flattening my hair in a manner that couldn't be attractive. But it was a table. And in a hot bar, on a Friday night in New York, you took a seat, wherever it was.

"HAVE YOU SEEN HIM?" Cammie yelled across the tiny table at me, her voice barely audible over the music and the wheezing air vent.

I shook my head, saving my voice.

"WE'RE NEVER GOING TO FIND HIM HERE," she continued, Benta covering her right ear as she shot Cammie an irritated look. The poor woman. Stuck in the middle of us, she'd be deaf by dawn.

"Who are you looking for?" The voice didn't have to shout; it spoke at my ear, the tickle of breath delicious against my skin, and I craned around, looking up into Carter's face. I smiled.

"Hey." My greeting got lost in the noise and he lowered his head, putting his ear to my mouth. "Hey," I repeated and wanted to bite into his neck and suck him into my soul. Someday, when we were babysitting grandchildren, this would be the story I'd tell. The day eloquent Grandma said "Hey," while stuffed into the corner of a crowded club.

"Been here long?"

I shook my head and my cheek hit his mouth. His hand reached out and settled on my bare knee, the touch electric. I tried to draw in a breath without shaking. God … his touch. It brought to mind his push of me back on his dining room table. The moment during the night when he trailed his fingers across my arm. His mouth, buried between my legs…

"Who are you looking for?" He repeated the question from earlier and I pulled back a little, tilting my head up and looking into his eyes.

I opened my mouth, and honesty fell out. "You."

His eyes smiled, and his mouth twitched. I gripped the edge of the table and kept myself from reaching for him. "Want to get out of here?"

"Yes." He couldn't have heard me but he read my lips and squeezed my knee, running his hand up to my hip, and he helped me off the stool. Leaning across the table he shook Benta's hand, then Cammie's, introducing himself while never letting go of me, his hand at my back, keeping me in place at his side.

"I'm stealing Chloe," I heard him shout to them. "Is that okay?"

"FOR TONIGHT?" Cammie hollered back.

He looked at me and grinned, a moment of silent connection, a moment where the din of the bar faded and we had—in that brief second—*something.* He looked back at Cammie and the connection was broken. Then he leaned into her, whispering something in her ear, and her eyes widened slightly at me, her hand passing over my phone.

I snuck a look at it as Carter shouldered through the crowd, a text from Cammie coming just as I dismissed the missed call alert from Vic.

> *He said "for as long as she'll let me." He'll steal you for as long as you'll let him. I think he's a keeper.*

I almost missed her second text, it coming through right as I went to lock my phone, and I smiled when I saw it.

P.S. Use protection. Hopefully Magnums.

49. Heartbreak Red

We stepped away from the club, his hand settling on my back, the slow caress of his fingers against my exposed skin sending shivers up my spine. He took on the role so easily, the Gentleman Who Behaves While Driving Women Crazy. I looked over at him and he spoke.

"Joey called me."

"He did?" I frowned, my heel catching on an uneven part of the sidewalk, and I gripped his arm tighter.

"Yep. Told me to stay away from you."

I laughed and glanced up at him. His face was serious, and his eyes stared straight ahead without a hint of humor. "What? Why?" I looked back down at my feet. Concentrated on putting one in front of the other without stumbling.

"He didn't really go into details … just said that you were seeing someone on set." I could feel the grip of his arm tighten, his muscles cording together in rigid strength.

"I'm not—that is so…" I growled under my breath as we came to a stop at a cross street, my hand letting go of his arm, my face hot with embarrassment.

"He also said he told you about Brit."

Brit. The fuckbuddy. "Yeah," I said curtly. "He told me about her."

"We're just friends." Carter turned to face me under the glow of the streetlamp, his eyes on mine. "I mean … we've fucked in the past. But it's just a physical thing. We wouldn't work in a relationship."

I wanted to follow up that cliffhanger with a jumble of questions, the first one being *why not*? But I didn't.

"It's not my business who you sleep with." I did the cool girl shrug, like I was chill with whatever. "It'd be different if we were … you know. Dating." I didn't know why I brought up *dating*. I had come there for a hookup. Right? An isolated event that might turn into a casual sex relationship with one of the sexiest men I'd ever met. Not a real relationship. Not with … my mind stuttered a little. *Not with a maintenance guy.* I'd thought it before. It just hadn't, in my mind, sounded so *bad* before. Why had I looked down on Carter? Just because I used to have rich parents? I shifted uncomfortably, another mark tallied in the *Chloe Was a Bitch* column.

"You wouldn't want me to hang out with her. As friends."

It took a moment for my mind to catch up. "Right." Regardless of whether Carter and I would ever be official, I didn't think I'd *ever* be okay with my boyfriend hanging out with someone he used to sleep with.

There was a break in traffic and we hurried across the road, my hand tucking back into his, his grip strong and reassuring as we turned the final corner before our building.

"So…" He squeezed my hand. "Nothing is going on with you and this guy on the set?"

"No." I looked up at him. "He's just an ex who showed up on set. Joey would love me to date him again, but…" I shook my head and looked away, down the street toward our building. "We're over." I tried not to think of Vic's mouth, skimming down my neck as he held me down and thrust inside of me.

Carter let out a low whistle as we crossed the street, just steps away from the building, just steps away from being alone. My body tightened in anticipation, my steps hurrying—

I stopped when I saw what he was whistling at, a low-slung red Maserati convertible parked on the curb, my mind immediately shuttering back to the past.

"That's your car?" Vic smirked at Mom's Mercedes station wagon. "You're going to show me around Miami in that?"

I rolled my eyes at him. "I got rid of mine when I moved to New York. Trust me, this isn't my vehicle of choice."

"And what would be?"

"That's easy," I teased, opening the door and stepping into the car. "A Maserati. Red. Like all the hearts I plan on breaking."

My breath caught in my throat. *Vic wouldn't have.* We stepped closer, Carter pulling on my hand, his eyes on the car, and I saw an envelope on its windshield, my name printed on the front in black calligraphy.

We stopped before it, and he followed my eyes, his arm reaching out and plucking the white envelope from the windshield.

"Chloe?" My name was a question on his lips, and I stepped back, away from the envelope, away from the question, away from this outrageous gift that would suck me close and run me over.

"Chloe?"

The second time he called my name I was already running inside, my heels loud on the lobby marble then silent on the carpet. I took the stairs, pulling off my stilettos and sprinting, my heart loud, breath hard, and I was winded by the time I got to my apartment and slammed the door shut.

I screamed. Hard and loud enough that a thump sounded from above. Three thumps. The kind a hard heel slammed into the floor makes. I stopped screaming and moved to the couch, punching pillows before grabbing a box of tissues and ripping off a handful. I blotted tears, blew my nose, and cursed Vic's name.

This car was nothing to him; it was a pawn in a chess match where my heart was the prize, and his strategy was so much better than mine. His strategy was born from a lifetime of having everything, including me. His strategy took risks because he had nothing to lose.

My strategy was to play defense and gamble nothing and protect myself, and I did a shitty job of that when I let him push up my skirt and fuck me in Joey's trailer.

The knock was soft and gentle. I almost missed it, the timing coinciding with an enormous blow of my nose. When he knocked a second time I stood, walking over to the peephole and looking through it. I sank against the door, almost relieved when I saw it was just Carter.

"Everything okay?" he called out.

"Yeah." I wiped at my eyes. "Sorry about that."

"No worries. I'll just remember, come your birthday, that you don't like cars."

I laughed.

"What should I do with the card?"

I should have told him to throw it away. I should have told him to rip it into tiny pieces and stuff it down a garbage disposal. "Can you slide it under my door?"

Through the peephole, I saw the playful grin that crossed his face. "No goodnight kiss?"

I smiled, and a fresh stream of tears leaked out. "Not tonight."

The white envelope slipped underneath the door. "Thanks," I said quietly.

"No problem. Good night, Chloe."

I smiled, then remembered he couldn't see me. "Good night, Carter."

He turned and left and for a long beat, I stared through the peephole at the empty hallway. Carter would never be able to buy me a Maserati. Did it matter? It felt like my old life was another person entirely. I didn't want the Maserati out front, not when it put me back with an unfaithful man, back in a life that suddenly felt hollow and superficial.

I bent down and picked up the envelope, running my fingers over the white parchment, my name jotted on its surface in a script that was familiar and one hundred percent Vic.

I ran a finger under the seal and opened the envelope. Pulled out a square card and, with a shaky hand, flipped it open.

This car is fast, like the beat of my heart when you smile. Fierce like your spirit. Incomparably gorgeous, like its new owner.

This is not a bribe or a lure. It is a stick shift, but you've never had trouble handling that before.

Enjoy it baby.

Paper-clipped to the back of the card, a folded piece of paper: a car title. I unfolded it carefully and saw my name on the owner's line, my new address below it.

Typical Vic. The man gave a gift that would be a pain in the ass to give back. My mind spun with all of the issues that having a car in

New York would bring. Parking. Insurance. Gas. I couldn't afford the damn thing, even when it was free. My hands reached for my cell, my fingers dialing Vic's number, then my brain kicked in and I stopped, and set down the phone, stepping away. I brought my hands to my head and took a deep breath. I needed help. Freakin' psychological help to stay away from this man. I stepped back to my phone and called the next best thing.

The girls were still at the club. I asked them to come over, and they didn't ask questions. "We'll be there in twenty," Benta said and—eighteen minutes later—she buzzed the front door.

Dante took a stool in the kitchen, Cammie went for the liquor, and I headed to the living room. "What'd he do?" Benta asked, plopping down on the chair, pulling off her heels and tucking her feet underneath her. "Do I need to kick his sexy ass or what?"

"It wasn't Carter." I sank into the couch.

"What the F is this?" The shout came from the kitchen and I didn't move, just closed my eyes and waited. Cammie had obviously found the card. From beside me, I heard the scurry of bare feet as Benta rushed to her side.

"Holy shit, Chloe," Benta said, her accent strong. "This is big, even for him."

I heard the screech of the stool as Dante stood. Great, a freaking party around words specifically designed to break my heart. "Smooth," he muttered and I heard the crinkle of the title as it passed hands.

"It's not smooth," Cammie snapped, and one of my kitchen drawers slammed shut. "It's pushy."

"And ridiculous," Benta chimed in.

"And pimp," Dante said. "And generous. And sweet."

"It's Vic," I said helplessly, watching Cammie enter the living room, her hands steady as she poured me a large shot of Patrón.

"What does that mean?" Dante asked from the kitchen.

"It means," Cammie said, passing me the glass. "That our little Chloe here is in trouble."

It's Vic. The girls understood. Three simple letters that make up a name. Three simple letters that spell

DOOM.

TROUBLE.

TEMPTATION.

I lifted the glass to my lips and downed it.

50. Fighting With the Past

ChloeMadisonNYU
HARRY WINSTON INC.
Rare Jewels of the World
133 likes
ChloeMadisonNYU Dear Harry,
I miss you. Let's cuddle sometime.

The next morning I called him.

"Hey babe." Vic sounded ridiculously cheerful. Carefree. He was probably back on a beach, drink in hand, his yacht floating nearby. I stood on a dismal New York street, rain tapping against the top of my umbrella, a hangover blazing, and stared at my his car. There was a parking ticket, stuck on its windshield, soaked by the rain.

"You can't do things like this."

"Of course I can." The confidence stretched through every syllable and why wouldn't it? He was right. He could do anything he wanted. In Vic's world there were no worries, no consequences, no ramifications.

"No, you can't. I don't *want* this car. Send one of your people to come pick it up." His people used to be my people. His employees had picked up my dry cleaning, grabbed my groceries, driven my drunk self home. It had been the opening act to the rest of my life, a life that never happened. A life that was shattered that one, terrible afternoon.

"The car is in your name, Chloe." His voice grew harder, more stubborn, the authoritativeness having the wrong effect on me.

"Put your hands on the wall."

I didn't question it, had put my hands on the gold-foil wall, my taupe nails digging into the surface when he ran his hands down my back, over the strings of my bathing suit and down to my ass, his fingers pulling my bathing suit to the side. We were in the Hamptons, at his family's estate, the din of a hundred friends floating up the staircase from downstairs. "Vic," I said softly, the word becoming a moan as his fingers pressed in between my legs.

"Shut up and face the wall. I can't see your body another second without having it."

"Someone will come upstairs," I protested.

"Then they will see me fucking my girl, won't they?" The words were as hard as his cock, the push of him taking my breath, my nails sliding down the wall, my fingers gripping the chair rail as he held my hips and eased himself out, then thrust back in.

"Say my name, Chloe. Tell me how much you love it."

"I love it," I gasped, my cries rising in volume as he let loose on me.

And I had loved it. I had loved when he'd ordered me around. Had loved it when he took control of my life and made it so easy for me. Had loved everything up until the moment I realized what it cost.

I swallowed hard and tried to concentrate. The car. That was what this was about. "I didn't put the car in my name, you did. Without asking me. So fix it."

"The only thing I'm fixing is us."

I closed my eyes. "You can't fix us, Vic. We're broken beyond that."

"I can fix anything."

"No Vic, you can't. You can't buy trust. You can't buy back what you did."

"I made a mistake. *One* mistake. I'll never do it again, Chloe. *Never.*" His voice broke on the last word, and I heard the sincerity in it. How easy it would be to forgive him. To walk away from this tiny apartment and my shitty job as Nicole's assistant and back into a life of luxury on Vic's arm.

Everything would be easy, and every day I'd wonder.

If he was really going where he said he was going.

If he really needed to have two cell phones.

If he could be trusted.

It hadn't been *one* mistake. I knew that in some place, deep in my soul.

"The car already has a parking ticket on it. I can't afford parking tickets, I can't afford insurance, I can't afford *anything* extra. Dammit, Vic, send one of your people to pick it up!" My voice was shrill, the words panicked and angry.

"Chloe, love, I'll buy a spot for you, I'll cover the expenses. I already spoke to Joey; he's going to get you a salary for your work on *Boston Love Letters*, that will help with—"

"Oh my God—STOP!" I screamed into the phone, my voice reaching a pitch it hadn't reached since I was a child. "STOP SCREWING WITH MY LIFE! I DON'T NEED YOU ANYMORE!" I gasped, gripping a nearby post for support and wanted to hang up, didn't want to hear his response, didn't want to hear anything but a dial tone.

There was only silence on the other end. I wet my lips and assumed a calmer tone. "Vic, please listen to me for once. I don't want any money from you; I don't want any gifts from you. I am asking you to *please* stay away from me. If you love me, if you've *ever* loved me, please respect the fact that I am not strong enough to always do what I should do. I shouldn't have hooked up with you in the trailer—God, I hate that I did. I shouldn't answer your calls; I shouldn't have even read your card. And I *definitely* shouldn't accept this car. Please stay away from me. Please do not call me. *Please.*" The last word was a final beg in a conversation that already had me on my knees.

When he finally spoke, it was a Vic I'd never heard before. One broken and quiet. "I can't stay away from you, Chloe. I've tried."

"Try harder." I sank against the nearest wall. "Please."

I needed him to stay away because I couldn't.

51. Table for Two

Carter was sitting on the front steps of our apartment building when I walked up. His shirt was off, the muscles in his back stretching as he tilted back a cold blue Gatorade. He saw me and finished the sip, standing up as he wiped his mouth with the back of his hand, his abs tightening with the motion, and my eyes dropped down on their own before lifting back to his eyes. He grinned. "Hey, big city. Surprised to see you during the day."

I shrugged, shifting my purse strap on my shoulder. "Got the afternoon off." A rare gift from Nicole, one that—I was pretty sure—was motivated by her desire for alone time with Paulo. Behind me, taunting me, the Maserati sat, now behind a gate, in a parking spot that Vic had, in some way, handled.

I smiled, and his mouth tugged up at the corners. I tried to keep my eyes on that smile, to avoid gaping at his shoulders, his sweaty chest, the tone and muscles of his arms as he rested his hands loosely on his hips. I could think of a thousand ways to waste the afternoon with him.

"Well then … given your free schedule, why don't I take you to lunch?"

Lunch. It'd be our first real date, one proposed entirely by him.

"I'd love that." I smiled, and he stood up, tossing the Gatorade bottle into the trash.

We made an interesting pair in the sandwich place two blocks over. He'd put on a shirt, the material damp and worn, clinging to his torso—the ensemble perfect for Hot Construction Worker porn. I stood close to him and looked at the menu, discreetly sniffing the air around him. He smelled amazing; masculinity rolled in grass and topped with sex. He had washed his hands when we arrived, the faint scent of lemon now chiming in on the delicious combination. Next to him, I wore skinny white cropped jeans with my Estella wedges and a silk navy top, diamond studs sparkling from my ears, my hair twisted back into a loose and messy knot. The cashier gave me a competitive once over before perking up and zeroing in on Carter.

"Hey Carter." She flashed a smile that would make a dentist swoon. I stared at her brilliant white teeth and swallowed the urge to ask her secret.

"Hey Monica. How's it going?"

"Great. You getting the usual?" Her teeth were almost freakish in their perfection. Absolutely straight. I would have suspected veneers if she hadn't been wearing camouflaged Crocs.

"You know it." He tossed an arm around my shoulder, and I was able to inhale his smell deeply without looking like a freak. God, forget the sandwiches. I wanted to go back to his place, right then, and work up some sweat of my own. It suddenly occurred to me that I'd never dated a manly man before. I'd always dated Clarke and Vic types—ones that wore suits and valeted their cars and grew muscles in the gym but couldn't actually swing a hammer. This type of man was an entirely different type of sexy, one that could build me a house, a fire, could protect me in a storm or on the street. "What are you getting, Chloe?"

I ordered a Cuban sandwich and lemonade, and followed Carter to a table. "So," he started, leaning forward, his eyes on mine. "What's up with the car?"

I shrugged. "My ex likes to woo. It didn't work. I'm trying to give it back." A year of turmoil, summed up in three sentences.

Carter nodded and picked up his meatball sandwich. I picked up my lemonade and took a big sip.

Good talk.

"So … you work as an assistant?"

I nodded, with a wince. "Yes. For Nicole Brantley." His face was blank, the man not up to date on socialites, and I hurried to explain. "She's an actress. And her family owns a prophylactic company."

The corner of his mouth twitched up, into a smile. "Prophylactic? Is that how she refers to it?"

My grin widened. "I honestly don't know if I've ever heard her say anything about it, but her mouth isn't above the word *condom*." That was the damn truth. The woman couldn't complete a sentence without a curse word being present—at least, not in her own home. Out in public, she hid her fangs well.

"Do you see yourself working for her for long?"

I huffed out a laugh. "God, I hope not." I told him about my tuition bill, leaving out the details that led to my financial troubles, and noticed his eyes, they stayed on me whenever I spoke—almost intimidating in their focus. He was actually listening to me, not just waiting for a chance to speak, his focus one hundred percent on me. It felt odd, a man paying such rapt attention to me, and I tried to remember the last time I had such complete attention, without eyes darting to a phone, or a sentence interrupted, details lost.

"So, once you pay your tuition, then what?"

I took a bite from my sandwich and chewed, thinking about the question. It was sad that I didn't know the answer. Ever since my eviction, all of my focus had been on surviving. Well … there'd been a pitiful couple of weeks when classes were wrapping up and during finals, where I mostly moped around—feeling sorry for myself. But once that had passed, I'd been so busy, so desperate, that I hadn't exactly thought through the next step. Would there be a next step? Would I ever save enough to pay off that bill? Or was I stuck, being Nicole's errand girl, for the rest of my life? I literally shuddered at the thought.

"You cold?" He glanced up at the fan, and I waved him off. Vic would have never noticed. And if he had, he'd have leaned forward and checked out the possibility of headlights in my shirt.

"I'm fine." I took a sip of my lemonade and noticed him still listening, waiting for my response. "I don't know what I'll do after I get my degree. I'll probably try to find a job in real estate. Something with a salary, maybe in development."

"You like the construction end of it?"

I let out a strangled laugh that sounded a little like a cry. "Honestly, I have no idea. I chose real estate as a major because my parents pushed me there." And that was the truth. Something I hadn't even confessed to myself. Something that—right there in that cheap deli—was terrifying. I was working my ass off to get proof of a degree in a field I didn't even really *like*. Or *know* if I liked. What if I hated it? What if I was terrible at it? I felt panic growing, my hands trembling a little in their reach of the sandwich.

"Chloe." His voice was strong and steady and I lifted my eyes to meet his. "It's okay if you don't know. That's what this time in your life is for—to figure it out."

"Is that what you're doing? Figuring it out?" Maybe he was actually an attorney, one on construction sabbatical, working on his hammering technique while his fat bank account accumulated interest.

His eyes crinkled a little at the edges, as if he could hear my pathetic inner monologue and found it humorous. "Not exactly. This is as figured out as it gets for me, right now."

My fantasies stopped their party and slunk back to the dormant recesses of my mind. "You like being a super?" The question came out poorly—like I couldn't imagine why anyone would want to do *that* for a living. I winced at the sound of it and hoped he wasn't offended.

He laughed. "I do. Plus, it has the occasional perks."

"Like?" A big bonus at the end of the year? Ten percent ownership of the building?

"Sexy tenants." He leaned forward. "There's this one girl—she's new—that I haven't been able to stop thinking about."

The heat rose in my cheeks, and I forced my smile into a scowl. "Really? I hope you're not talking about the blonde in B4, because I heard she's a snobby bitch. One who parties *constantly*. With really loud friends."

"Who loses her keys often?" He grinned and god, his smile was perfect.

"I heard that's just an excuse she uses to get inside single men's apartments." I widened my eyes and he leaned forward, the two of us sharing the secret.

"She's not a snobby bitch." He whispered. "But she *does* have really loud friends."

I giggled, and we were close enough to kiss.

"Do you think I have a chance with her?" he said softly.

My cheeks hurt from smiling so much. "Yeah." I said softly. "I think you do."

He closed the gap, his lips soft to mine, then we were suddenly standing, his hands quick, our sandwiches shoved into a bag in seconds. "Let's go." The words were a growl, his fingers wrapping around my wrist and pulling, the frantic step of him to the door causing a smile to tear across my face.

Yes. Let's go. Please.

52. "Please."

We slammed through the door of his apartment, our lunch tossed in the general direction of the kitchen, his hands pushing on my shoulders, back against the wall, lifting off me long enough to pull off my shirt, tear at the clasp of my bra, and yank down the straps. When I was topless, my bare shoulders against the textured wall, he stopped. His movements slow, he ran both palms up my stomach and cupped my breasts, squeezing them gently, his large hands holding each one easily, my name a reverent whisper off his lips.

"Carter," I begged. "Please."

"Wait," he said and lowered his mouth to my breasts, his tongue and lips depositing soft kisses, sucks, and gentle bites across my sensitive skin, my back arching, my hands finding their way to his head, pulling at his hair. I wanted more yet didn't want him to stop; the need between my legs competed with the pleasure his mouth was giving. He took my nipple into his mouth, and I whimpered, my hands grabbing at his soft shirt and pulling it, his head lifting, his T-shirt coming off so I could finally touch his skin.

I grabbed his shoulders and his hands dropped lower, to the button of my jeans, the pop of restriction lifted, the zipper loud in the room, his fingertips dipping under the material, pulling my panties and jeans over my hips.

"Damn skinny jeans," he chuckled against my neck. "I hate these."

I pushed on his shoulders and he dropped to his knees, peeling off the jeans, his hands on my shoes, and then I was completely naked and he was leaning forward, his hands sliding to the back of my thighs and up, his mouth cupping me as his fingers bit into my ass. His tongue was confident and talented, the man unafraid of my body, my taste. He sucked on my clit gently, and my knees gave out when his tongue dipped inside of me. My weight sagged into his strong hands, unintelligible sounds coming out as I gripped the wall and tried to stay sane.

I didn't stay sane. I don't know why I even tried. I clawed at the wall and melted against his mouth, coming hard, then stumbling after him toward the bed. I lay back on his sheet, his eyes meeting mine as he knelt in between my legs and had the sense to put on a condom. I watched him, strong fingers sure of their actions, foil tossed aside, one hand gripping his cock as he rolled the latex over it. My first sight of him and I propped up, my glimpse quick before he lifted my legs around his neck and propped himself above me, my eyes lifting to his. He held my gaze until the moment that he leaned down for a kiss and pushed himself inside. That moment, it was perfect. So tender, so caring. Even as it hurt, my body adjusting to his size, my breath catching for the briefest of moments. I wrapped my arms around him and he started thrusting. Slowly and tenderly but somewhere, somewhere after my first orgasm and before the second, he lost control. Sat back on his heels, held on to my hips and started a furious, mad rhythm of fucking, his grip on me hard, possessive, and hot.

After the second orgasm and before the third, he rolled me onto my side, continuing the pleasure, his mouth coming down and kissing, biting, whispering things into my neck.

You make me so hard

I've wanted this for so long

You feel incredible

I can't … I can't hold off.

Oh my God, Chloe. Chloe. I'm coming…

And somewhere between my third orgasm and his first, I forgot about trying to hold back. I forgot about protecting my heart. I got over all of my hang-ups. And I fell a little bit in like with him.

53. God Bless Presa Little

I rolled over in Carter's bed and stretched, kicking off the covers, the smell of coffee dragging me out of sleep. I smiled, remembering the night before. It had officially been the Greatest Sex of My Life. I had the perverse urge to go online and gloat, hashtag *SuckItVic*. Instead, I eyed the bathroom door, hearing the sound of a shower. Glancing at my naked body, I wondered if I had time to run to his kitchen for a cup of coffee before he got out. As great as my three pilates DVD workouts had gone, I didn't feel up to a naked dash in front of Carter's ripped ass.

I ran for it, spilling some coffee in my pour and stealing a piece of toast off a plate in the kitchen. I was darting past the fridge when I stopped, distracted by a ticket stuck under a Mets magnet. What the … I peered closer. Yep. A Presa Damn Little ticket. A ticket that matched the two stuffed in my wallet, which I'd received from Nicole. I heard the shower turn off and booked it, my butt hitting the bed just in time to pull the sheet over me before the door opened. A barely covered, dripping wet Carter stepped out, a towel wrapped around his waist. "Good morning."

I took a sip of coffee and smiled, still trying to work through the ticket I had just seen. I hadn't even wanted to go to the event, preferring to avoid Nicole at all opportunities. But on the other hand, this *was* Presa Little. One of the most revered and most private artists of the century. She hadn't been photographed in public since Lady Gaga wore meat. An opportunity to meet her wasn't something I wanted to give up.

I swallowed the sip of coffee, watching him walk to the closet. He opened the door, and my question from our first hookup was answered. Absolute organization. His T-shirts were hung and sorted by damn color. "I saw your ticket to the Presa Little event."

"Yeah." He nodded, reaching up and grabbing a shirt.

I tried again. "So … how do you know her again?"

"She's a friend of my parents. I knew her growing up." He pulled his shirt on and turned toward me, boxer briefs in hand. I settled further back against the pillows, lifting my eyebrows at him when he reached for the towel. He dropped it, and I giggled despite myself, his face scowling as he stepped into his underwear. "Never laugh," he muttered, kneeling on the bed and crawling toward me.

"I'm sorry," I whispered behind my coffee mug. "It's a nervous reaction."

"So is this." He grinned, taking my coffee cup away and pushing me back, his mouth nuzzling under the sheet and nipping at my neck.

"She must have been a good friend," I mumbled, my eyes falling back on the giant canvas original above his bed. He pulled the sheet lower and I grabbed at it, giggling again when his mouth found its way to my newly exposed breasts. My parents' friends were all stuffy investment types, not Presa Little—a beautiful older woman who *People* once called the Most Interesting Woman Alive. She had homes in Australia, South Africa, and Paris. How could she know *Carter's* parents? "What do your parents do?" I suddenly realized how little I knew about the man on top of me.

"God, your mind jumps. You really want to talk about my parents right now?"

"I have tickets to the show too," I explained. "I was thinking about inviting you. You know, since you know her."

"I'll go to the show with you." His mouth moved lower, on my stomach, and I felt his hand slide under the sheet and up my bare thigh.

"Really?"

"Do I get to glare at your boss with judgment in my eyes?" He pulled the sheet lower and my legs apart, settling between them.

I giggled at the scrape of his stubble against my thigh. "Yes. Please do."

"One final stipulation."

"What?" I gasped out the word, his mouth brushing across me, his tongue taking a teasingly slow path over my clit.

"Right now, I get to make you scream so hard the McMullins on the fifth floor will hear you."

"Why them?" I shuddered beneath his mouth, and his hands held me down.

"They're deaf," he whispered, and the hot pass of his words was another sensation I loved.

"Deal," I groaned, and my hands twisted in the sheets as he lowered his mouth.

When I came it was loud. It was long. It was amazing.

And our date was set.

God Bless Presa Little.

54. *Just the Two of Us*

ChloeMadisonNYU
197 likes
ChloeMadisonNYU Caviar has been replaced. My taste buds aren't complaining. #lunch #LongIsland #Nathans

I eyed the truck skeptically. "This is yours?"

Carter leaned over the bed's side and grinned at me. "Yep. There a problem?"

"It's a truck." I said carefully. An *old* truck. Rusty, with paint peeling from its trim, it had to be from the nineties. I glanced in the window and saw a rip in the bench seat, tan padding pushing through.

"Yes." He tilted his head. "You can back out. Won't hurt my feelings."

I gripped the door's handle, a thick silver piece with a button on it. Pushing the button, I yanked open the heavy door and looked inside. At least it was clean. I glanced down at my pale blue pants. I shut the door. "Just … let me change. Two minutes," I promised, backing up from the truck, careful not to touch my clothes.

He chuckled. "Okay."

I took the stairs, leaving the garage and heading up to my apartment, washing my hands the minute I got inside. I wouldn't make the two-minute promise, but I tried my best, digging through my closet until I found a ripped up pair of jeans and a Yankee T-shirt. I grabbed a baseball cap, tossed my sandals for tennis shoes, and grabbed some bottled waters from the fridge. By the time I got back downstairs, he'd turned on the truck and I pushed aside any hesitation, opening the door and climbing in.

"Better?" he asked.

"Better." I smiled. "I think I was a little overdressed."

The edge of his mouth turned up, a dimple showing. "Nah."

He shifted into reverse and I buckled my seatbelt, holding on to its strap as the truck jerked into motion. No airbags in sight. I braced my feet against the floor and prayed he was a good driver.

"Turn here," I argued, looking down at my phone.

"I can't get around to the loading dock if I go that way."

"Well the next road is a one-way." I let out an irritated breath and he laughed. "What?" I growled.

"I'm just curious if you have ever, in your life, been to Long Island."

I rolled my eyes. "I've been to Long Island."

"Really."

"Yeah. *Really.*" Granted, my trips had been a long way from the industrial area we were lost in.

"Let me guess…" He took a left, in a direction that went against everything that Google Maps suggested. "To the beach." He glanced my way. "And the theatre?"

"There's also a vineyard," I pointed out, pursing my lips to stop a smile.

He turned down a side street and parked, somehow right in front of the tile store we'd been headed to. I glared at the sign. *Dammit.*

My purpose in tagging along with Carter had been to help him pick out materials. I had readily agreed, thinking it would be easy to pair a backsplash with granite, especially for someone as stylish as myself. I stared at the countertop before me, at the eighteen different options I had pulled for review, and my confidence wavered. I glanced out the window, at the truck, where Carter was helping load a vanity. His T-shirt tight, his biceps bulging, he pulled the heavy piece up into the bed. The picture was so utterly male that I almost fanned myself. I watched him as long as I could, my eyes darting away in the moment before he pulled open the store's front door, his steps echoing across the floor toward me. "Pick something?" he asked, wiping his hands on the front of his jeans and I looked up from the options, my breath catching in my throat as I saw the damp cling of his T-shirt to his chest, the wide grin of his smile, the way his eyes even smiled at me. The man looked at me as if I were something *special*, a look so foreign that a part of me wanted to cry. How long could that look last? How many women had gotten it?

I wasn't special. I wasn't even—the more I got to know myself—that great. But that look, that smile—it made me want to be more. I smiled back at him. "Yeah," I said. "I found the perfect thing."

"Awesome." He stepped closer and leaned in, pressing his lips to mine softly, then pulled back. "Meet you at the register?"

"Yeah." I mumbled, already wanting more. "I'll be there."

He walked off, and I stared down at my mess of tiles.

I needed to stop overthinking it and just make a decision. It was two colors that some renter would never notice.

I grabbed two samples and headed for the counter.

55. She's a Monet.

Presa Little's show was at the Gagosian Gallery in Chelsea, *the* place for anyone to hold anything. I debated for a good hour over what to wear, finally opting for a silk T-shirt dress that, paired with heels, worked as well for a cocktail party as for a formal event. When Carter knocked at my door at eight, I smiled at the view—him in a suit. A *very* nice suit, one his build filled out perfectly.

"Nice threads," I mused, running my hand over his lapel before tilting my head up for a kiss.

"Thank you. You look stunning."

"Thanks. Ready?"

"If you are." His face was tight, and I felt my first bit of unease as I grabbed my purse.

"Are you feeling okay?"

"Yeah." He smiled. "Just a long day."

I bet. There'd been plumbing vans parked out front all day, men in uniforms carrying things up and down our stairs, all with urgency in their steps. Nothing like that to stress me out every time I flushed the toilet. "Is everything okay? I saw workers…"

He shrugged. "A leak on an upper floor. It was a beast to get to. Sucked up the whole day."

Glamorous stuff, our conversation. I nodded and stepped into the cab, double-checking my wallet for the tickets.

"I should probably warn you about Presa…" Carter glanced out the window, and I looked up at him, suddenly alert.

"What about?"

"She can be territorial. Aggressive," he corrected himself. "Unfriendly."

I blinked, surprised at the string of adjectives, none of which matched the worldly ambassador I had pictured. "Territorial? Over *what*?"

"She's known me a long time. With girls I've dated in the past … she can come on a little strong. Protective."

"Like a momma bear with her cub?" I tried to follow his train of thought.

He grimaced. "No. Like…"

Our conversation was interrupted by an accident, two cars ahead of us colliding, our cab slamming on the brakes, throwing us both forward. Carter's hand reached out to protect me, my eyes rolling as he took advantage, his fingers caressing me through my dress. I swatted his hand and reached for the handle.

By the time we stepped out, there was already a full-fledged New York City argument going on between the drivers over what looked, to my untrained eye, like a big scratch. He slipped the cabbie a ten and we decided to walk the remaining four blocks to the gallery.

When we approached, there was a crowd outside, paparazzi clustered, a few looks shot our way and then we were ignored, his hand in mine as we entered the already crowded show. Inside was pure eye candy, brilliantly lit canvases everywhere, my eyes jumping from one to another as we moved deeper inside. "Want a drink?" Carter offered.

"Yes please. Champagne."

"Wait here so I don't lose you." He pressed a gentle kiss on my neck and I smiled.

I was studying *Peace of Heart*—a red and pink wonder, tiny veins flowing through the large abstract, when I was bumped from behind and turned. Across the room, my eyes caught sight of Carter, his hand resting on the bar, his head tilted down toward the woman who stood close by his side. Presa Little. I recognized her immediately, her jet-black hair pulled back and pinned up, her stance strong and in control. The woman once had a lion as a pet. I still remember the 2005 *Vogue* cover where she stretched naked over its back. As I watched, she ran a hand over Carter's arm and my gaze narrowed.

I knew nothing about love and less about succeeding in life. But I knew what a woman on the prowl looked like. Presa Little angled her head up to Carter, and I saw the history in every ounce of their interaction. *A friend of his parents?* Bullshit.

Carter moved his arm away, but it was too late. When he glanced over, our eyes met, and I raised my eyebrows. I ignored Carter's directive to stay put and walked through the crowd, watching as her head turned to me, a smile crossing her face.

I hoped, when I approached fifty, to look like this woman. Even through jealousy, I saw her beauty. The woman was worldly, sophisticated, and utterly comfortable in her own skin. When she shook my hand, her shake was strong and confident, and I felt incredibly young and naïve.

"Presa, this is my girlfriend." Carter ran his hand down my back and cupped my waist. "Chloe."

Girlfriend. It was such an unexpected title that I mentally stuttered. I tried my best to smile. "It's a pleasure to meet you. I'm a big fan of your work … have been for a long time."

"Thank you, Chloe." She smiled at Carter. "It's so great to see my Carter *settling.* I thought it would never happen."

Her accent was full of rolled Rs and elongated vowels. I could tell that she wasn't a native English speaker, but she was adept enough to know the difference between "settling down" and "settling." Oh, and *my* Carter. I caught the possession. Saw it in the way her eyes sharpened as she looked at him, verbal claws of ownership digging in and taking hold. It pissed me off and I swallowed a retort, mentally counting to three before I responded.

"How do you two know each other?" I smiled when I asked the question but it still came out a little sharp. She turned to me, her eyes lighting, feeding on my insecurity.

"God, I met Carter when he was … what? Nineteen?" She glanced at him and he nodded warily. "His parents were some of my most loyal clients. Carter worked at my studio, assembling canvases and packaging up my sales. He's always been good with his hands." She smiled at me. "But I'm sure you know that."

My face blushed hot, and I felt off balance. If I were Benta, I'd snap off a witty comeback. Cammie would simply smile, with eyes that killed. Me? I wasn't qualified, not to spar with the likes of Presa Little. Not to fight over a man I didn't really have ownership of. I returned her smile weakly.

"Ms. Little?" A tall man in a suit appeared at her right. "We are ready for you at the podium."

Presa nodded and turned to Carter. "I've got to run. It was wonderful to see you and to get a chance to meet you, Chloe." She hugged Carter, a hug that lasted a few seconds too long. She smiled sweetly and, in a swish of fabrics, left.

I looked up at Carter. "Well?" I asked.

He groaned and reached for my hand. "Let's find someplace to talk."

56. Mrs. Robinson is a Bitch.

We stepped outside, navigating around the incoming stream of people and walked west. Aside from the gallery, we were in the industrial part of Chelsea, an area virtually abandoned at night. We didn't have to go far to be alone, stopping at a bare spot alongside a wall. I leaned against the rough brick and he faced me, his hands tucked into his front pockets, his eyes glancing back to the event before focusing on me.

"When I started working for Presa, I was pretty much just hormones and attitude." He shrugged. "I was nineteen and she was … I don't know. Thirty-five? Forty? One night, I worked late and…" His shoulders lifted, and he looked at me like he wasn't going to finish the sentence, like that dangling morsel was all I was going to get.

"You worked late and?" I pressed.

He ran a hand roughly through his hair. "And she came into the back room in nothing but her underwear, and I fucked her over a crate of paintings."

I blinked. "Had you had sex before?"

He raised his eyebrow at me. "Yeah. I'd had sex with a few different girls. But Presa…" His hand moved up, rubbing his neck. "Presa was different. Sex with her was different. She taught me a lot, about women, what they like. And about relationships."

I crossed my arms over my chest. "So … she was your sexual mentor?"

He pursed his lips. "If you want to call her that."

"For how long?"

"About a year. Give or take."

I sorted through my feelings. "Did you love her?"

Before he even answered, I found the root of my unease. It wasn't because he'd been nineteen, and she'd been two decades older. It was because she was PRESA LITTLE and I was little ol' broke Chloe. They'd probably had a sophisticated, sex-filled, worldly affair, while I spent Saturday nights in my apartment crying over gifts from my ex-boyfriend. In the back of my mind, an insecure part of me suggested that Carter only brought me there as a way to rekindle his romance with Presa.

He nodded. "I did."

"Do you love her now?"

Another response, without pause. "No."

It was a good answer but I would have loved a few sentences of clarification. Preferably a few lines about how much my killer bedroom skills trumped hers. *That* would have been a good response.

I bit my bottom lip and looked away. "I didn't mean to be nosy."

He shrugged. "It's not the first time a girl has wanted to know."

Girl. Not girlfriend. I wanted to chase down the distinction and stab it with the heel of my Tom Ford stilettos. Had he called me his girlfriend because that was what he wanted, or was it to ward off Presa? And at the same time, did I *want* to be his girlfriend? Was I ready for that step?

I liked him—a lot. Almost too much. There was still so much I didn't know about him, and so much he didn't know about me.

"Want to go home?"

He held out his hand and I took it, thinking about how I hadn't yet seen Nicole. I didn't want to, couldn't stomach her hanging on Clarke, playing the part of loving wife. Not tonight. And even though we'd only been there fifteen minutes, the thought of seeing any more of Presa made me gag. I smiled up at him. "Yeah."

Home. I liked the sound of that.

57. Getting Clean Never Felt So Dirty

He stripped me in the bedroom, taking his time, his fingers skimming off my dress, then my bra. I covered myself with my hands, and he smirked, clicking his tongue and shaking his head. Then he dropped to his knees, pulling my thong over my hips and down to the floor, my hands holding his shoulders as he pulled off one of my heels, then the other. "Get in the shower." He turned me toward his bathroom and grabbed my ass, then growled and smacked it. It was just hard enough to make me jump, just hard enough to make me wet. I glanced over my shoulder as I headed to the bathroom, his eyes on me as he loosened his tie, his belt already undone, dress shoes being kicked off.

I came to a stop at the entrance to his bathroom. My last visit, I had found the bathroom half asleep in the middle of the night with an urgent need to pee. Now, I saw everything I had missed. The shower, big enough for two, a bench on one side, a rain head and a wide window that looked out on the city. Much fancier than mine.

He stepped behind me, reaching past and twisting the shower nozzles, his mouth nipping at my neck as the water came on in a rush. "Wait." He stopped me from stepping in, his hand testing it, his other hand taking delicious liberties between my legs. I was panting by the time he nudged me forward, under the spray.

It wasn't fair to compare two men, but Vic and Carter were there, in my mind, almost constantly. And Vic never made love to me like this. Carter *worshiped* me in that shower. He took his time, his fingers gentle, running over every bit of me, his mouth constantly on mine, or on my skin. He sat me down on the bench and knelt before me, his hot mouth settling in between my legs, his total attention on me.

I was close to coming when he stood up, and HARD was not enough of a description for his cock. Good Lord. Talk about absolute beauty. It stuck straight out and I reached for it, missing. "Wait," he breathed, his hand yanking the handheld attachment off the wall and rolling the control left, adjusting the spray until it gently pulsed and then he knelt, holding it in between my legs, adjusting the angle and the setting until I gasped. "Right there?" he asked, his eyes on mine, concentration lining his face.

"Yes." The word hiccupped out of me, the water pulsing on my clit, a drumming patter of liquid that already had my thighs tightening. My eyes followed Carter as he stood back up and put his hands on the back of my head, his cock at a perfect level for what was next.

"Please," he asked and, really, it was a waste of a word. I grabbed at his waist, pulling him forward and, for the first time, put him in my mouth.

I saw a video once on giving a grapefruit blowjob. It was mind-blowing. Quite possibly the best thing I had ever seen. I didn't have a grapefruit in Carter's shower but if I had, I'd have squeegeed the hell out of his perfect, delicious dick with that grapefruit.

So, I had no grapefruit, and I was a little distracted by the water's stream, a mind-blowing orgasm lifting me off the bench mid-blowjob. But I don't think Carter minded. In fact, right after I came, he pulled out of my mouth, his breath hard, a moment of pause between us, before he offered it back. "I don't want to come," he swore, "but *fuck* you give amazing head."

That's right, bitches. I couldn't balance my checkbook and didn't know the capital of Iowa but I apparently gave amazing head. I could die a happy sexpot. I contained my pride and resumed my incredible blowjob skills. And a few minutes later, he knelt back down, pulling me to the edge of the bench, and put that gorgeous cock inside of me. I wrapped my legs around him but he pulled them off. Lifted my feet and put them flat on the bench, so I looked like some squatting catcher but when he pushed back in, I understood the change in position. I also understood that he was a sexual freak of nature, and I should never ever ever ever let him go.

“Can I—?” he gasped out the words and I understood the question.

“Yes.” I grabbed him, held him close, suddenly frantic for him to come inside me. He pushed deeper, groaning when he came, his grip almost painful on my skin. When he finished, he sank against the wall and turned to me, his eyes heavy, his hand reaching out and he pulled me to my feet and against his chest. “Fuck,” he mumbled, pressing his mouth to the top of my wet head. “That was insane.”

I didn’t have enough intelligent thought to form a response, just smiled against his chest, placing a kiss on his skin. We moved out of the shower and he dried me off, then lifted me, carrying me to his bed and dropping me onto the covers. I rolled over, keeping the towel with me, and watched him, studiously avoiding the giant canvas stretched above my head. Now that I knew his connection to Presa Little, his art collection was no longer impressive. Now, it was just a reminder of their relationship.

It wasn’t my place to ask him to take it down. I knew that. Especially not at this stage of whatever we were. Still, the thought of it being the first and last thing he saw every day irked me. “Have you ever thought about selling these?” I waved a hand in the general direction of the masterpiece above the bed.

Carter chuckled, pulling open a dresser drawer and taking out a white T-shirt, tossing it my way. “No.”

Short. Concise. I started to follow up the answer with a follow up question, but right then, at 10:49 PM, his doorbell rang. And any questions I had stalled.

58. Late Night Booty Call

I stayed in place on his bed, still naked, the sheet clutched to my chest, and listened. The one good thing about a New York apartment's tiny size: ease in eavesdropping. I heard clearly the moment when he opened the door, and I heard the surprise in his voice when he said her name.

"Presa?"

I didn't know why he was surprised. I saw the way she looked at him. More importantly, I saw the way she looked at *me*. Like I was an annoyance, something to squash just for the fun of it. I stood up and quietly walked to the door, my hand on the doorknob. I peeked through the crack and saw Carter, his boxer briefs and nothing else on. All I could see of Presa was the elaborate skirt of her dress.

"It's not a good time," Carter spoke quietly. "Which I'm sure you know."

"Don't be silly. I came by for a drink. It was so nice to see you tonight."

"Chloe is here. My girlfriend? You met her tonight."

The girlfriend reference again.

"Oh. The little blonde."

That irritated me. Even more than the middle-of-the-night booty call. I looked for my dress but it was on the other side of the bedroom, hanging off a chair.

"You should go. It's inappropriate, you being here." He moved a little, as if to usher her out.

"I thought you liked a party." Her voice sounded as if she hadn't moved an inch. "She doesn't like to share?"

"*I* don't want to share. Or *be* shared. I'm not going back into that world with you, Presa." He sounded tired. Poor guy. Discussing threesomes was probably exhausting. "Please leave."

Yes Presa, I thought. Please leave before I run out of this room, completely naked, and smack that entitled smirk off your face. They were into threesomes? Any sexual confidence from our shower faded.

"Stop," Carter spoke, and the word was muffled. I stuck my head out of the door to try and see what was happening, could hear the sounds of feet scuffling across the floor, and as I craned my neck, I could see Carter trying to push her through the door. With a yelp of indignation, Presa finally reached the hall, his hand shutting the door quickly, the latch flapped shut, and when he turned to me, I stared in shock at her lipstick, bright red on his mouth.

As a woman, I didn't always act rationally, especially when it was a week before my period, my brain was still strung out from orgasms, and I was looking at another woman's lipstick on my man.

And yes, Carter was my man. That was the first order of business that I was determined, right there in the middle of the night, to set straight.

"You told her I was your girlfriend." The words came out like an accusation, and I could see the wariness in his eyes when he responded.

"Yes."

"Am I?"

"Do you *want* to be?"

"Yes!" I snarled the words and he looked confused. I didn't really blame the man. Most discussions of commitment came after champagne and roses and hot sex. And usually the person asking about the commitment didn't sound like she was ready to join the WWE. "Do you *want* to be my boyfriend?" I stepped forward, my hands clenched at my side and his eyes dropped, for a minute, from my face. It hadn't been my plan to have this fight while naked; in fact, it hadn't been my plan to have a fight at all, but I didn't bother to cover up. "Do you want to be my boyfriend?" I repeated, my words all but a threat.

"Yes?" The answer was a question, a healthy amount of fear in his eyes.

"Good." I turned and stalked back to the bedroom, and it was around the time that I slammed the door, my bare feet stomping over to the bed, that I realized how mental I was acting. Had I really just gained a relationship? Or had I just beaten a distracted man into submission?

I crawled into his bed and heard the sink come on in the bathroom, some splashing. He was probably washing off her lipstick. I heard the sound of teeth brushing, and I felt relieved and irritated, all at the same time.

I realized, staring up at the ceiling, that my feelings were a little irrational. I couldn't be pissed at him for Presa Little showing up at midnight. Not when Vic would have done the exact same thing. In fact, Vic *had* done the same thing, in Joey Plazen's trailer, and I'd let him take it so much further. Granted, Carter couldn't have had sex with her, not with me watching. I guess the real question was—if he'd been alone, would he have still pushed her out of his door?

I didn't know the man well enough to know the answer to that question. Hell, I didn't know *myself* well enough to answer that question. If I opened my door in the middle of the night and Vic was standing there, could I say with one hundred percent certainty that I wouldn't kiss him? Or worse? Falling for one man didn't safeguard us from the feelings we might have for another. If anything, the forbidden could just make temptation stronger.

I didn't want to talk when Carter came back from the bathroom. There was just too much going on in my head. I closed my eyes and pretended to be asleep. Did some mumbly groan thing when he gently touched my shoulder.

It was weak. I should have sat up in bed and had a conversation like an adult. Discussed whether he really wanted to be in a relationship or whether we should keep it casual a little longer.

Instead, I kept my eyes closed and my breathing regular and then, I really was asleep.

October

It was so different being with Carter. The only real relationship I could compare it to was with Vic, and it was so different from that. Now, I wasn't even sure that I ever loved Vic. The man who'd broken my heart, who I'd struggled against for over a year, and it might not have even been true love. It was a scary thought. Because of this—if what Carter and I had was stronger, then that meant the fall would be harder. And right now, I felt so brittle. So exposed. So afraid.

In this state, I understood why I always ran back to Vic. His world was safe and easy. This new one was terrifying. Beautiful. Liberating. I swallowed my fears and moved toward it.

Too bad for pesky loose ends. They tangled up my steps.

59. So Much for Male Loyalties

ChloeMadisonNYU
94 likes
ChloeMadisonNYU
Slackers.
#BostonLoveLetters
#crew #notimeforrest

The sun was actually shining. After days of rain, it was worthy of a celebration. Or a free breakfast, courtesy of my favorite actor in the world. I walked into Joey's trailer, all sunshine and happiness and encountered a face that, very clearly, communicated his lack of love toward me.

"What? No love?" I dropped my arms, which had been outstretched in prep for a hug.

"I heard you're dating Carter." He all but bared his teeth at me.

News traveled fast. "Yes." I stole a croissant from a box on his counter. Seriously, I could live in his trailer. Meals and snacks delivered four times a day, a masseuse on call, a giant bed for naps … I'd be set and happy.

"I thought you were getting back with Vic Worth."

My mouth never made it to the pastry. "What? Who said *that*?"

"*He* said that. To me. After our last production meeting."

"Well, he's an idiot," I sputtered. "I have no interest in getting back with him. None." I took a bite of the croissant and closed my eyes. It was hot. So freaking good. I cracked an eye long enough to reach for the minibar handle and grab a juice. Yes. I could definitely live here. "Aren't you and Carter friends?" I mumbled the question through a delicious combination of orange juice and flaky sugar.

"Yeah." He dismissed any history with Carter with one shrug of his shoulder. "But you were with Vic first. You need to reconsider this, Chloe." He stood from the couch and paced. PACED. Like we were discussing a nuclear agreement and not a nonexistent relationship with my ex.

"Why do you care?" I sat down in the closest chair, the breakfast box in my lap and looked through my other options. Not a lot unless I wanted to go in the cream cheese direction.

"I want you to be happy. Vic is settled, he has a good job, spoils you rotten…"

"Has a dick that finds every blonde in town…" I finished off his list and tossed the box onto the coffee table. "I know you can act better than this. Shut the F up and tell me the truth. What's in it for you if I date Vic?"

He stopped pacing. "We need more money."

I about fell out of my chair. "*Already*? It's been a month!"

"We have another three weeks left to film, Nicole says she's tapped, every other investor has bailed, and it's not much—just another five million."

Nicole says she's tapped. I almost snorted at the absurdity of the statement. Clarke had to be the one stopping that financial hemorrhage. I shrugged. "Well, I'm not this film's hooker. And I'm not yours either. If *BLL* needs money, make some cuts to the budget. Your afternoon massage, for example." His eyes narrowed, as I wiped my mouth. "I shouldn't have to date an asshole just so your movie gets made."

"Does Carter know?"

I looked up. "Know what?"

"About you and Vic." He nodded in the general vicinity where Vic had had me.

About you and Vic. The words were so simple, yet so ugly. I looked up at his face, everything in me going still. "Are you going somewhere with this?" I asked.

He shrugged. "Maybe someone should tell him."

The threat was clear. It was also stupid.

"Wait." I stood. "You want me to break up with Carter, or else you'll try and break us up by telling him about Vic?" My voice rose and fell enough times in that question that I hoped Joey saw the stupidity in his logic.

"It's not about me wanting you to date Vic. It's about me not wanting my friend to get hurt." Joey's bullshit response lit me on FIRE. If he didn't want Carter to get hurt, he wouldn't be pushing me to … UGH. I was in a conversation with a crazy person.

"You're right." I tried a different tack, Joey raising his eyebrows warily. "I think Carter should know about Vic. About…" I gestured in the direction of the sex and wondered how much Vic had told him. Vic had loved to talk about our sex life, to his friends, to complete strangers…

"She is, she's absolutely incredible." His hand ran up my bare thigh and under the hem of my dress. "You are, you know that baby?" I smiled when he nuzzled my neck, his watch heavy and cold on my thigh and I felt his fingers sneak around the edge of my panties.

"Vic," I whispered. "Stop."

"We fucked on the way here." He turned away from my neck and toward the guy at the next stool, some Wall Street yuppie who was staring at us like he wanted to toss aside his martini and wade right in. "You wouldn't think that, from looking at her, right? All innocence until the car door closes." He tugged a little on my panties, and I put a hand on his chest and pushed. Hard. When he released me, his hand taking an exploratory route home, and leaned back, he winked at me. I frowned and reached for my drink, wanting a distraction, something to keep my eyes away from the stranger.

Part of it had turned me on. Vic bragging, other men wanting. It was an aphrodisiac that had him ripping off my clothes as soon as we found a bit of privacy. But it was just as often a source of arguments, a breach of trust. And right now, with my mistake shoved in my face, I *hated* Vic for sharing that with Joey.

I stood and grabbed my purse. "I'll tell Carter." I smiled at Joey, and his eyes narrowed. "Tonight. So you won't have to worry about his precious little heart."

And just like that, the threat of blackmail was gone.

In its place, my anxiety spiked.

60. My Middle Name is Classy

The Psych Myself Up to Tell My New Boyfriend About Sleeping With My Ex Party was well underway. Granted, it was a little light on party guests. But I'd had quite an interesting time downing half of a pizza and three beers on my own, a meal that put me solidly in the drunk category. Not the best place to be when trying to coherently confess your soul.

I'd also turned just a teensy bit emotional. Maybe it was the hit I took off the joint that I found in one of my old purses. Or it was post-period hormones but whatever the reason, by the time Carter knocked on my door, I was half crying, half panicked.

I shouldn't have been so freaked out. Except that Carter was the first guy I'd liked in a long time. And he wasn't damaged or an asshole, which was a new thing for me.

I opened the door, and Carter swayed a little. Oh, wait. No. That was me. I swayed a little and my hand tightened on the door. "Are you okay?" His eyes concerned, his brow furrowed, and he stepped forward and grabbed my arms, sort of holding me up.

"I'm fine." I giggled. I didn't know why I giggled. I was nervous, and my stomach was in knots and a fifteen-year-old girl's giggle came out of me. He smiled a little, and I wanted to kiss him for it.

"I take it we're not going to dinner." He eyed my pizza and the empty bottles, which I swore I had thrown away but nope, they were sitting right there, on my coffee table, giant pieces of evidence. And oh shit, he was right; we were supposed to go out for sushi. The pizza had been a frozen one that I had planned to heat up as just a snack. One piece, that was all I'd have, something to tide me over until dinner. The beer had started the same way. One tiny piece of pizza and one beer, just to calm my nerves and pacify my stomach. Then … my eyes drifted over the train wreck on my coffee table. I didn't handle stress well.

There'd been a speech I'd planned. I closed my eyes and tried to remember it. Something that started with my history with Vic. It'd been a good speech. I'd practiced it twice. Carter's hands were holding me up by my biceps, I glanced down at them and the words just blurted out, without introduction or warning.

"I slept with my ex. In Joey Plazen's trailer. The night before he gave me the car."

Then … with his hands still wrapped around my arms, I leaned forward and vomited.

Super. Classy.

I know.

I opened my eyes and blinked, my alarm clock coming into fuzzy focus. I rolled over carefully, stilling when I realized I wasn't alone, Carter next to me, stretched out on top of the covers, jeans on, a couch pillow squashed underneath his head. I closed my eyes and did a self-assessment.

Foul taste in my mouth? Yep.

A little sweaty underneath the hot blankets? Oh yeah.

Knot in my stomach? Gone.

Shame of my actions? Non-existent.

Hmmm. I felt brave enough to prop up on my elbows and look around. I was pretty certain, given his full dress and … I peeked under the covers … my own jeans and top, that we didn't have sex. Or get even close to it. I closed my eyes and tried to remember more. The memory came fuzzy through the grip of a headache.

I'd told Carter about Vic and me. Then, I'd vomited. Apologized while … crawling to the bathroom? I winced, and Carter shifted. He opened his eyes and saw me.

"Chloe." His hand lifted, rubbing over his face. "Good morning."

"I slept with Vic. In Joey Plazen's trailer." It was like my vomit from last night. It just wouldn't stop coming out.

He smiled. "Yes. I know. You mentioned that, several times."

"And you're okay with it?"

He considered me for a long moment. "I wasn't. But … you're pretty hard to stay mad at when you're bent over a toilet."

I winced. "Sorry."

"You said that a lot last night." He met my eyes. "But you also told me it was over, with you and him."

"It is." My words were firm, no hesitation in my gaze. "Definitely." The words rolled out strong and confident. And I was sure of myself, positive that I *wanted* it to be over. What I wasn't as confident about was if it actually *was* over. It took two to tango, but it also took two to part.

"Why do you seem surprised that I'm not mad?"

"Well…" I kicked off a tangle of sheets. "It was after we hooked up. That'd bother some guys." It definitely would have bothered Vic.

"I didn't exactly walk away from that night expecting loyalty." He reached for me, but I rolled away. Mainly because I was pretty sure my morning breath was horrific. But also because he was *so* casual about this that it was raising my own questions.

"Did you have someone like that? An ex who was still around? Or who still is?"

"You mean, like Presa?" he raised his eyebrows and I fidgeted with the edge of the sheet. "Before that show, I hadn't seen Presa in months."

Months? I would have preferred *years*. "Anyone else?" The memory of the brunette—Brit—came to mind.

"Someone who gives me exorbitant gifts and drags me into isolated places for impromptu sex?" He shook his head with a smile. "No."

"I'm serious." I faced him squarely, wanting a straight answer. "Do you?"

"No." He pulled at the front of my shirt and I was forced into a kiss.

"I don't. You're it."

"Vic and I are over." I said the sentence a second time, because surely that would make it true.

Something flickered in his eyes. "I think you should tell him that." The suggestion was simple, no edge to the words, but they still cut me to the bone. I couldn't think of anything I'd rather do less.

"No." I stood up and headed to the bathroom, beelining for my toothbrush.

"Chloe." There was enough command in his voice to cause me to look over. "You tell me that it's over, but I've tripped over this guy since I met you. That car … you hooking up with him…" He took a deep breath. "Speaking as a man, I can tell you that we are dense. We miss subtle clues and tend to ignore things we don't want to hear."

I frowned. "Then he'll just ignore everything I say." Perfect logic.

"Talk to him." He pushed the subject, ignoring my logic, and I looked away, giving full concentration to the application of my toothpaste in a proper manner.

"Okay?" He poked me, and I looked up with a snarl.

"Fine." I stuck the toothbrush in my mouth with a scowl, and the conversation was over.

My stress, on the other hand, was just beginning.

61. Is Closure Really Necessary?

"It's unnecessary." I shook my strawberry shake, trying to unclog my straw. "Why do we need a conversation to confirm the fact that we broke up? He *knows* we broke up."

"It's *absolutely* necessary," Cammie interjected from across the table. "Especially after you let him…" She eyed me. "You know."

"Chloe can't handle it," Benta said. "It's asking for disaster. That man will give her one wink and BAM." She slammed her hand on the table, and Cammie and I flinched.

"Jesus, Benta," Cammie chided. "You're gonna break the table."

"He can wink his damn eye off," I stated. "It won't matter." It was one thing falling for Vic when I was single. But now, in a relationship with Carter, everything was different. Loyalty in a relationship—especially for me, especially after what I'd been through with Vic—was sacred. Which was just one of the reasons I was struggling so hard with Nicole's affair.

"Oh. Right," Benta said. "Forgive us. I didn't realize that so much had changed in … what? A month?"

"She did give back the car," Cammie pointed out.

"Hey!" I said sharply. "*She* is right here. And yes, things have changed. I'm with Carter."

"Okay, but *he* doesn't know they've changed," Cammie said slowly. "Which is why you need to tell him. *Clearly* and in person. So the idiot gets it."

"In person is stupid. You should just call him." Benta argued, and my gaze darted between them before landing on my phone. A call certainly would be easier. And risk-free.

"Chloe can handle a face-to-face without falling on the man's dick," Cammie snapped. "Short and sweet." She set down her milkshake and gave me her full attention. "Just tell him you're exclusive with Carter and that he needs to back the F up. Forever."

"Forever," Benta repeated, and they both stared me down.

I straightened in my seat. "Okay." I could do this. A clear face-to-face conversation where I would end any lingering expectations on Vic's part, part ways amicably, and emphasize we would never-ever-ever get back together. *cue Taylor Swift* I set down my empty milkshake cup. "I think I should do it in person," I decided.

Benta leaned forward, pushing my cell toward me. "So set it up."

"Right now?" I shouldn't have drunk that milkshake so fast. I felt nauseated.

"It's noon. The pretty boy will be awake." She nodded to the phone. "Call him."

My eyes jumped from her to Cammie, not one ounce of sympathy in either face. I groaned, grabbed my phone, and stood.

"Fine. But stay here. I'll call him from outside."

I leaned against the brick of the building and closed my eyes. Went through a breathing exercise, which didn't help at all, then tried a pep talk.

The call wouldn't need to be long. Short and simple would work just fine. We'd agree on the time and location, then hang up. Morning would be best, and I would keep the meeting short. There was a French cafe just off Central Park that would work. I scrolled down to Vic's number and took a deep breath. Then, my finger hesitant, I placed the call.

62. Calling the Enemy

"Hey baby." So casual, so confident. Vic's familiar greeting was painful, and I swallowed the urge to point out that I was not his *baby* anymore.

"Hi Vic," I spoke quickly, my fingers picking at the seam of my shirt. "Are you in town?" I held my breath, half hoping he wasn't, our interaction pushed off further.

"Nope. Blue marlin are hitting in the South Pacific, so we're going out. I'll be back in Fiji by the first, then back in the States by the fifth. Why?" His voice sharpened. "You need anything? I can have Jake there—"

"No." I tried to collect my thoughts. "I just wanted to talk. In person. We can do it when you get back."

"Is everything okay? I can fly back today."

"NO." I took a deep breath. "No, that's not necessary. I just wanted to…" This was stupid. A face-to-face wasn't needed. Discussing it right now was a better idea. "I'm seeing someone. I just wanted to tell you about it. And talk through it."

"Oh, yeah. The handyman." I could hear the smirk on his face, and it pissed me off.

"Just call me when you get back in town," I snapped. "We can talk then."

"I'll be back on the fifth. Let's meet then. My club. Ten o'clock."

"No." I sputtered. "I was thinking breakfast. In Central Park."

"Breakfast isn't good for me. And you said it was important. So let's knock it out as soon as I get back. Ten o'clock."

"I can't meet you at ten at night, Vic. That doesn't … *work* for me." I let out a hard breath and dug harder on the seam, finding a loose thread.

"For you or for the insecure boy you're dating?"

I frowned.

"Ten on the fifth. Wear something hot."

And before I could find a response, he hung up.

63. Negotiation Works Best Naked

ChloeMadisonNYU
103 likes
ChloeMadisonNYU Chanel is officially ready for Halloween. #boo #twoweekstogo

I knocked on Carter's door. Glanced at my watch. Tried a second time. No answer.

I eyed the stairwell and took that route, jogging down the stairs and into the basement. Carter had an office there, a tiny box stacked so high with items you could barely get inside. I had about forty-five minutes before Nicole would get out of her spa appointment and was hoping for lunch with my—I swallowed hard—boyfriend. That word still seemed foreign in my throat. Especially now, when I entered the dirty bottom floor, a place my prior boyfriends would never set foot in.

His office was empty, but the engine room door was cracked. I peeked in, the room cool and dark, and saw him. His shirt was off, the giant mechanics of our building behind him. We were talking rough big machines framing his tan, muscular skin, and I couldn't help but step inside, my hand pulling the door shut behind me, my sandals smacking against the floor.

He looked up, a wrench in hand, and rubbed at his nose with the back of his hand. Saw the look in my eyes, and stood, setting down the wrench. I forgot all about eating.

He picked me up under my arms, carrying me backward, my feet hanging limp, a huff of breath leaving me as he pushed me against the wall. My red sundress got shoved up, his pants quickly unzipped, and then he was inside me. Concrete cool and hard against my back, his grip biting into my ass, the grunt of his thrusts hot in my ear. He fucked me against that wall, and when I came, I screamed, the yell lost in the loud rumblings of the machines. When he finished it was sudden, his grip on my skin tightening, and I felt the shudder of him right before he pulled out.

That night, I told him about my attempt to call Vic and the disaster it had become. He listened quietly, his eyes darkening when I didn't sugarcoat the ending and told him exactly what Vic had said. How he'd called him insecure. How he'd wanted to meet me at night. Carter had looked away, a pulse in his jaw ticking, then back at me.

"I didn't want to force you to meet him. That wasn't what it was about."

"I know." We sat on his couch, my feet in his lap, his thumb rubbing gentle pressure into the soles of my feet. I rested my head on the arm of the couch and looked at the ceiling. "And I do think I should talk to him. Just to clear the air. Just so there's no doubt, in his mind, that we're over. I want him to stop everything he's doing."

"So then meet him. What difference is morning or night?" Carter's thumb resumed its massage.

I shrugged. "It's a control thing, really. I guess I don't like him dictating the place." My lie came out perfectly. It wasn't really the place, or the time that bothered me. It was the thought of seeing him. I wanted to put Vic in a box and pretend he didn't exist. I didn't want to look up into his face and see our history there. Even scarier, any regret on his face.

"It's the last time you'll have to see him." Carter ran his hand up the entire length of my leg, and I shifted, giving him better access.

"Right." I was starting to lose my train of thought, his fingers sliding along the inside of my thigh.

He watched me squirm and his eyes darkened. "I don't want you to meet him alone. Make sure there will be other people there." There was possession in his words and it was unbelievably hot, his face tightening, hands a little rougher on my legs. My mind flashed back to our second encounter, in the hall of my apartment, when he'd been pissed. I'd thought that look on him was hot. A possessive Carter was even hotter.

I slid deeper into the couch and pushed my foot into his crotch suggestively. "I'll think about it." I grinned when he crawled on top of me, his eyes narrowing.

"You do that, Ms. Madison."

"Or what?" I challenged him.

His hands settled on the clasps of my shorts.

His fingers pulled at my thong.

His head dropped between my legs.

And our conversation officially ended.

64. Six Tons of Oh Shit

I sat next to Dante, my laptop out, fingers quick as Nicole barked things from the backseat. Good thing I took typing in high school. I needed every bit of my 50-words-per-minute ability when dealing with Nicole's demands.

"And tell him that if he can't tell forsythia from winter jasmine that it's his damn fault, and I'm not paying for it." She paused and I heard the crack of a Diet Pepsi opening. "Did you run that background check on our new neighbors yet?"

"Yes. Just a second, I'll pull it up." I opened the file and turned in my seat, glancing back at her. Later, they would say that that small movement, my shift to the center of the car, saved my neck. All I knew was when the airbag exploded, it knocked me sideways in between the two front seats. And when we were hit a second time, six tons of moving truck slamming into the back of the SUV, our eyes met for one horrific split second.

A split second where Nicole wasn't bitchy or demanding or unfaithful.

A split second where she was confused. Then, smoke was everywhere, and I didn't see her at all.

I couldn't breathe. It was hot and dusty, clouds of smoke coming from the airbags, and I clawed at the door, trying to get it open. My hand finally found the handle and I pushed it open, gulping at the fresh air, the cab clearing. I heard Dante cough my name and turned to look at him, his hand pushing at the airbag, his own door cracking. "I'm fine," I called, fumbling for my belt, the hot metal of the other truck close, glass everywhere, and I wanted to look in the backseat, wanted to know … but I couldn't, I didn't.

65. I Should Have Seen This Coming

Nicole was not a person I'd ever felt affection for, yet there was this lump in my throat at the thought of her hurt. A bigger swell of emotion for Clarke. I didn't know why he loved that rotten woman, but he did. If she was hurt or dying … I didn't know how he would react. I stared at the carnage that was our vehicle and started to shake. The front hood was smashed, nothing incredibly major but enough to have stopped the Escalade in the middle of the street. It was the giant truck stuck into the back of the vehicle that was the problem. A collision that had eaten Nicole's seat in the crunch.

"She doesn't wear a seat belt." I looked up into the EMT's face. "Nicole doesn't wear a seatbelt." Clarke used to get on to her about it, all the time, an old argument played on repeat between them.

"Do you know what day it is?" The woman held my chin and shone a light in my eyes.

"Wednesday." I pulled away from her. "I'm fine. Do you know anything about Nicole?"

"No. I'm sorry." She didn't look sorry. She looked irritated, her hand quick and impersonal when she yanked the cuff off my arm. I looked for Dante, pushing off the hood of the car, a stranger's car, and she held me down. "Don't move."

"Chloe." Dante was there, a burn on his face, blood across his cheek but he was okay and I hugged him tightly. "They're getting Nicole out now."

"Is she okay?" I thought of when it hit. Her face. Her eyes on mine.

"I think she's okay. Be glad she was sitting behind me, your side got the worst of it." His eyes held mine, and I almost cried with relief. "Do you have your cell? Mine's still in the truck."

My cell. I reached into the pocket of my blazer. "Here."

"Thanks. I'm calling Clarke now."

I nodded, numbly noticing the cameras that had already shown up, the crowd starting, a few paparazzi present. Nicole would be crushed that she missed it, this opportunity in the spotlight. No … not crushed. I swallowed hard at my slip.

"Do you feel dizzy? Nauseous?" the woman asked, and I shook my head.

"Is there a chance you are pregnant?" I shook my head again, my birth control shot the one appointment I never missed.

She dabbed a cut on my arm, and I flinched. Then, above the blare of a siren and the sounds of the city, I heard the most perfect sound: Nicole bitching.

I pushed to my feet, ignoring the EMT's protests and ran through strangers, toward Nicole's voice. She was strapped onto a stretcher and *yelling*, one arm waving, a man grabbing the wrist and securing it down. I came closer, and her eyes zeroed in on me.

"You!" I swear there was an accusation in her voice, and I raised my hands in innocence, my eyes darting over her. She looked filthy, her white sheath covered with air bag powder and dirt, her hair coming out of her ponytail, her makeup a mess. Combine all that with the panic on her face and she looked deranged, but, thankfully, very much alive. She jerked her head toward me. "Come here!" she hissed, and I stepped forward cautiously, her voice dropping and eyes darting, like she was about to share a secret. "I need you to go to the car, right now, and get my handbag. It was on the floorboard. These *IDIOTS*—" that word screamed at full force in the direction of the medics—"won't get it for me."

"Your purse?" I asked blankly, glancing over my shoulder at the remains of the SUV, which seemed likely to burst into flames at any second.

"Yes. It's a black Birkin. Get it and keep it with you. Do you understand?" She pinned me with a look, as if her ten-thousand-dollar purse contained the cure for cancer.

"Yeah," I managed. "Yes," I corrected.

She stared at me blankly. "NOW!" she screamed, her good arm jerking.

"Sorry." I nodded to Nicole, and turned back to the car, dodging my overbearing EMT and carefully approaching the wreck. I was stopped five feet away.

"Where are you going?" It was a cop, his face no-nonsense, no pity given to my injuries.

"I was in the crash." I gestured toward it, in case he was confused. "I just need to get my boss's purse."

The guy's head was already shaking before I finished the request, and I swallowed any explanations of a Birkin's expense or the heights of Nicole's fury before I looked like an idiot. "It has her insulin shots in it," I bluffed. "The medics need it. If I could just have thirty seconds." I did the begging hands, jumping up and down routine and felt the edge of my bandage pop off. His eyes darted to the stretcher, Nicole's curses audible. "Please."

"Thirty seconds," he said gruffly. "Go."

"Thank you," I whispered, moving as quickly as I could, and pulled open the front door, the back one too mangled, and crawled over the center console, my eyes scanning the backseat floorboard. I let out a sigh of relief when I saw her purse, lying on its side. Its contents had spilled everywhere, and I leaned farther in, trying not to bump against anything, my hands grabbing at items and stuffing them quickly inside. Her iPhone, the screen cracked. Her moisturizer, then her keys. A few items had rolled under the seat and I stretched my arm, my nails digging into the edge of something plastic and I grimaced, sliding the object closer to me until I could finally get my fingers around it.

As soon as I saw it, I dropped it, a gasp slipping out, the stick rolling and I grabbed it before I lost it again.

So many memories, so many personal emotions tied to that simple white plastic piece, its window facing away. Just holding it felt like such a violation.

"Just do it already." Vic banged on the bathroom door, his voice irritated. I said nothing in response, my butt bare on the porcelain seat, the expensive tile of his parents' bathroom stretching before me. "It'll be fine, whatever it is. Just do it."

It didn't feel fine. It felt like a war of emotions. It felt like I was between two different life paths and whatever was on that stick would, literally, change my life. I had unwrapped the package with trembling fingers. Read the instructions twice. Let out a shaky breath as I had completed the steps.

My test had been negative and I had learned a lesson from it, getting on birth control the very next week.

Now, even though it wasn't my pregnancy test, I felt that same drop in my stomach. That same jittery moment of hesitation when I didn't really want to know the results. I looked down, my hand closed around the stick.

It wasn't my business to know. I should put the stick in her purse; gather up any other items, and leave.

I should forget that I even saw it.

Instead, I opened my palm and looked at it.

66. *Out of the ClearBlue Sky*

It was a ClearBlue pregnancy test, which made everything easy. No lines, no online instruction manual to hunt down. Just a simple word displayed across the top. PREGNANT. I had expected it, had known somewhere deep inside, what it would say, but I still inhaled sharply, my hand shaky as I gripped the stick harder.

"Time's up." The voice came from behind me, and I jumped, turning to see the cop. "You got to get out."

I hid the stick in my hand. "Just a minute." His face hardened. "Five seconds," I promised, my hands skating over the floor, making sure that nothing else had fallen. I stuffed it all, including the test, into her purse and closed the top flap, sliding my hand through the straps and crawling back into the front seat. At the last moment, I had the good sense to grab my own clutch. "Okay, I'm done."

Nicole was pregnant. No wonder she was so frantic for me to get her purse. If someone else had found the test, if word and photos had leaked out … I thought of Clarke and of his reaction. I thought of Paulo, and my world got a little darker.

Who was the father? Did she know? There really wasn't any math to do, the timeframe worked for either of them. Somewhere there'd be a joke about the condom queen getting pregnant. I gripped the handle of her Birkin tightly and stepped away from the crash. Spied them loading Nicole into an ambulance and headed that way.

Babies should be celebrated. Loved and treasured. I should be excited for her.

Instead, watching the ambulance's door slam, I felt sick.

67. Dropping the L Bomb

"Here." Dante held out my phone and I took it, watching Nicole's ambulance pull away. "Clarke's going to meet us at the hospital."

"Which one?"

"Langone." He watched me closely. "Are you okay?"

"Yeah." I shifted Nicole's purse to my other hand. Either it weighed a ton, or guilt and secrets added pounds. I was terrible with secrets. Vic used to sniff them out immediately. I'd say *hey* and he'd start an interrogation. Cammie and Benta could spot my tells too. Apparently, my whole persona changed—voice, face, and actions. The more I tried to act normally, the more awkward I was. Strangers, acquaintances, they didn't see it. Hopefully, when I returned her pregnancy-test purse, Nicole wouldn't see it either.

"I'm so sorry, Chloe. The asshole in front of me slammed on the brakes." He looked over at the wreck with a grimace.

I waved off his apologies. "Don't apologize. It was an accident."

He blew out a breath. "Want me to get you home?"

"No. I should get to the hospital." I glanced down at my phone. Three missed calls and two texts, both from Carter. I opened the first.

> *Joey called. Said he heard Nicole got in a bad car accident. Please tell me you are okay.*

I swore under my breath, the text sent ten minutes earlier. I almost didn't open his second text, anxious to call him and let him know I was okay. But I did.

> *I love you. I need you. Please be okay.*

I stared at the words. Love? My emotional stability trotted to the closest cliff and jumped off. Between Nicole's pregnancy news and the accident, I couldn't have an *I Love You* conversation with Carter right now. Did I love him? I thought so. But my emotions were all over the place. And he thought I might be hurt. Who knew what kind of false emotions he was dealing with?

I was torn, trying to decide how to respond, when I heard my name called. I looked up, Dante waving me toward a taxi. I took a deep breath and looked back at my phone, typing out a quick reply.

> *I'm okay. I'm sorry you were worried. I have to visit Nicole at the hospital. I'll call you shortly.*

It wasn't romantic. It didn't address his *I love you* at all. But hopefully it would calm his fears and stop any panic.

I saw dots appear, his response, and started toward Dante.

> *Thank God. Be careful and call me when you can. I love you.*

That again. I felt a burst of happiness. It felt strange, being happy on such a horrible day, and I locked the phone, feeling guilty, and tried to swallow my smile as I stepped into the cab.

68. Wounds Aren't the Only Superficial Things

Nicole's skinny arm reached out from under the hospital bed's sheet, waving for the purse. "Chloe!" she barked, and Clarke turned, his worried eyes meeting mine. I stepped into the hospital room and passed it over, her eyes meeting mine. "Did you get everything?" she asked pointedly and I nodded. "*Everything*?" she repeated.

"Yes. *Everything.*" I emphasized the word and I think she got the point, pulling the bag from my hands and peeking under the flap of it.

Clarke stepped toward me, lowering his voice. "She has some bad surface wounds," he said. "But everything is superficial."

"Really?" I glanced at Nicole, who closed her purse and clutched it against her chest like she might never let it go.

"She's refusing X-rays," he continued, and I nodded, unsurprised.

"I'm RIGHT HERE," Nicole yelled. "And I'm FINE. Chloe, call the studio and let them know I can't film today. And if I need a doctor, find one who will make house calls." She tried to run a hand over the top of her hair, and I saw the tremble of her fingers.

"You're not going to be able to film *today*?" Clarke turned to face her. "Nicki, you need to rest. Have you seen your face? You'll have bruises, swelling—" I put my hand on his shoulder and stopped him, Nicole's eyes widening as she lifted a hand to her face. Stupid man. He should know how much a threat to this woman's looks would freak her out.

"Don't worry about it." I smiled in my best attempt at reassurance. "I'll call them."

"Good," she snapped. "And get me a doctor. I want to be released from this hellhole now."

I took her order and escaped, finding a nurse and communicated her demand. And, forty-five minutes later, she was released.

I leaned against a column in the parking garage and watched as Clarke and Dante carefully helped her into a car, her purse still in a death grip against her chest.

"We've got it from here," Clarke said, shutting the door and looking at me. "You've had a hard day. Why don't you head home?"

I nodded without argument, waving goodbye and watching them pull out of the garage and into the sunlight. I wondered, as I stepped into a cab, what more could possibly go wrong.

As it turned out? A lot.

69. *Was I Brave Enough to Love?*

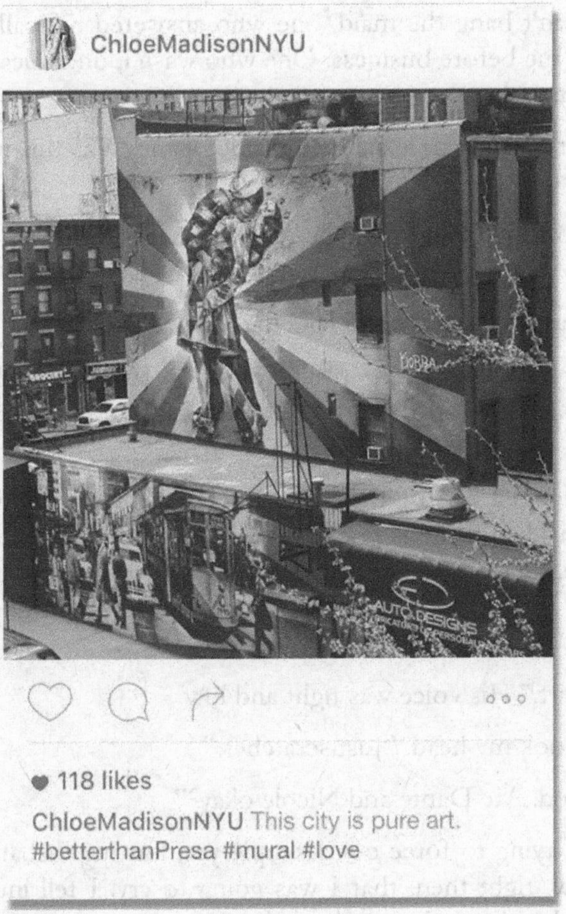

ChloeMadisonNYU
AUTO DESIGNS
118 likes
ChloeMadisonNYU This city is pure art.
#betterthanPresa #mural #love

The pregnancy news ate at me, devouring every spare brain cell, nothing else computing as I sat in the back of a filthy cab and tried to think. I needed to talk to someone, needed feedback, and my options were the girls or Carter.

Shit. *Carter.* I had forgotten all about him and the *I love you* texts.

It scared me, knowing that he might feel as strongly for me as I felt for him. Talk about a stupid fear to have. We were all running around this giant city trying to find love, trying to find soulmates. Looking for an all-encompassing, scary love just *like* this one. I should be jumping up and down in my Brian Atwoods and speed-dialing Carter's number. Proclaiming my love to him and embracing the fact that—for once—I was experiencing this love with a *nice* guy. One who wouldn't bang the maid, one who answered my calls, one who would put me before business. One who wasn't, underneath all of his sexiness, an asshole.

A small bit of happiness sparked inside of me. Was this it? Could he be my person?

Could I do this? Could I be the girl who ran toward right instead of wrong?

I could swallow my fears and take the jump. I could.

The driver knocked on the plastic partition and I looked up, seeing our building. "Oh. Sorry." I fumbled for cash and passed it forward. "Thanks."

When I stepped out of the car, Carter was there, standing on the sidewalk, his hands in his pockets, shoulders hunched forward. When he saw me, he relaxed, stepping forward and pulling me toward him, his hands gentle as they touched me, his eyes darting over my injuries.

"You're hurt." His voice was tight and low.

"No." I shook my head. "Just scratches."

"Thank God. Are Dante and Nicole okay?"

I nodded, trying to force out a simple yes, but my throat felt so full and I knew, right then, that I was going to cry. I fell into his chest and sobbed with no clear reason why. His arms wrapped around me, and he murmured my name into my hair, telling me it was going to be okay, telling me that I was strong and beautiful and amazing.

He brought me inside and ran a bath. I watched the water and thought of the dust, tiny particles moving around the cab of the truck. He carefully undressed me and cleaned my wounds, his touch careful, his eyes concerned. I remembered the squeal of brakes, a honk, Dante's shout. He'd shouted my name. The impact had been so loud. I could hear it, hours later. Without talking, without questions, Carter put me to bed, curling up behind me, one gentle kiss placed on the back of my neck.

It was exactly what I needed.

I did love him. I really believed that. I just didn't know if I was ready to admit it.

70. My Mouth is Big

I kept Nicole's secret for all of sixteen hours. Anything past that would have been impossible, it was just too great for me to sit on alone. Which was why, at seven in the morning, I woke Cammie up with an enthusiastic use of her buzzer. Lucky for me, I was in a car accident the day before, so I got a free pass. Once we covered my injuries and got some coffee brewing, we sat on her couch, whispering so as not to wake Dante, and I spilled everything.

"Shut up." Cammie's eyebrows raised in evil glee. "She's *pregnant*?"

"Yes." I giggled despite myself. It wasn't funny. But for all of the shit I'd watched Nicole get away with, the woman had it coming. I composed my face and tried my best serious face. "It's not funny," I admonished.

"It's *kinda* funny," Cammie mused, lifting her coffee mug for a sip. "Have you told Benta?"

"No. Don't."

She raised a hand in surrender. "No worries there." Benta, God love her, couldn't keep a secret for shit. You told her anything juicy and she'd have a *Times* billboard rented before the end of the hour.

It felt good to let it out. To have a sounding board. And, let's face it, it felt great to hear her gasp of shock, to have someone who truly understood and appreciated the magnitude of the fact that NICOLE WAS PREGNANT. Cammie all but whipped out a calendar, trying to figure out ovulation windows and the probability of whose sperm was luckiest. Or rather, unluckiest. I tried to picture a pregnant, hormonal Nicole and saw absolute disaster. When I thought of her as a mother … well. I already felt bad for Chanel.

We talked for over an hour, and produced absolutely no game plan on how to handle the pregnancy test. I left with promises to keep her updated. So for right now, I was sitting on the information and trying to pretend I didn't know it, and trying my best not to think about it.

Talk about an impossible task.

November

I knew from the news that my parents' noose was tightening, their legal fight running out of options and funding. When I called on his birthday, Dad actually answered. We chatted about the Dolphins and then he shared a moment of truth, his voice tight and irritated.

"We just thought we had more time, Chloe. They came in so fast … they took everything. If I had known, things would have been different. The investigation wouldn't have mattered."

A bundle of sentences that took any remaining respect I had for my father and ground it to dust. I didn't want parents who squirreled away money and then ran. I didn't want to come from that stock. I wanted a dad who apologized to me. Who hugged me and told me that he screwed up. That he was sorry for not supporting me through the last year. Who said *something* that validated all of my love for him. On that call, he didn't even tell me he loved me. It was as though my parents had only known how to show love through gifts and—without their money—had no feelings left for me.

71. Distracted by the D

I knocked on Carter's door with one goal in mind: To Confess Love. He opened the door, and I didn't even get out a greeting. He hooked a finger through my belt loop and pulled me into his chest. His mouth came down on mine, his other hand pushing the door closed and then I felt the full palm of his hand on my butt, squeezing hard. He gripped me like he thought I might slip away, his kiss deepening as we stood in place, my bag dropping through my fingers, my hands reaching up to grip his hair.

Any chance of talking disappeared in the pull of his mouth off mine, his hand pushing me back, and as my shoulders hit the door, his knees hit the floor, his fingers at the top of my leggings. His name was a question off my lips and he ignored it, pulling at the waist of my pants and my panties, and then they were skimmed down my legs and around my feet.

He was a man on a mission, and my flats were off, my left thigh lifted over his shoulder, and then his mouth was between my legs, my hands skittering over the door as I tried to hold on to something. "Carter," I gasped his name around the time that his tongue found *that* spot, the one he discovered one morning and could barely hold me down after. It wasn't my clit, it was further back … and when he flicked his tongue over it, I was gone. I collapsed against the door, my hands weak on his shoulders, my weight on him, his hands holding me up as he worshiped me with his mouth.

Light flutters, so light and constant and perfect—at that spot then up to my clit, his fingers biting into my bare ass, a guttural groan humming over my sensitive skin and spelling out his enjoyment. I wanted to move, wanted to not be standing, two wants that got lost in the swell of pleasure. When I came, my nails dug into his shoulders, my foot braced against the floor, my thighs tightened around his head, and everything in my mind went black.

I had a vague recollection of him lifting me up. Of him carrying me to his bed. I found my bearings around the time that my back hit the sheets. I helped him pull off my shirt and watched as he yanked at his, his abs flexing as he threw it into the corner of the room, his fingers quick as they worked at his pants. He was *so* freaking hot. So strong, the cut of his muscles showing in the simple act of shedding his clothes. His eyes were on mine the entire time and when he crawled onto the bed, hard and ready for me, I was ready for him.

I was *so* ready for him.

"You need more furniture." I picked up a shrimp with my chopsticks and gestured to his bare bones room.

"I don't like clutter," he remarked, scooping fried rice onto his plate.

"Yeah—I've seen your closet. I could tell." I popped the shrimp in my mouth and chewed, watching him crack open a Coke.

He glanced my way. "You prefer your men messy?"

"Not at all." I thought of Vic, who tossed his clothes on the floor, a maid picking them up the minute our back was turned. "I'm just jealous I wasn't born with that gene."

"I don't know if I was born with it or if it was beaten into me." He made a whip motion with his hand, and I raised my eyebrows.

"Please tell me it wasn't by Presa." I made a face and he laughed.

"No, no. My mom. She wouldn't let me eat unless everything was in its place."

I smiled at the image, one so different than my childhood. I could picture him, a miniature heartbreaker, then a lanky teenager, put into place by a bossy mother. "I wish my mom had been more like that. Maybe then…" Maybe then I'd be a lot different. Maybe then I wouldn't have struggled so much when the rug was yanked out from beneath me.

He shrugged. "It's one of those things that you hate as a kid but learn to appreciate the benefits of later. I think they did a pretty good job of raising me."

"Was your Dad strict too?"

He nodded, scooping out some noodles and holding them out for me. "Do you want kids?"

Kids? That wasn't something I hadn't thought about. Literally. I had always assumed I'd have them, just hadn't ever really thought if I had wanted them. Vic had wanted five boys. So that had always been that. Discussion over, damn whatever sperm or Chloe had to say about the matter. "I don't know," I said, taking a sip of my tea.

"I think you'd make a great mom." I almost asked him to repeat himself, wanted to hear the words one more time.

"Really?" I scrunched up my face. "I can't even handle myself."

"The best parents are those that try. And that can admit their mistakes."

Well, wasn't that the truth. Maybe, if my parents admitted their own shortgivings, I would have seen more of my own. "So…" I said slowly, setting down the box of food and sitting back in my chair. "You're saying that because I'm a train wreck, I'll be a great mom?" I narrowed my eyes at him and he smiled.

"I'm saying that Chloe Madison doesn't seem to do anything half ass." He stood and walked around the table, leaning over and resting his weight on the arms of my chair.

"That sounds like a challenge," I mused, grinning wickedly up at him.

He laughed and pressed his lips to mine. "You up for it?"

I was up for it. And as it turned out, so was he.

72. Closure: Is it Really Necessary?

The alarm blared, jerking me out of sleep, an insistent beep that was impossible to ignore, especially not at five in the morning.

I rolled over, pulling a pillow over my head and listened to him silence it. I fell asleep around the time that his shower started and woke up again when he whispered my name, his mouth kissing my neck. He asked if my alarm was set, and I grunted out a yes. Then he was gone.

My meeting with Vic loomed, just one day away. I dreaded it. I had always done better with Vic when I didn't see him. There was something about us being face-to-face … it had, in the past, weakened all of my barriers. This time needed to be different.

"You know, you don't need Carter as a reason to say goodbye to Vic." Benta reached over, stabbing her fork into one of my grapes and stealing it. "Cutting ties with Vic has been overdue, regardless of anything else."

"I know." Benta caught the eye of the waiter, and I snuck a glance at my watch. Our lunch had been impromptu, the stars aligning to give us a forty-five minute window of time to inhale salads and pregame my meeting with Vic.

"You broke up with him for a reason," Cammie added.

"I *know*," I repeated, pulling my plate closer and warding off a second attempt by Benta.

"You know what I think?" Cammie mused, taking a long and dramatic sip of ice water.

"I think … you better hurry up because I have to get back to work?" Benta drawled.

"I think," Cammie said, shooting Benta a glare, "that Chloe's a saboteur." She looked at me. "You know you have a good thing with Carter, and it scares you. So you're tempted by Vic purely because you want an excuse for your relationship to fail."

"But she's not tempted by Vic," Benta argued. "Right?" She looked at me.

"It's Vic's money," Cammie interrupted me before I could speak. "That's what she's struggling with."

"I'm not tempted by Vic." I swallowed. "And I'm over his money." I looked down at my plate, thinking of every horrible thought that had crossed my mind, back when I'd first met Carter. How much money and future lifestyles had ruled my decisions back then.

Benta laughed. "Really? The same Chloe Madison who balked at our Spring Break trip because she was too fancy for Carnival Cruise lines?"

Cammie leaned forward with a smile, because it was apparently Make Fun of Chloe Day. "The same Chloe Madison who had *daily* maid service at your old apartment?"

"That was Vic's maid," I pointed out.

"And you loved it."

I rolled my eyes. "Who *wouldn't* love daily maid service? That's a stupid statement."

But I did. I'd loved it. I'd loved everything about that life. And maybe that *was* what I'd struggled with so much in terms of Vic. Maybe it hadn't been him, but his money, his lifestyle—a distinction that turned my year of struggle from being lovestruck to just being materialistic. *Ouch.*

"Chloe's right." Benta's comment dragged me back to the conversation. "I would *love* daily maid service."

"Let's not talk about Vic and maids," I groaned. "Please."

Cammie raised an eyebrow at me. "Oh, I'm sorry," she said. "How terrible of us to remind you of his cheating right before you end things with him."

"I already ended things with him," I shot back, standing and gathering up my trash. "This is just closure."

Closure. Such an odd concept. Did relationships really need it? Or was it just an excuse for one last glimpse at what could have been?

I didn't ask them the question. They were, at times, a little too honest for my heart's sake. But I thought Benta and Cammie were both right.

I needed to kiss Vic's ass goodbye because it was the right thing to do and it was about damn time.

I needed to embrace my relationship with Carter and stop being a wimp. Whether I'd told him so or not, I loved him. He made me realize how empty my old life had been. And in his eyes, I saw a future that I wanted more of, a future where I was a better person.

Wow. I might have just become a grown-up.

73. *Drinks With the Devil*

ChloeMadisonNYU
189 likes
ChloeMadisonNYU Waiting for the devil to arrive and eyeing my barmate's drink.
#closure #liquidcouragevsdietcoke

I met Vic in the downstairs bar, instead of his upstairs office. I'd been in that office too many times. Bent over that desk, on top of liquor invoices and payroll docs. Pressed up against the window, my cheek to the glass, his hips pumping against my ass. Vic loved that office. I didn't want to think about how many women, both during and after me, he'd had up there.

I got there first, finding a stool at the bar and pulling out my phone, returning a text to Cammie.

"Can I get you a drink?"

I looked up at the bartender. A drink. Ha. Alcohol was the one thing I *didn't* need to add to this situation. "Diet Coke," I said. The man winced, but grabbed a glassful of ice.

It took fifteen minutes for Vic to show up. When he did, it was in a dark gray suit, a blue shirt underneath, his jacket unbuttoned, his tie loose around his neck. His hair was neat, his skin tan from his fishing trip. He smiled at me as he approached and my hand tightened on my glass. The problem with not drinking? You lost the careless steel it could give your spine.

I started to speak, and he cut me off, leaning forward, so close I could smell his cologne. "Cute outfit."

"Thank you." I'd dressed casually, knowing it would irritate him, especially in this club, an establishment that prided itself on an unbendable dress code. My jeans and V-neck had made the doorman shake his head as soon as I had stepped up, his mouth souring into a scowl when I flashed the gold card that Vic had given me. There were only a handful of them in the city, some VIP bullshit that Vic printed up that gave carte blanche at any of his places. I hadn't ever used it when we'd dated, everyone knowing who I was but now, eighteen months later, all of the faces were different, the city of New York one that changed often and easily forgot.

Vic pulled his stool forward and it was then I realized that the bar had emptied, the bartender gone, the velvet curtain to its entrance pulled shut.

We were alone and God, I hated it when he did shit like that.

Well, now I hated it. I used to love it.

74. Hit Me With Your Best Shot

His stool was near enough that his knee brushed the inside of my thigh, his huff of breath close enough that the hair on my skin rose in response. I pushed my drink away and stood, needing space. Being that close to Vic never led anywhere productive.

"Vic." I swallowed. Short and sweet. I could do this. "You've got to stop … reaching out." He sat back, his elbows on the bar, his body completely relaxed, his mouth twitching a little as if he was holding back a smile. "I mean it." I narrowed my eyes and stood a little straighter, wishing for a moment that I wore something more commanding than flats and Hudsons. "You and I are done. I'm in love with Carter." It was the first time I'd said the words aloud, and they came out flat and uncertain, almost like I was posing it as a question.

"Really," Vic drawled out the words. "Love?"

"Yes." I lifted my chin and met his eyes.

"Do you even know what love is, Chloe?" Funny that the man who'd tainted the word for me could speak so confidently about it.

I lifted my shoulders in a shrug. "I'm figuring it out."

He didn't like that. I saw the tighten of his lips, the clench of his jaw, the curl of his fingers around the lip of the bar's edge. "So it's the same? As it was with me?"

"No." The next part was cruel and hard but true and necessary and the words fell out painfully. "It's better. It's a real relationship. I trust him. I don't know if I ever trusted you." So many nights, waiting up for his calls, wondering where he was. So many trips taken without me, Instagram pics on other girls' accounts, his jet in the background, their smiles where mine should have been.

"And how well could he treat you, Chloe?" His loose position was gone, his stool empty. He was on his feet and stepping closer, one of his hands wrapping around my arm and squeezing. "Does he let you super-size your fast food order? Get a popcorn at the budget movies?"

"Don't be an ass." I yanked my arm and turned, stepping away, wanting some distance, some space, less of him and more of me. I raised my arms to my head and breathed deeply. Willed myself to relax.

He kept his distance, thank God. I heard the screech of a stool and looked over, seeing him push my purse aside, his hand on my glass and he met my eyes, lifting it to his lips. He scowled at the taste and set it back down. "What—you stop drinking too?"

I squared my shoulders and met his eyes. "I love him." I watched him shove at my glass, the tumbler slick on its slide across the counter, and I winced when it went over the edge, turning away when it hit the tile floor, the crash loud and painful.

"Bullshit, Chloe. I know you. You don't *love* him. And I'm different now. I've learned from my mistakes. I'm the only one who can give you the life you deserve." At one time, that threat would have affected me. Now, it was laughable.

"You're wrong. I love him." Each time I said it, I found more truth in it.

"Stop saying that!" There was another crash of glass and he was on his feet again, stepping toward me, and I flinched, my hands coming up in protection.

There was a growl from the doorway in the moment before Vic's hands latched onto me.

I didn't know how long Carter had been standing there, or what he had heard but I knew when Vic's hands grabbed me, Carter moved—a fluid burst of masculinity, his impact with Vic flinging me free, my side hitting a table's edge. A burst of pain flared in my ribs and I clutched my mid-section, my head whipping to the two men who, at different moments in time, owned my heart.

Carter got to his feet, his hand tight on Vic's shirt. Vic lifted his head, a manic laugh bubbling out. "Go ahead," he spat out. "Give me your best shot."

"Carter," I spoke quietly but he looked up, his arms bulging as he held up Vic's weight. I nodded to the three men standing in the doorway, Vic's security team, men with guns underneath their jackets and itchy trigger fingers. "Let's go."

Vic's fist swung upward as Carter let him go. It was a cheap shot, unsurprising, but I heard the connection and winced. Carter stood, his hand wiping at his mouth, his eyes dark, and looked at me. I hurried past him and grabbed my purse. It had fallen to its side, and I shoved its loose contents inside, my hands quick, steps quicker, and then we were outside, the night air warm, our exit lost in the madness that was a city at night.

We stepped into a curbside taxi, my butt sliding across the vinyl seat, my hand tightly grasped by Carter, nothing said between us until the cab pulled off, bumping over a pothole in its exit.

"Are you okay?" Carter ran a finger over his lip, blood smearing, and he frowned.

"I'm fine. He wouldn't have … he wouldn't have done anything." Vic's temper had flared a hundred times. The worst he'd ever done was throw things at me. Things that could be ducked, his fist hitting the wall beside my head something that scared but didn't hurt. "I had it covered," I said the words for myself as much as I did for Carter.

"You shouldn't have met him alone like that. I told you not to." His tone was low and judgmental, and I bristled.

"It wasn't supposed to be alone. I didn't realize he'd clear the bar. Why were you there?"

He laughed. "Is this what this is gonna be? You're pissed at me for showing up?"

"I've been followed before. Checked up on. I don't like it." I looked out the window.

"I didn't follow you because I didn't trust you. You told me where you'd be—"

"And I was there," I said, cutting him off.

"I was waiting for you in the entrance. Just in case. I heard a shout; I came in. Don't make it into anything else."

I didn't know what to think. Didn't know if I was sensitive from my time with Vic, time where I was constantly monitored, his paranoia trumped only by his jealousy. Carter had never acted that way, had been more than cool with all of Vic's bullshit, including the set up of this meeting to begin with. I felt the knot in my back begin to relax, and I turned to look at him, reaching out my hand. "The only reason I met him was because you asked me to."

"I know, and maybe I shouldn't have insisted. I'm sorry I didn't knock him out." He grimaced.

I thought about how he'd looked, his muscles tense, the blur of his movement, the protective rush to my aid … it had been, in the whirlwind of it all, pretty hot. I smiled. "You didn't do so bad. That's probably the closest Vic's ever come to a beating. He's normally got his guys close by. But I hate that he sucker-punched you."

Carter shrugged. "Hey, I got the girl. It was worth it." He leaned over, burrowing his head into my shoulder and inhaled deeply, relaxing into me. "A kiss would help," he whispered.

I obliged. It was the least I could do, the soft brush of my lips against his split lip, his bruised jaw.

It wasn't until later that I realized the problem. After our shower, after his gentle towel dry of my hair, after a long and sweet session in between the sheets, after I flipped off the bedroom light, and reached down into my purse for my phone to plug it in.

My hand skated over a compact, lip-gloss, and my wallet. Fumbled behind a half-eaten Snickers bar and my earbuds. My heart started beating and I turned on the bedside light, looking again, more frantic this time.

My phone. It was gone.

75. Five-Fingered Prick

My missing phone wasn't an accident and it wasn't my fault. I knew that instinctively, my stomach twisting as I slowly shut the purse and set it down. This was Vic.

I heard the screech of his stool and looked over, seeing him push my purse aside, his hand on my drink and he met my eyes, lifting it to his lips.

Shit. I imagined him, sitting at home, his fingers across my screen, flipping through my photos, reading my texts … I had the insane urge to get dressed and run back to his bar, or his penthouse, or wherever the damn man was. Find him and rip my phone back from his freshly manicured fingers.

I punched on the bed with a hard fist, Carter sitting up, his hand touching my elbow, asking if everything was okay. "It's fine." I tried to smile, turned and crawled under the covers, my body sliding alongside his. I kissed his neck and burrowed into his side.

Right then, I should have told him about my missing phone. Full disclosure, open communication, and all that good-for-relationship stuff. But with his lip freshly split from Vic's punch, our minds finally off the night's events, I just couldn't. Instead, I laid my head against his chest and stewed. Pretended to be asleep while, inside, my mind went crazy.

I never wanted to see Vic again. Not even for my phone. But then, I thought of everything on it, the personal invasion of him pawing through it…

As soon as Carter fell asleep, I crawled out of bed. Borrowed his cell and called Cammie from the bathroom. She was awake and cut me off mid-sentence, as soon as she understood the dilemma.

"Wipe your phone." She spat out the directive as if it was simple.

"What?"

"He knows your passcode, right?"

My passcode. The four-digit code I'd used since high school. "Yeah," I said glumly.

"Remotely wipe it. Now. You can do it through iCloud."

iCloud. The thing I'd cursed so many times before… could it actually be my savior? I winced at the thought of the last time I'd backed up my phone. At what I'd lose in the wipe.

"Now, Chloe. Before he gets every naked selfie off it." Cammie's voice broke through. *Naked photos.* My mind tripped and fell over every sexy pic I'd taken in the two years I'd had that phone. I should have known my vanity would have come back to bite me.

I cracked the bathroom door and eyed Carter's laptop, one I didn't have a password for. "Can you do it? I'm at Carter's."

She jumped into action and a few minutes later, my phone, wherever it was, had been completely erased. I would have the headache of paying for a new phone. But the satisfaction of not having to call Vic? To not go crawling back to him, hand out, asking for it back? *That* was worth it. That felt better than anything else.

That night, for the first time all week, I slept soundly.

76. Breaking up with Balenciaga

ChloeMadisonNYU
149 likes
ChloeMadisonNYU Had a threesome in Brooklyn today. Me, Ben, and Jerry. #BostonLoveLetters #shooting #movie

A woman in New York City couldn't survive without a cell phone. It was a fact. Especially not a woman working for Nicole Brantley. My old self would have marched into the closest Verizon and walked out with a shiny new phone. My new self had to wait three days for my phone insurance to ship out a refurbished replacement. My new self agonized over the two-hundred-dollar fee. I hated Vic a little more with every inconvenience caused.

My job probably wouldn't have survived the three-day period if not for the set walkies—a giant radio that hung on my hip, a cord running from it up to an equally sexy headpiece that Nicole insisted I wear. I looked ridiculous but could hear Nicole's voice loud and clear when she barked. And she barked constantly. It turned out pregnancy was hell on a bitch's hormones. Her taste buds had gone crazy too. She'd been demanding the weirdest food. Olives, coffee-flavored ice cream, feta cheese, and banana popsicles. Try and track down *banana* popsicles. It was impossible. I called seventeen stores before she decided she'd rather have cherry.

There was one benefit of the constantly affixed headgear. I could tune into the general set chatter, which was usually snooze-worthy except for today, when a PA mentioned that Victor Worth was on set. I immediately ducked into Wardrobe and hid, my butt settled down behind racks of clothes, my fingers picking absentmindedly through the fabrics. I was stuck there for the forty-five minutes it took for word to finally circulate that he'd left.

When I returned to Nicole's trailer, there was a box for me, too big to hold just a phone, and I growled a little under my breath. I ripped at the ribbon with angry hands, the white lid yanked off to reveal the purse—a Balenciaga City Bag—black, with a card hanging off one strap. I flipped open the card, steeling myself for the message, ready for something sexual and inappropriate, as was Vic's style.

This one zips shut. Better for not losing things.

I had to roll my eyes at that. Peeking in the bag, I spied my phone.

So he had returned it. No face-to-face meeting required, no lording the phone over me in exchange for contact.

Call me paranoid, but I didn't necessarily want it back. Not when it had been in his hands. Not when he could have gotten his geek squad to do God-knows-what to it. Tracking software? Keylogger programs? Remote access? Probably all of the above. I opened up the lid to the trash and ditched the phone, hearing the thud of it hit the bottom. One problem solved.

The bag … I ran my hand slowly over the supple leather, its clean and beautiful lines. Then I opened an upper cabinet and pushed the bag inside, hiding it behind all of Nicole's junk. There was a limit to pride, and it stopped at insanity.

77. The Thing I Didn't Want to Talk About

Parents. The one word no relationship needs. Carter said it and I took my time chewing my bite of salad. Beside me, my new phone chilled on the tabletop, freshly synced, my life back in order. Or rather, it was. Until Carter brought up his parents. And dinner with them.

"Saturday night," he continued. "They suggested a French restaurant on Park." He speared a piece of fish and looked up at me. "Do you like French food?"

"Yes…" I said cautiously.

"You don't have to come." He shrugged. "I know it's been a crazy week for you with work … and with it raining tonight…" His words got lost in another bite of food and I set down my fork. It wasn't *that* crazy of a week at work. And what did the rain have to do with anything?

"I can come." My curiosity spoke for me, something about the casual invite; coupled with the reluctance of his voice … I was suddenly dying to meet them. How bad could parents be? I warmed to the idea, my head nodding. "I'd love to meet your parents."

"You would?" Carter looked wary.

"Yeah." I stabbed at another piece of salad. "I love parents."

"Have you told yours about us?"

I slid the fork slowly out of my mouth, chewing the bite, trying to think of the proper response. "No," I finally said. "I—I haven't spoken to my parents in a while." I stared down at my bowl, picking through the mixed greens. Our last contact had been my dad's birthday. Since then, I'd left four or five messages, all unreturned. After the last, I hadn't had the heart to try again. And that had been almost two weeks ago.

Odd that Carter and I had discussed almost everything but our parents. I'd planned to tell him about mine. *Next week* I'd kept thinking. The *next weeks* had piled up on themselves and turned into … God. Five months. Five months since we'd first met. And now … I shifted in my seat. It didn't seem the time. Not when I'd asked him so little about his. I knew they'd been strict. Neat freaks who withheld sustenance. Nothing else. "Your uh—parents. They're still married?"

"Yeah," he said, watching me. "Yours?"

"Yeah."

"You don't like to talk about them?" he asked.

I managed a laugh. "Not really. You?"

He shrugged. "You know a little. My parents are … grouchy." He grimaced. "To be honest, I'm a little worried that they'll scare you off."

I looked up, meeting his eyes. "They won't." I couldn't think of anything that would scare me away from this man.

He chuckled. "You sure about that? They've always been difficult with anyone I've dated."

I was.

Turned out, I might have underestimated the situation.

78. I Hate These People

I checked my reflection for the tenth time in the mirror above my sink. Smoothing down my hair, I checked my teeth. I was dressed conservatively, but cute—a Krisa jumpsuit paired with jeweled flats. Carter called my name, and I swallowed. "Coming!" I called, running the sink for a moment to buy some time. I shouldn't be so nervous. Parents loved me. And why wouldn't they? Carter could have done a lot worse. I tossed some lipstick in the clutch and snapped it shut. Gave myself one last look in the mirror and then pulled open the door.

"Ready?" Carter leaned against the wall, his eyes lifting to me and he smiled. "You look beautiful."

"Thank you." I let out a nervous breath. "I'm a little stressed," I confessed.

He smiled, pulling me to him and pressing his lips to mine. "Come on," he said. "We're going to be late."

"You're supposed to tell me I have nothing to be nervous about," I scolded playfully, shrugging into my jacket and following him into the hall.

"You'll do fine," he said, checking his watch.

Still not the words I wanted. I took the hand he offered, and we stepped into the elevator. I blamed the drop of my heart on the quick descent, my nerves humming.

Something was off.

We stepped in the small restaurant, Carter giving our name to the maître d', my heart sinking when I saw, seated just a few tables inside, the older couple who had interviewed interrogated me for the apartment. The woman's back was as stiff as it had been in my interview, the man's face just as dour. I grabbed Carter's arm and hoped he'd veer right, to the bar, but he saw them too. I'd forgotten for a moment that they were his employers, him recognizing them also.

He steered me in their direction and they looked up at our approach, the woman's eyes skipping past Carter and landing on me, a glint of recognition in her eyes. I smiled politely and looked away, to the other tables, wondering if Carter's parents were already there, absently trying to remember the last name of the couple in front of me, in case this chat turned into actual conversation.

But then Carter hugged the woman, and I heard the word *Mom* cross his lips. And everything stopped in the heartbeat it took for my sluggish brain to put two and two together and finally understand it all.

Carter's connection to Presa Little.

His job.

His apartment, so much nicer than mine.

He wasn't just the super. He was the *owner*. This old couple who had barely let me rent an apartment—he was their son. I snapped to attention and put a little more into my smile, my efforts dampening under their withering stare.

Carter turned, pulling out the closest seat. "Chloe?" he offered, his eyes meeting mine cautiously.

I wanted to kill him. I wanted to grab his shirt and drag him outside and yell every question coursing through my mind at him until he confessed everything.

But I didn't. I smiled graciously and took my seat. I placed my napkin in my lap and nodded a hello to his parents. I sat through the painful first moments where no one spoke and ice water settled in glasses and waiters hovered.

And then, the silence was over. Carter's mother opened her mouth, and hell poured out.

I'd sat through a few painful dinners in my life. This was the worst. It was my interview, times five. The questions didn't stop; they peppered at me from across the table, and I wanted to duck for cover, wanted a bathroom break, wished I smoked just for an excuse to escape.

When his father asked about my parents, I paused, glanced down at my menus, this hell not even half over, and debated about my answer. Tried to weigh truthfulness over first impressions. Knew, no matter what happened with Carter and me, they would eventually find out the truth.

"My parents?" I stalled.

"Yes. They work with investment portfolios, isn't that correct?" Carter's mother tilted her head and peered at me as if I was a specimen to be cut open.

I considered dodging the question. I hadn't even told Carter about my parents and their situation. But I didn't. "He *did* work with investment portfolios," I said carefully. "But the SEC has suspended his license. I'm not sure what my father will do now, assuming that he avoids jail time."

That shut them up. His mother's mouth fell open a little, her eyes widening. Beside me, Carter inhaled, and his father set down his drink, the glass hitting the table with a loud clink.

I didn't stop. I told them everything, wincing a little at how cold I sounded when I spoke about my parents. I couldn't help it. If the last year had shown me anything, it was that my self-centeredness was an inherited trait, and that every *I love you* from their mouths had been a lie.

"So…" his mother said primly. "Your parents are criminals and you are an … *assistant*." She stretched out the final word in such a way that made my job sound as bad as my parents' crimes.

"Yes." I took a deep sip of wine, finishing it off. "That's correct."

"I see. And the chances of your parents being exonerated are…?" She raised an eyebrow at my empty wine glass, then at me.

"Pretty much nil." I shrugged.

She sighed, and I glanced at Carter's father, who had stopped talking about fifteen minutes earlier. His face was stiff, and I looked to his son. It was a mistake. Carter looked hurt, and I couldn't help but glare a little in response. I wasn't the only one who'd been secretive about my parents. I had spent our entire relationship with this image in my head of Carter's life, his upbringing, his future. It certainly hadn't involved a mother wearing Chanel with a four-carat diamond on her finger, her nose raised higher in the air than Nicole at a staff meeting. Everything I had envisioned … a rough youth, clawing his way to financial independence … all of that was false. The damn man had probably attended a better prep school than me.

And it was right about then, with my dinner plate carefully set down before me, that I realized two things. First, that any worries I'd had over Carter and his future prospects were unfounded.

Second, I wasn't relieved by that realization. Instead, I was … I stared down at my dinner and tried to process my feelings. I was *disappointed.* Disenchanted. Not just with Carter, but with myself. I was no longer the fallen society girl who had fallen in love with a poor boy and tossed away her materialism. I was the fallen society girl who would climb right back into her old life, clawing up the chest of her sexy boyfriend.

Much more fairytale. Much less inspirational.

I picked up my fork and tried to find my appetite. Tried to perk up by telling myself that the worst of the evening was over.

Famous last words.

79. Walking the Plank

We left the restaurant, my hand stiff in Carter's firm grip, his parents huddling together against the wind. I breathed it in with relief, grateful for fresh air after the tension-filled dinner, his mother's judgment choking me the entire meal. She thought I was a gold digger, had all but called me one during the meal, multiple insinuations made that I was with Carter for his inheritance. An inheritance I hadn't even known about. It was ridiculous.

I couldn't wait to get home, was almost distracted enough by the idea to miss his mom inviting themselves over. I blinked, turning my head against the wind, toward their conversation, just in time to hear Carter politely push them off.

His mother, damn her soul, didn't back down. "Don't be silly, Carter. I haven't seen the building since … gosh. Since we interviewed Chloe. Let us check in on our investment, sweetie. It's the *least* you can do." Her eyes glowed at me, and I wanted to throw up my hands in frustration.

"*You* don't mind, do you Chloe?" Oh … the witch. Bringing me into it.

I gave my best smile. "Of course not."

She eyed me with suspicion. "Well. Let's go before it gets too late."

Oh yes. One thing I agreed with. Let's move this disaster along as quickly as possible.

We walked the few blocks home, Carter and I following behind his parents, their slow shuffle painful to follow. I gripped Carter's arm and watched the street, the road bumper-to-bumper, an odd occurrence at 10 PM on a weeknight. I looked up ahead, trying to see past the mess of traffic, hoping to see the source of the problem. Probably an accident. Maybe a brazen New Yorker jaywalker got hit. It was a wonder we didn't all end up splattered on these dirty streets. I glanced up at Carter, wanting to whisper an apology, wanting to laugh about this ridiculous situation, but his body was tense, his eyes straight ahead, and I didn't.

Just across from our apartment building, his parents suddenly stopped, right in the middle of a crosswalk. I swallowed a response, pulling on Carter's arm to go around the suicidal couple. It was then, stepping around them, that I saw what had slowed traffic, the face of our building transformed, and I stopped, my eyes darting in a hundred places at once.

I saw our building through wisps of my breath in the crisp night air. Beside me, my silent boyfriend, a man who had been tense all evening, something I had attributed to stress over his parents, then anger over my secrets. I hadn't even considered something else. Something like *this*. When had he done it all?

The trees before our building were wrapped and draped in white lights, white rose petals lining the front walkway, our front planters suddenly overflowing with jasmine, orchids and roses. But the real impact was the building itself, the white brick illuminated with a light show, images dancing across its surface, the production impressive in its detail and clarity, the twelve stories a giant canvas of all things Chloe.

Me, as a child, in pigtails, running through the Miami surf, my head thrown back in a laugh. The image dissolved into a more recent one, me sipping a drink, my eyes on the camera, my mouth curved into a smile. I tried to place the image but then it was gone, replaced with a slow-motion shot of me, spinning in the New York snow, my arms outstretched. I remembered the day, Cammie and Benta and me in Central Park. It was a couple of years ago, and I smiled at the memory. I snuck a glance at Carter but couldn't read his expression, his face in shadow.

Across the street, the parking lot had been emptied, all the cars gone—all except my gleaming Maserati—music started. Lilting, haunting music, and I stepped forward to get a better look, moving through the stalled traffic, everything unreal, as if I was in a dream.

A grand piano. There was a grand piano in the empty lot, a woman in a red evening gown seated before it, her hands quick on the keys. Beside her, a man in a tux stepped forward, his steps confident and strong toward me, and I stopped, suddenly understanding everything about this situation.

This wasn't a dream, a romantic surprise orchestrated by Carter.

This was a nightmare, dressed in Armani and striding closer.

I turned and found Carter. He was still on the sidewalk, his mother's mouth in his ear, his head forward, ignoring her words, his eyes on mine. The building's display changed, a new image of me, and the transition lit his face, giving me a brief peek at the confused hurt there.

"Chloe." I turned on reflex, and dropped my eyes to Vic, who knelt on one knee before me. "Will you marry me?"

"What?" The word sputtered out of me. I darted my eyes to Carter, stepping back, and Vic caught my wrist.

"I know." He said the words softly, almost tenderly, his voice hushed as if he had a secret, his tone so serious that I stopped.

"You know what?" My mind flashed through all the things that he *could* know. About my embarrassing pant-rip incident in Sephora on Tuesday? My one, super-quick spin around the block in the car he bought me because I just couldn't help myself?

"About the baby." He pulled on my hand and stood, his eyes on mine, warm and loving, the man before me a Vic I had never seen. He looked at me as if he worshipped me, excitement radiating from him, his hands moving to cup my shoulders.

"The baby?" I repeated blankly. I was vaguely aware of the crowd growing around us, a crowd that included Carter and his parents. In the city that never slept, that loved a show, the attention had strayed from the hundred-foot light show and turned to us, hushed whispers darting from the crowd, camera phones out, and … somewhere … a girl *awwed.* I wanted to find her swoon and break it in half. Grab her shoulders and shake some sense into her. Tell her that roses and giant displays of affection didn't equate to real love or good decisions.

I tried to step back and he held on. "I know you're pregnant," he said softly. "And I know it's mine."

"You're *pregnant*?" Carter suddenly spoke up, stepping closer. He was angry, I could hear it in his voice, and I looked from Angry Carter to Loving Vic, the role reversal strange.

"No!" I pulled at Vic's hands, prying them off my shoulders and stepping back, turning to Carter, giving him my full attention and ignoring Vic altogether. "I'm *not* pregnant."

"Yes she is." Vic spoke with such authority that I almost believed him, my mind skipping back to my last period, trying to do a rush job of figuring out if pregnancy *was* a viable possibility.

"How do *you* know?" Carter turned to Vic, and as I watched his fists clench, I was transported back in time to the bar, to their fight, and steeled myself for a repeat. I watched with dread as a confident smile spread across Vic's face.

He had something, *knew* something. And I was both terrified and fascinated to find out what it was.

80. My Big Fat Mouth

Vic pulled out his cell phone. Held it up and read a line aloud.

"Day 3 and counting. I don't know what to do. I still don't know who the father is." Someone in the crowd gasped and Vic glanced their way and winked. The asshole was enjoying this, all eyes on him. He looked from Carter to me, made sure we were all listening in, and then continued.

"To which Cammie replied, 'Just wait it out. Don't tell anyone.'" Vic dropped the hand holding the phone and smiled at me. "Right, Chloe? Isn't that what you texted her? That you didn't know who the father was?"

Cammie? Texts? Suddenly I got it, my irritation with his stealing my phone and documenting my texts trumped by the fact that his stupid misunderstanding caused all of *this*. A gigantic spectacle over *nothing*. I laughed and waved my hand at Carter, hoping to dispel his panic, my words not coming out fast enough to stop this train wreck. "That's not about me," I scoffed. "It's about *Nicole*."

"Nicole?" Vic's voice finally held a hint of doubt. He cocked his head at me, no recognition of the name.

"YES. Nicole Brantley, my boss? The star of the film you just financed?" I stopped myself before I wasted any more time than necessary clueing in a man who didn't deserve an explanation to begin with.

I grabbed Carter's hand, trying to make my next words clear enough to end this.

"Vic, go home. I am not pregnant. That text wasn't about me. I'm not marrying you, we are *over*." I spoke clearly, enunciating every word, hoping that Carter's parents were following all of this.

"It was. You are—" He frowned, his dense skull still not getting it. "I saw the text messages…" he protested.

"About my boss," I repeated, and I think he saw the truth in my eyes. "She's pregnant. It was about her."

"Not you?" He sounded almost disappointed.

"No." I stepped away from him. "Go home," I repeated, a little gentler.

I turned to Carter and noticed the crowd. Still watching, still listening, their faces rapt, their phones out, probably Periscoping the whole thing. My eyes dragged over them and I tried to remember what I had just said, how loud I had said it, and my stomach dropped.

Suddenly, I felt queasy. But it didn't have anything to do with being pregnant and everything to do with the fact that I might have just broken Nicole's pregnancy, *and* her affair, to the world.

81. The Worst Kind of Goodbye

I ignored the crowd and stepped close to Carter, wrapping my arms around his neck. I whispered an apology into his ear and pulled him down for a kiss.

He resisted, his mouth stiff when it connected with mine, his hands wooden on my hips, and I had a moment of desperation before he softened. When his mouth finally yielded, fingers digging into my waist, I sighed against his kiss.

There was a loud clear of a very old throat, and Carter pulled his head up, our kiss breaking. We turned and saw his parents, twin visions of disapproval, both staring at me as if I were the devil.

"I'm afraid I don't feel up for seeing the building after all," his mother said stiffly. "All of *this* has left a rather bad taste in my mouth." She gestured to the light show, which was still running, a hundred-foot image of Vic and me kissing now front and center. It would have been funny if I'd been an innocent bystander. Now, with the image towering above us, on the side of *their* building … it was terrible.

"Goodnight, Mother." Carter didn't apologize, and I knew I should step forward and say something … the right thing, something that would put all of this behind us.

I drew a complete blank. I tried to hug the woman, and she stepped back. I revised the approach and held out my hand to his father. He shook my hand quickly, pulling his palm back as if I was diseased. "I'm so sorry," I said helplessly. "I'm really not pregnant."

Wow. If there was a list of things you didn't want to say to your boyfriend's parents during an initial meet-and-greet, that would be it. *I'm really not pregnant.* Super classy stuff. I tried again. "It was nice to see you both again. Maybe we could have lunch next week."

"I don't think so," his mother sniffed. *Ouch.* You'd think, given my night, she could have let me down gently, hid at least *some* of her disdain.

I watched as Carter hugged them both, and then they left, practically running to an awaiting car, the tires almost screeching on the pavement in their haste to head back uptown.

My stomach dropped as I watched them go, and I wondered if this was IT. The end of everything—my job, my apartment, and my relationship.

82. Finally Saying the Words

The crowd dispersed, someone turned off the Chloe lightshow, and Vic sped away with a glower. Carter and I made it to my door, and then just stared at each other: two awkward people with no clear direction.

"So," he finally said.

"Yeah." That was my brilliant response. I felt too tired and too emotional to discuss it all. A part of me was still upset about his lies, or omissions—the fact that he never told me that his parents owned the building we lived in, that he'd grown up just as pampered as I had. Along with being tired, I was vulnerable, rubbed raw by Vic's public display of affection—an incredibly romantic proposal from a man I had once loved deeply.

"I'm gonna head in," I finally said.

He didn't like that. His mouth tightened, his hand came up and yanked through his hair, a sigh hard off his lips. "Chloe," he said, and it was the end of the sentence, neither of us eloquent.

"I'm going to bed." I unlocked my door and hoped he'd stop me. Rolled the strap of my purse over my shoulder, and gave him a moment of opening, plenty of time for something to be said. But he stayed quiet, and I stepped inside, then the door was shut and I was alone.

Truly alone.

Vic was fully gone from my life. I had seen it in the sag of his shoulders, the moment he had finally understood that I wasn't his responsibility anymore. It saddened me that he'd gotten excited over the idea of a baby. That he had planned that big proposal with the thoughts that we could start a family—a life—together. Six months ago, it would have made my heart sing. Of course he'd assumed it was a Worth child. That was the type of man he was. Confident that, in the race of sperm, his would always win. But something had died between us, out on the street. Maybe it was the public humiliation of my snub, maybe it was seeing me turning to Carter and physically choosing between the two of them—I don't know what it'd been, but something changed. I searched for feelings of regret, but there was none, only relief at the end of that chapter.

It made me a little nostalgic, a big chapter of my life to close, a chapter in which I changed a lot, grew up a lot.

I skipped a shower and changed into pajamas, crawling into bed, all of the lights off, the television dark. I lay there for a long time, waiting for sleep, trying to drown out my thoughts, so many *what ifs* floating through my head, trying to find places to settle.

I hoped for his knock, and when it came, I was out of the bed and ready, swinging open the door, my voice quiet considering the screaming of my heart.

Carter stood there, pajama pants low on his hips, his shirt off, every muscle on his torso tense as he stopped mid-knock. He looked at me and said nothing.

I stepped back and waved him in.

That night was one of our first without sex. He pulled back the covers and climbed in, pulling me beside him and close to his chest. Hugging me tight, his arm around my chest, his legs hooked through mine and he said only one thing, his breath against my neck, his heart beating a hard rhythm against my back.

"I love you."

"I love you too." It was my first time saying the words out loud, and they almost rushed from my lips. His arms tightened a little around me, and I felt the relief in his grip, a moment of hold before we both relaxed. I fell asleep there, in his arms, the murmur of the city loud outside the window, my body warm in his embrace.

Below us, on the floor where I'd carelessly dropped it, was my purse. Inside, my phone vibrated with each new tweet and Instagram post that mentioned me. As Carter and I slept, social media exploded.

83. Aren't Visitors Supposed to Call First?

Someone hammered on my door. The pounds were hard enough to wake us, the door shaking against its jamb. Carter jumped from the bed, moving to the door, and I groped for my phone, pulling the sheet around me, trying to figure out through a haze of sleep what day it was, where I was, and who the demon in the hall might be.

Carter spoke, his hands on the door, eye to the peephole. "It's a woman."

I found my purse, then my phone, and didn't bother unlocking it, seeing a chorus of missed calls from Dante and Nicole. "Oh God," I mumbled.

"She's not going anywhere," Carter remarked, the door shaking with a fresh round of knocks.

I tossed the phone on the bed and walked to the door, waving Carter aside and steeling myself. I pulled opened the door.

I'd seen fury in human form. I'd never seen *this* before. Dante stood behind Nicole with a warning on his face, but none was needed. Not when the woman before me sizzled with emotion. She glared at me, and I could see the edges of her psyche breaking. She was as close to killing me as sobbing in my arms.

"You… *bitch*." The words spat from her mouth and I flinched.

"Nicole, I don't know what—"

"Shut up!" she seethed, pushing forward, a sharp fingernail jabbing my shoulder. "Do you know what you've *done*?" She screamed the words, her voice shaking on the final syllables.

I didn't feel like guessing. Paulo? Her pregnancy? The fact that I'd been sneaking Chanel non-organic treats?

"I've got the studio on my ass, the press on my ass, a heartbroken husband and Paulo is flipping his *shit*, Chloe."

Ouch. So her pregnancy *had* leaked, as had her affair. "I'm sorry Nicole, it was a bad situation. No one should have overheard—"

"Overheard?" she seethed. "Not just *overheard*. There are a dozen different *videos* of you blabbing about my personal business. You've spelled out my entire life for anyone with an internet connection; you wouldn't shut up."

I got her point. Realized my fuck-up. And there, in my pajamas on a Saturday morning, finally decided that I didn't care. Not about this woman. Not about her issues. Not about the consequences of her actions. I met her eyes and said, for the first time since she hired me, what I really thought. "You got yourself in this situation. You shouldn't have cheated on Clarke. And you should have told him yourself that you were pregnant."

She stepped closer, fully inside my apartment, and slammed the door shut on Dante's face. I stayed in place and met her murderous stare.

Then, her mouth trembled and, oh my God … she was about to cry.

"Do you know how long Clarke and I have been trying?" she whispered. "All of the doctors, the fertility treatments…" Her words died, and she looked away, swallowing hard. She suddenly looked, in the harsh morning light of my apartment, old. Like she'd been up for hours, her eyes puffy, wrinkles not covered by makeup, dark shadows not covered with concealer. "Clarke would have been so happy to find out I was pregnant. That was *our* moment, Chloe. One for us to celebrate, one we've waited for seven years for."

"If it's *his*," I pointed out. "Paulo—"

"Paulo had a vasectomy five years ago," she snapped, her eyes hardening. "Not that *that's* any of your business."

Very rarely had I felt as much of an asshole as I did right then. And that was before I read all of the gossip articles, the tweets, and posts. That was before Nicole stiffened, her hand grabbing at her stomach, her face going pale. I watched her grope for the wall, her eyes darting to me in panic, and I barely caught her before she crumpled.

"I'll call an ambulance." Carter grabbed his phone and I sank to the floor, propping Nicole's head up on one of my pumpkin pajama legs and shushing her. I didn't know why I *shushed.* I thought it was, for some reason, soothing.

It wasn't. For one, her cursing drowned out any effective soothing qualities. For another, Carter held the phone away from his mouth, mid-directions to 911, and told me to shut up.

So I did. I shut up and let Nicole curse me. I held her in my arms, and I prayed that her baby was all right. I had already messed this up. I couldn't take any more consequences from my actions.

In the distance, there was the wail of a siren, the sound almost swallowed by its city.

84. Loose Lips Sink Everything

I sat on the floor of the ambulance and stared at my shoes. Pink Nikes. They clashed horribly with my pajama pants. And I wasn't wearing a bra, my nipples standing out in the cold air of the vehicle. In between my knees, my phone buzzed, Joey calling. I stopped its vibration and wondered what I would tell him and Hannah. Wondered if the secret of Paulo's involvement would keep. I wouldn't be the one to spill it. I had already, in the last twelve hours, done more than enough damage.

I didn't know anything about babies or pregnancy. But I did know that the Moment You Tell the Father was a pretty big deal. So was the Moment You Tell Your Friends … and Your Mother … and Everyone Else. There were a hundred websites devoted to helping you break the news. Some people put plastic babies in cakes for an unsuspecting relative to break a tooth on. Some put a literal bun in the oven and hope someone gets the witty reference. Some flew banner planes, some rented billboards, but NO ONE wanted the news broke via an assistant's blabby mouth on YouTube. No one wanted a thousand gossip sites running the headline *Who Is Nicole Brantley's Baby Daddy*? I thought of all of the people that news hit. Clarke, her husband who didn't even know about her affair. Her friends, those social maggots who would feast on this for years. Her parents, those society mavens who had earned all of their fortune on condoms, yet got all a flutter if her table settings didn't include a fish knife. All of those people, everyone in her life, got her joyous baby news in that horrific fashion. Something ten years in the making … and I had ruined it.

I felt terrible. Even worse once I found out that Paulo wasn't the dad. All of my texts back and forth with Cammie, all my soul-searching and inner debates … wasted. I had a moment of guilt over some gleeful moments where we had made fun of her predicament. Nicole probably wasn't even *with* Paulo anymore. She probably got pregnant and kissed goodbye to that affair—fully focused on her new future.

The ambulance went over a pothole and I winced, my head hitting the side of the vehicle, my nerves past shot. Nicole held out her hand, asking for mine, and I took it. I held her hand and realized, my mind spinning through everything, that I was going to quit. In that moment, while gripping the hand of a woman I didn't like, praying for her baby, the ambulance rough as it fought for its place in a city that didn't budge, the right decision was clear. Life was too short, morals were too important, and I flat out didn't like my job. I'd rather be back on Cammie's couch, working for minimum wage, than be her assistant.

I didn't say anything to Nicole. I figured it wasn't exactly the time. With everything the poor woman had going on, she might need one dramaless moment.

We finally arrived, and I was sent to the waiting room. Clarke and Dante showed up and we sat there, the weirdest threesome ever, in the corner of the hell that was an NYC emergency room.

I watched Clarke as he sat in his seat, beside Dante, his elbows resting on his knees, his shoulders hunched, pulling the lines of his shirt tight. I didn't know what to say to him. I felt like I should say *something*, but the shitstorm of drama that I had caused seemed too big, too impossible to resolve in the time that stretched before us.

He lifted his head and looked at me, and I saw the thin edge of emotion that he straddled. "The newspapers…" He swallowed, his beautiful mouth tightening for a beat. "They said that you said you didn't know who the father was."

The conversation that I had dreaded for a year was finally here. "Yes," I managed, hoping he would stop talking, hoping we would go back to silence.

"Why?" He adjusted the end of one shirtsleeve, pulling it tight, his eyes dropping briefly. "Why wouldn't it be me? Who else could it be?"

When he looked back at me, it was two sets of eyes in total. Dante also watched, every muscle in his body ready to pounce. This was a test. I realized it instantly. Not from Clarke. Poor, beautiful Clarke just wanted to know what the hell was happening in his life. But Dante, he watched to see what I was made of. I wished I knew. I looked down at my pink Nikes and bought a sliver of time.

I had always hoped that Nicole would be the one to confess. If I took away that option, telling Clarke about Paulo, would it ruin any chance of him trusting Nicole again? Or had I already ruined that moment by bringing up the paternity at all? It was pretty much assumed, from my quick glance at social media, that Nicole was the Unfaithful Slut of the Week.

"It was Paulo."

85. Spilling the Beans

"It was Paulo."

That bomb didn't come from me; it came from Dante, who muttered the words, his voice dark. My head snapped to him, my eyes widening, any inner debate over spilling the beans on Nicole's lover ended. Clarke's attention turned from me and zeroed in on Dante.

"Paulo?" Clarke sounded surprised.

"This *couldn't* have been a surprise." Dante stood and faced him. "How often was he at your house? And her getting this role?"

I didn't know why Dante was getting so self-rightous. He had kept the secret, same as me, all of us guilty in this situation except Clarke. Clarke sank back in his seat, his head resting against the wall. He looked beaten. Lost. I watched his brow pinch and wondered if I had looked that defeated and broken, in the aftermath of discovering Vic's affair. But then, I'd been caught completely off guard. Clarke, he'd spent almost a day sitting, waiting for the guillotine to fall.

Waiting to find out who the executioner was.

86. *She Doesn't Deserve Children*

Clarke clammed up. I watched him sink against his seat, his gaze shuttering, his arms crossing, his mouth narrowing into a thin line. Our group fell back into silence, nothing said until a nurse walked out and asked for me.

"I'm Chloe." I stood up, hesitantly raising a hand.

"Mrs. Brantley has asked for you."

I glanced at Clarke, then back at the nurse, who had already turned, her scrubs pushing through the double doors. I grabbed my purse and darted after her, worried about being left. I didn't glance at Clarke when I scurried past. Didn't want to see the questions in his eyes. I didn't want to know why she had asked for me, didn't want to see her, was too terrified of a negative outcome to ask the nurse about the baby.

"The baby is fine." The nurse spoke over her shoulder, waiting on a hospital bed to cross our path.

"It's fine?" A swell of emotion filled my chest at the news, and I sent a silent *thank you* up to heaven.

"Yes. Mrs. Brantley has an ulcer, one that flared, probably due to stress and a daily ibuprofen habit. But she's stable now. Still in some pain, but the medicine will kick in soon."

She stopped outside a room and nodded me forward. I steeled myself and stepped into the room, ready for battle. Instead, I found a different woman. Not the enraged, screaming banshee from hours earlier; Nicole had sunk into a large bed, tiny among all of the IVs and equipment. Her room had a window and she looked out it, her gaze barely flicking to me when I entered.

"Does Clarke know about Paulo?" she asked quietly.

"Yes." I didn't bother telling her that it was Dante who shared the news, or that Clarke had pulled it out of us. At that moment, she didn't seem to care and I was running out of the energy to deal with all of this.

"I don't want to talk to him," she whispered the words and wrapped her hands around her stomach. "I'm just so tired. Of everything."

Well, *that* made two of us. I sank into a recliner next to her bed and closed my eyes. The last few days had been such a whirlwind; I'd hardly had a moment to rest. I wondered where all of her friends were. Then again … I wasn't sure Nicole really had any friends. Acquaintances? Yes. Fellow social maggots? Yes. True friends? No. Another domino on top of Nicole's stack of sadness. I had a fleeting thought of Chanel and wondered where she was.

"Is he staying?" Nicole's question was so subdued, so quiet and naked in its vulnerability, I almost missed it.

"Who? Clarke?" It seemed like a ridiculous question. "Here at the hospital? Yeah, he's in the waiting room." *Wanting to see you.* An addition I should have added, but I was chicken.

"He should leave me," she mumbled. "After everything…"

I didn't know what to say. I completely agreed with her. During the last year, I'd asked myself a dozen times why the damn man stayed. On one hand, it was endearing, his commitment and devotion. On the other hand, it was stupid. But what did I know? I'd stayed with Vic for two years. There were probably plenty in his inner circle who had laughed behind my back, who had questioned my intelligence level. I couldn't really judge Clarke for anything. "This could be a fresh start for you two." I ventured. "You could be honest with him. Faithful."

She snorted, a little taste of old Nicole fighting to the surface. "Like I have a choice?" She scowled. "My body is going to be shot after *this*."

This. That was her reference to the baby. I swallowed every response that bubbled in my throat and mentally circled, in bold red pen, my date of resignation. Next Monday. She should be out of the hospital by then. Maybe I could kidnap Chanel on my way out. With all the baby and affair drama, they probably wouldn't even notice.

I glanced at my watch and decided to move this pity party along. "I've got to run." I stood, snagging my purse off of the floor. "I'll send Clarke back."

Her head lifted off the pillow. "Where are *you* going? What is more important than *this*?"

"I'm sorry. An appointment," I lied, moving for the door quickly, before she had a chance to retort.

Her last words were shouted at me, the demand slipping through the door right before it shut. "Don't send Clarke back here!"

I considered the order, and then, in one of my final acts as Assistant to Nicole, discarded it

87. Back Where I Belonged

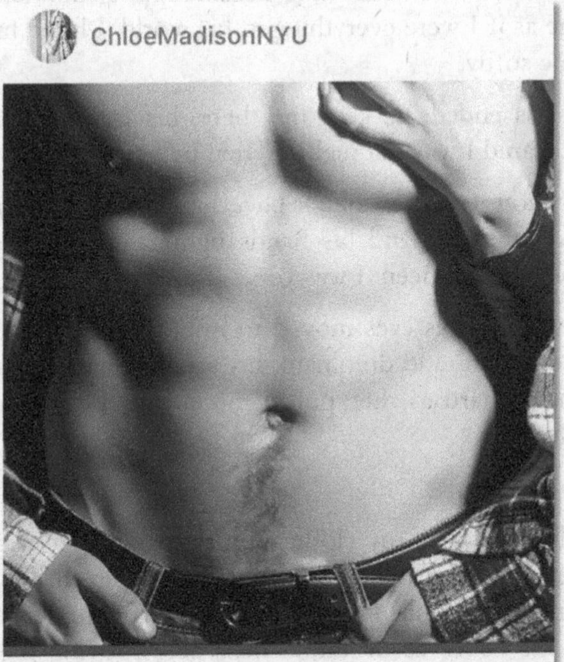
ChloeMadisonNYU
49 likes
ChloeMadisonNYU Manly is my new weakness. #movingon #C9

I saw Carter the minute I stepped from the taxi. He stood on the front steps of our building, his hands in his back pockets, the pose accenting the tight fit of his shirt on his shoulders, the muscles of his arms, a slight peek of abs visible above the low hang of his jeans.

I stopped before him and looked up into his face. "Hey."

"I love you." The best response in the whole world. I smiled bigger.

"I love you too."

"I can't decide if I want to carry you to my bedroom or to lunch."

"Bed," I said immediately, and he laughed, dropping his arms and stepping down a few steps, pulling me against his chest and looking down at me for a moment—one heart-stopping moment where he stared at me as if I were everything in his world. I lifted my chin, and he kissed me softly.

When the kiss ended, he kept me there, his face serious. "Do you know how scared I was last night? When he proposed?"

Last night. How could so much have happened in just twenty-four hours? I wet my lips, and his hands tightened a little on my hips. "You shouldn't have been. I was yours the entire time."

He swallowed and his eyes moved to my mouth, then he kissed me again, this kiss hard and dominant, his tongue diving in and claiming me, his fingers hard as they pulled me close. "Bed," he whispered, and I nodded.

"Now."

My bag fell in his hall, my clothes got lost along the way, and I lay back on his bed and watched him yank at his shirt, his abs stretching and popping as he pulled it over his head and tossed it aside. He kicked off his shoes as he undid his jeans, shoving them over his hips, taking his boxer briefs along with them, and then he was naked—fully naked—the sun coming in the window and showcasing the utter perfection of the man. Already hard, he took his time walking over to the bed, his hand gripping his cock, moving in slow and delicious strokes. I hated to glance away from the scene, but then he spoke, and I looked up to his face and there … I was a goner. Intense heat in those eyes, he looked at me with such need that I was instantly addicted, never wanting to look away from his face again.

"Spread your legs, baby. Let me see you." He stroked himself, his voice hoarse and I slid my feet along the bed, my knees parting, nothing hidden from his eyes.

He stopped at the foot of the bed and stood, his legs slightly spread, and stared. "Touch yourself, baby. Put your fingers everywhere that you want my mouth."

If I was wet before, I was soaked by the time I ran my tentative fingers in between my legs. And with him there, his chest flexing, arm moving, breath hard, I showed him exactly what I wanted him to do.

And then, he did it better.

I knew I'd said it before, but I loved this man.

88. Chanel No. WTF

If I ran fast enough through life, I couldn't see its cracks.

Nicole's drama.

My looming unemployment.

Carter's parents.

Vic.

In the moments since that horrible night when Vic proposed—I'd run fast, and love had blurred my vision. Carter and I fit so perfectly together, in this new relationship of *I love yous* and *orgasms* and *God you're beautifuls* that I managed, for almost a week, to ignore everything else.

Then real life came calling.

Cammie was coming over, and late. I eyed the clock and sipped my wine, turning up my playlist. The buzzer sounded and I skipped the speaker, letting her in without complaint, my hand swinging open the door at the first sign of a knock, my buzz kicking, pajama pants imperfectly paired with a Current-Elliot top. We were going to make cupcakes, drink wine, and watch a movie. Plans that stalled when I saw the couple at my door.

"Mom?" I almost checked my wine glass, to see if I had chugged it all, had slipped in pills, had done *something* to imagine my mother, her arm slipped carelessly through a Gucci crocodile bag, my father towering behind her. I hadn't seen them in over a year, and yet, somehow, they looked exactly the same. No extra wrinkles from stress, no salt and pepper roots betraying the months since a proper dye job, no worn suitcase in hand. Mother was in a St. John suit, her hair perfect, smile wide, a mink stole around her shoulders. My father was in his typical garb: an oxford shirt tucked into dress pants, sunglasses perched on his thick head of hair despite the late hour. As handsome as ever, they looked like a million bucks. A million highly illegal bucks.

"Chloe, where are your manners?" She scowled at me as if she still owned my dwelling, her hand pushing open my door, and as she swept past, the scent of Chanel No. 5 catching me, a thousand memories tied to the smell.

"Chloe." My father nodded stiffly and I nodded back.

"What are you guys doing here?" I didn't close the door, just pivoted in place, a little wine sloshing out, and stared at them. Mom didn't respond, too busy surveying my apartment, her lip curled in a manner that clearly indicated her disapproval. Something inside of me snapped.

"What are you doing here?" I repeated. "Aren't you both under house arrest?"

"Oh," she said airily, waving her hand. "Nothing so barbaric as that. I mean … the hearing is tomorrow morning. *Then* we'll probably be restricted to the house."

"If the judge doesn't send us straight to jail." My father said the statement mildly, lifting up my bottle of wine and examining the label.

"It's turned into such a mess, it's really quiet humorous." Mom turned back to me, her eyebrows raised, and she grinned at me, as if we were teenage girls sharing a delicious secret.

"You have a hearing *tomorrow*?" I tried to follow this.

"Yes." She stepped forward and wrapped her arms around my neck, hugging me tightly. "We came all the way up here just to see you, Chloe. You should really act happier to see us."

I didn't have a response. I patted her back awkwardly and looked to my father, who was busy tipping back a glass of my cheap wine. "So … you fly home tonight?"

"Oh, I'm not sure." Mom pulled back and reached in her bag, finding a tube of lipstick and pulling it out. "We may do a little traveling. We tried to deal with the investigators, but…" She waved a hand in the air like the FBI was a pesky little kid who was stomping through her hibiscus.

Then it hit me, and the only thing that really surprised me was that they had stopped in New York first. "You're *running*?"

It was a waste of words. I knew, before my dad even coughed on my wine, the answer.

89. Cupcakes Heal Most Wounds

ChloeMadisonNYU
82 likes
ChloeMadisonNYU Haters gonna hate, bakers gonna bake. #cupcakemadness #girlsnight

Twenty minutes. That was how long they stayed. How long I got to say goodbye. Long enough for a glass of wine, some critical comments on my apartment, a lot of evasive answers, and a brief set of hugs before they left. And when they did, I swore I smelled relief in their departure.

They missed Cammie by minutes. I met her in the lobby, my wine glass still in hand. I managed a hello then burst into tears. I didn't know why I was crying. Why, after all this time, did I expect more from them? What did I want? A mention that they were proud of me? Recognition that I found my own way, got on my own two feet? They didn't even ask if I was seeing someone. They didn't even tell me they loved me.

Cammie got me upstairs, found a box of tissues, and refilled my wine glass.

"I'm sorry," I sniffed, leaning into her arms, us side-by-side on the couch.

"Don't be," she chided. "You were overdue for this."

I sobbed out a laugh. "You damn bloodhound. You must have smelled my tears." Benta and I used to joke with her about it. If you were ever going to have a breakdown, do it with Cammie. She'd kick your ass into shape while feeding, nursing, and loving you through your pain. She sensed emotional weakness, and she came running.

She smiled. "It was good timing."

I wished I had Cammie's parents. They would have stayed longer than twenty minutes. Then again, they wouldn't be on the run. They wouldn't have broken the law.

"I can't believe they are running." I grabbed the tissue Cammie offered and blew my nose. I shouldn't have been surprised. I should have known. Mother wouldn't do prison. Father would probably come apart at the seams. And both of them, regardless of their actions, seemed to think they were above punishment. And they must, despite all of my thoughts to the contrary, still have money. When I'd walked them outside, I'd watched their designer shoes clip right into a chauffeured Mercedes. No taxi for Mom and Dad.

"It just seems unfair," I continued. "They aren't getting punished *at all.* And I'm here, trying to pay off my tuition and…" And Mom was sashaying around town with a twenty-thousand dollar purse. It was so unfair that they were headed to a new life and so frustrating to know that any chance of us regaining a relationship was disappearing in that flight.

"Chloe." Cammie pushed me upright. "Not to be bitchy, but I think this was actually good for you."

"What?"

"You were pretty entitled before." She shrugged. "You've changed from all this."

"Entitled?" I raised my eyebrows at her. "You aren't exactly scraping by on your Tahitian vacations."

She leveled me with a look. "You were spoiled."

"We were *all* spoiled."

"But you're *nicer* now," she said gently. "You're smarter. You see things differently. Before, you wouldn't have given Carter the time of day."

I laughed into a fresh tissue. "I kinda didn't. Not in the beginning."

"I'm sorry about your parents." She said the words quietly and I hated the change in topic, the return to this ugly reality.

"Thanks," I said flatly. "I just don't know what to do with them." I didn't even think of calling the police. It seemed, no matter how flawed family may be, they were still that: family. They still required your love, your acceptance, your protection. Or maybe I'd just watched too many episodes of *The Sopranos*.

I crawled into bed that night and lay in the dark, the room spinning a little from the wine. Was I happy they had stopped by to say goodbye? I couldn't, through all of my emotions, decide.

90. Was I Reading Too Much Into This?

I sat in the backseat of the Brantleys' SUV, Chanel in my lap, and stared at the text from Carter.

> *We should talk. Dinner tonight?*

Hmm. My first instinct was to run in the opposite direction. *We should talk*?

I hadn't told him about my parents' visit. Had sworn Cammie to secrecy so it was a non-event, something that had never happened. If the cops or FBI ever showed up, I wanted his statement to be truthful *and* non-discriminating. And it wasn't like I was lying to him. I was just excluding facts.

Which … was kind of exactly what he did with me. Like how he conveniently failed to mention his parents' wealth or their eight-million-dollar Fifth Avenue penthouse (Benta's research, not mine). Granted, I really should have asked more questions. Or any questions. The ironic thing was, a few weeks ago, I didn't really *want* details, assuming that his poor upbringing would make me feel guilty for mine. HA. Silly me.

I glanced up, toward Dante, the SUV idling at a red light. "I just got a text from Carter. He wants *to talk*." The clear enunciation of the last two words would have had any female lifting her head in interest, eyes widening, full understanding instant. Dante simply sat there. Silent.

I leaned forward. "Did you hear me?"

"So?"

"So?" I repeated. A typical man's response. "*So* what should I do? What could he want to talk about?"

"Why don't you just ask him?" He said the words slowly, as if my brain might not process words spoken at any other rate of speed.

"Right now?"

"Yes."

I hesitated, my fingers over the phone. What a simple and novel idea. One that might reduce my stress in the six or seven hours before dinner and This Talk. I blew out a breath, Chanel jumping up, her tongue licking at my jaw, and I smiled despite myself.

What do you want to talk about?

I stared at the question, then sent it, my text bouncing off satellites and landing before him, three little dots indicating an impending response.

My parents. The things I haven't told you.

Oh thank God. I let out a sigh of relief and saw Dante's eyes flick to me in the rearview mirror. "It's nothing," I blurted out. "I thought it was about me." Or us. Or something Vic did. Or breaking us. Or a hundred other things because it seemed like all I'd done lately was mess up.

He coughed out a laugh. "Girls are so weird."

I smiled despite the insult. It was kinda true. We are, in a million complex and unexplainable ways, weird.

But at least this dinner would be about him. I pulled my notebook from my purse and started to write down a list of Carter questions that I still needed answered.

Not just weird. We were organized. And procrastinators. Speaking of which, I still needed to quit. Dante pulled up to the Brantleys' and I glanced up, deciding to put it off just a *few* more days.

91. A Grown-Up Conversation

"I didn't mean to lie to you." Carter pushed aside his bread plate and looked at me, the restaurant quiet, warm light from the candle between us flickering over his features.

"It wasn't really a lie. More an omission." He was too serious, his face drawn, and I watched him, trying to find the source of his tension.

"I knew what you thought, and I didn't dissuade you. I'm sorry for that."

"Was it a test?" That had been one of the first things I'd wanted to ask him. "Were you wanting to know if I was dating you because of your money?"

"I don't really *have* money, Chloe." He leaned forward. "My parents pay me a salary for my work at the apartment. And for the other two that I super. It's not a lot."

"But you will." He was an only child, one thing I knew. And there had to be *something* to protect, his Mother all but accusing me of stealing her family fortune.

He nodded slowly. "When I'm thirty-five I gain access to my trust. My apartment—it's part of that. As are a few other things."

"Okay." I shifted in my seat, unsure of why this conversation was so stiff. Unsure of, really, why we needed to have this whole production at all. He could have just shared this, over coffee in his kitchen, at some stolen point in the last three days.

"My mother called me. I wanted to talk to you about it, apologize to you properly for her actions at dinner."

I didn't know how I missed all of the clues. His excellent diction. His manners, almost formal at times. The way he held a glass, a fork. Maybe it was because I'd seen these things, men like him, my entire life and was blind to their traits. Maybe it was because a part of me *liked* the thought that he wasn't like the boys I grew up with. Maybe I'd invented an alternative Carter in my mind and formed him into a rough creature he wasn't.

Because the man before me was all polish and tact. Showing his breeding, his training, the expensive education. Then I remembered Vic's bar, Carter's launch into the room, the fists, the blood. I remembered being in the engine room with him, the dirt on his hands, the sweat on his chest, the grunt in his throat when he fucked me against the wall.

He wasn't pure gentleman, not the silver spoon assholes of my past. He had the fine edges but was something more, stronger. Maybe it was his mother, making him earn his keep, her stingy fingers tight on the purse-strings, this age-thirty-five rule a good one, one that shaped him into the complex man who sat before me.

"It's okay." I smiled, suddenly warming to the idea of his mother. I leaned forward and linked my fingers through his. "She's protective of you. I get that."

He looked at me warily, his next sentence stiff. "She hired a private investigator, Chloe. I just found out this morning."

I pulled back my hand. "What?"

"She wants to know more about you. He's been following you." He leaned forward. "I'm so sorry. I've told her that I won't—"

"For how long?" I saw spots between us, bits of black, my head spinning with everything that…

"I'm not sure. Two weeks at least." His jaw was tight, eyes apologetic, but all I could think about was hugging my parents outside our building. Them getting in their car and making their escape. This investigator *seeing it all.*

"Are you mad?"

"I wouldn't say that I am mad…" I said carefully. I swallowed and met his eyes. "What happens if she doesn't like the investigator's report?"

He didn't look away. "If she doesn't like you, I lose my trust fund." The words came out matter-of-factly, as if his whole future wasn't tied up in their vowels.

It was so unexpected; an outcome I had never imagined. I might have fallen in love with a poor man after all. And I might be the reason he loses everything.

92. Oh. You Guys Again.

ChloeMadisonNYU
81 likes
ChloeMadisonNYU I'm ready for summer.

My phone rang as I opened the door, and I answered it, stuffing it against my shoulder as I lifted out Nicole's groceries.

"Chloe Madison?" a stiff male voice asked.

"Yes?" I said warily.

"This is Agent Peter Hertslem. I'm calling about your parents."

I shouldered the door closed and leaned against it, my hands full with bags, my heart beating hard in my chest. "I don't know where they are," I lied. Dad had pulled me aside before they left, whispering their itinerary, which had included a stop in the Hamptons before their flight to Dubai.

"I'm not calling for that, Ms. Madison. We know where they are."

"You do?" Dante paused, and I waved him on, my chest growing tight, the life of a fugitives' daughter stressful.

"Oh yes," he said, with an air of superiority. "I'm looking at them right now."

The FBI picked up my parents at the airport just an hour after they'd left my apartment. Yet, it took four days to get that call from the FBI, one that was apparently "just for courtesy" to inform me of their detainment.

Four days since they had been arrested and flown back to Florida, and that call was the *only* one I'd received. One from a smug stranger. Didn't prisoners get phone calls? They must have made theirs to someone else.

I wondered, for a day or so, if they thought that *I'd* turned them in, if that was the reason for their silence. But if they thought I was a daughter who'd snitch, they wouldn't have come to say goodbye. And they certainly wouldn't have told me their plans—my mind stalled, bits of the agent's conversation coming to mind. The airport. Wait. Mom and Dad wouldn't have *flown* to the Hamptons. They would have driven. Much less inconspicuous, much less chance of being caught—plus Mom loves that drive. And the Hamptons were northeast of the city, not south. They wouldn't have been at the airport unless…

It took me longer to connect the dots than it should have. For the last hours, my mind had just conveniently skipped over the fact that my father had completely lied to me about their itinerary. Either as a safety measure in case I ratted, or as a way to throw the cops off their trail in the expectation that I *would* rat. Both options dismal signs of my parents' faith in me.

Inside, I felt one of the last bonds between me and my parents break.

December

I was torn. I wanted to be selfish, to hold Carter tightly to me and never let him go. But then I'd be responsible for him losing his inheritance. How could I do that to someone I loved? Wasn't the sign of true love putting the other person's needs before your own?

A part of me was egotistic enough to think he'd be happier with me than with his trust fund. I looked at how much better my own life was without my parents' money, and how much richer I was with him in my life.

Regardless, it wasn't my decision to make. It was his.

93. *Coercion is a Dish Best Served Wet*

"Move in with me."

The words didn't register. Maybe because my head was tilted back, hard against the pillow, my nails scraping against the top sheet, trying to find something to hold on to. Or maybe the issue was the fact that his mouth was so far away, the heat of his words hot against my naked skin, his tongue finishing off the final syllable with a flick across my sensitive clit.

"Oh God," I groaned when his tongue changed, from a flick to a flutter, soft and hot, the constant pressing going faster and faster, bringing me closer and closer…

I arched off the mattress, pushing myself harder into his mouth…

And he stopped. "Move in with me."

My body yearned, the need intense, my hands reaching down, in between my legs, just a touch needed to…

He grabbed both of my wrists and slid forward, pinning them to either side of my head, my sexual haze lifting as I blinked at him. "Chloe."

"Carter," I shot back, struggling against his grip, my hips bucking off the bed, the orgasm still right there, just needing the right touch…

His body was now on top of me, a fine stretch of muscles that—at any other point in time—would have been celebrated. But right then, I could only think of one thing: my rapidly fading orgasm.

"Will you move in with me? You can have the big closet."

"I'm so close." I worked my legs free and wrapped them around his waist. Talk about sexy—having him huge and hard against me, each minute shift of his body a giant reminder of how lucky I was. "Please," I begged.

I couldn't even process his request. Couldn't decide whether to be happy or freaked out. When a man like Carter moved his bare cock along your body, you didn't think. You didn't do anything but beg.

I tightened my legs and tried to change our angle.

I reached down and tried to grab him, to wrap my hand around his girth.

"Say yes," he whispered, his weight on his hands, his head dropping down to brush over my lips.

"Why don't you make me scream it instead?" The words were a challenge and I watched his eyes when they hit, the darken of his stare one that filled me with anticipation.

He sat up, his torso moving away and gripped my hips, positioning himself in between my legs, and I couldn't help but whimper in relief as his fingers dug into me, his initial thrust slow and deep and perfectly in control.

After that, nothing about our sex was controlled. And my *YES* was a scream. A loud and long scream, followed by fifty or so short, concise versions, coming quicker and quicker before … I curled forward, my hands gripping at his shoulders, my body stiff as everything turned the most perfect shade of orgasm.

When I came down, limp against the mattress, it was settled. *Moving in together*. I steeled myself for panic, but there was none.

94. To Pack or Not to Pack?

"Maybe this is a mistake." I said. "Moving in together?" Something I never did with Vic. I'd never lived with anyone, save those months with Cammie.

"Why?" Cammie asked, sipping a red Starbucks cup, her elbow knocking Benta's arm when she reached for her cookie. "You guys've been together, what … three months?"

"Two and a half, exclusively." I corrected. "But we've dated since…" I scrunched up my face and tried to think. "July."

"Carlos moved in with me after three months," Benta unhelpfully supplied.

"Exactly. And we all remember how well *that* social experiment turned out." Benta and Carlos lasted three weeks after he moved into her place. It took that long for them to come to the conclusion that they, in fact, hated each other.

"You know what the issue was?" Cammie asked, pointing a navy fingernail in Benta's direction. I waited for this gem of knowledge with all the excitement of a root canal. "Carlos moved into *your* place. I think it works better when the girl moves in with the guy. Otherwise, you feel like he's a freeloader."

"Didn't you guys split the rent?" I looked at Benta, who nodded through a mouthful of—damn her—my cookie.

"It doesn't matter," Cammie said. "Call it tradition, patriarchy, whatever. A woman wants a provider, and you don't feel that way if he's suddenly taking over half your closet." This coming from a woman who'd never lived with anyone other than me. "You guys won't have that problem, since you're moving in with him. And plus…" she popped a peppermint into her mouth, "you'll save on rent!" She beamed, like she had ever once worried over a rent payment.

But … she did have a point. Now that Nicole was back home and settled, the plan was for me to quit on Monday. I'd offer to work a final two weeks, but Nicole would most likely kick me out the door. Unemployed just in time for the holidays. JOY. It *would* help the situation if I didn't have to worry about rent. But was that really a reason to move in with a guy? I voiced the question.

"What you need to think about," Benta reasoned, "is if you would move in with him if your rent stayed the same. If the answer is yes," she shrugged, "then you're good to go."

It was kind of a stupid hypothetical because I couldn't even decide if I should move in with him and my rent *wasn't* staying the same, but I understood her point.

"It's the next step," Cammie said. "Either you and Carter are serious about each other or you aren't. If you are, then you need to know if you can live together." She blinked at me as if it was so obvious, and I eyed her eyelashes suspiciously. The girl got extensions. She had to. She wasn't that lash-blessed before. I swallowed the observation and tried to focus on her advice. She was right. It was the next step. Did I want a future with him? It was a question that took a minute to answer, a decision that I wanted to be absolutely sure about. And the answer, after three long sips of my coffee and a lot of time staring out the window, was yes.

I *loved* him. I fell in love with him thinking that he had nothing. And I wanted a future with him. The man was willing to risk his entire financial future on me … I could certainly risk the next step with him.

I wanted to try. I wanted more. And if the next step toward our future was moving in together, then I wanted to take that step. I swallowed hard and looked away from the window. "You're right," I nodded. "I'm going to do it."

I didn't know why they squealed, coming forward and hugging me tightly. But the celebration was what I needed. Validation that gaining a relationship didn't jeopardize this friendship. "I'm proud of you," Cammie whispered against my ear.

"Thanks." I released them and sat back, glancing at Cammie one more time before I decided to risk her wrath. "Now, what the hell did you do to your lashes?"

95. We Are All Worthy of Love

Two weeks after Nicole's hospitalization, I slowly climbed the steps to the Brantleys', my eyes on the toes of my Jimmy Choos, my heart hiding somewhere in my chest. I stared at their front door and remembered, a year ago, how desperate I felt, ringing their doorbell. When I looked back at that woman, I barely recognized myself. Cammie was right. I had changed. Everything in my life had changed. I inserted my key and turned it in that lock for one last time.

Maybe I should have rung the bell.

I opened the door and stepped into a fight. Clarke and Paulo, standing toe to toe in the foyer, a maid standing in front of me, her mouth half-open, a broom in hand, her steps hurriedly moving to the side to let me in. The director's shirt was gripped in Clarke's fist, Clarke's dark and angry face growling out something too soft for me to hear.

The New York wind sucked the front door shut with a loud slam that announced my presence. I winced at the sound, but neither man moved, their eyes locked.

"Where's Nicole?" I whispered to the maid.

"In bed."

"Does she know about this?" I watched Paulo attempt to push Clarke away, his struggle against solid muscle worthless.

"No." The answer was a hushed whisper and almost lost in the loud crash. I'd heard that sound before. The sound of expense and turned to see Paulo bent backward over the foyer table, the glass centerpiece—one that replaced my broken one—now in a thousand pieces on the marble floor, Paulo's hands frantic as he attempted to hold off Clarke.

"I'm going to tell you a final time," Clarke threatened, "and then you're going to get the hell out of my house. Stay away from my wife."

"Easy." Paulo's squeak was embarrassingly feminine, and I didn't move, as fascinated by this train wreck as I was horrified. "I just wanted to tell you it wasn't mine. I got snipped five years ago. I just thought you'd want to know. And she and I—we're done. We've been done. She broke it off when she found out about the baby."

Clarke shoved off the man, Paulo's body rolling to the side, his arms failing to catch his fall, his knees landing in the crystal and he wheezed out a cry. Clarke stepped another pace back, his breath hard, emotions barely controlled, his hands on his hips as if he were resting from a sprint.

I needed to go upstairs. None of this was my business. It was too personal, the emotion on Clarke's face too raw, for me to witness. Yet, my feet couldn't move, my eyes watching as Paulo made it to his feet, carefully limping toward the door.

"We still have to film," Paulo said. "Just a few press things. Shouldn't take but a day or two per week."

"That's fine." Clarke spat out. "I'll be there with her."

"Seriously," Paulo said, shuffling the last step to the door. "We're through. I just thought you'd like to know."

Clarke said nothing and the scrawny man made his exit, my attempt to sneak by thwarted by a loud crunch of crystal underfoot. Clarke's eyes met mine and my heart sank at the sadness there.

"I'm sorry." I said, my shoulders falling. "I wanted to tell you. I just…" I swallowed. "I just kept hoping she would."

His jaw tightened and he glanced upstairs, to their bedroom. "I wish she had."

"Why are you still with her?" The question I'd sat on for so long jumped, uninvited, off my tongue. I stumbled after it. "I'm sorry. It's none of my business—"

"It's fine." He interrupted me. "It's a valid question." He tilted his head at me, considering his words. "Nicole … there's a part of her that's broken. But that doesn't mean that she isn't worthy of being loved. Everyone is worthy of that. And, for some reason or another, my heart chose her." He shrugged, his eyes unfocused as he stared at the broken crystal. "Another woman would have been easier to live with, to love. But another woman wasn't in my cards. Nicole was." He looked at me. "Do you understand?"

I sort of did. Unfortunately, when I looked at Carter and myself, there were certainly some parallels—consistencies that put me squarely in Nicole's role. Part of me was broken. I had a hundred pieces I was trying to fix. And there were certainly other women Carter could have picked, ones that would be easier to deal with. I looked back up at Clarke.

"I do." I stepped toward the staircase. "I've got to talk to Nicole."

"Leaving us?" There was a wisdom in his eyes that I couldn't lie to.

"Yeah."

"Good for you." He smiled and I relaxed a little. He was such a good man. He really was. I think the reason I fell so quickly for Carter was because I saw Clarke in him. Both of them solid and steady. Both of them trustworthy and loyal. Both of them so far removed from the superficial world that Nicole and I lived in.

I nodded a goodbye and took the first step, my climb up the giant staircase increasing in speed the higher I got.

Quitting. One chapter in this crazy journey, finally coming to an end.

96. My Penniless Ass is FREE

I ducked when she threw the pillow, her face red, lungs already hoarse from screaming. I watched it bounce off the dresser, and Chanel instantly growled, pouncing on it with excitement, her ferocious play of it taking any air out of Nicole's hissy fit.

"I'll work a final two weeks," I offered. "I'll train a replacement—"

"You scheming bitch!" she hollered, looking for a new pillow, and I eased to the door before she made her way to the alarm clock. One good thing about quitting now—her immobility gave me a degree of safety. Looking at the rage on her face … if she could get up and strangle me, I think she would have.

"So … you want me to leave now?" I reached for the knob.

"Fuck you!" she seethed.

"I'll leave everything in the office, with instructions—"

"Stick them up your penniless ass!" Her groping hands found the remote, and I didn't move fast enough, it catching me in the shoulder and stinging like a bitch.

I swallowed any parting niceties and darted out the door, Chanel quick on my heels, both of us hightailing it down the stairs. I was almost glad for her fury. No guilt from a final sniffling memory of Nicole begging me to stay. On the downside, I was pretty sure, scooping Chanel up in my arms and kissing her goodbye, that my chance of a recommendation letter was toast.

I waved at the maid, the crystal pieces almost fully gone, and gently set Chanel down, all but skipping out the front door. I wanted to jump up and down when I hit the sidewalk. Wanted to grab the closest stranger and shake them with joy. I was actually FREE. Free of that woman and her drama. A taxi turned down their street, and I flagged it down, glancing at my watch as I hurried to the curb and opened the door.

Chirping out a hello to the impassive driver, I gave him the address to the *BLL* set and settled back in the seat.

I did feel sorry for her unborn child. I felt sorry for Chanel, hated pulling away and knowing that she was still stuck there, in her puppy booties and designer dog sunglasses. The taxi turned a corner, and I thought of Clarke, the tension in his shoulders, the sorrow on his face. It looked like he and Nicole would make it through this. Especially with the baby coming. Clarke would be a great father. And maybe the birth would change Nicole for the better. I was just glad I wouldn't have anything to do with any of it.

Warm sun came through the window, and I pushed any lingering thoughts of Nicole out of my mind. I smiled like a crazy person, and pulled my sunglasses out of my bag, pushing them on. Unemployment, so far, felt *great.*

97. Senior Citizen Kink

"I'm sorry, Chloe. We can't let you in."

I stopped, mid-text to Carter, and looked up at Fred. Dear sweet Fred, who shared his banana bread with me when I got grouchy. Dear sweet Fred, who had stepped *out* of the security shack and now stood in front of me. "You're kidding."

"Nope." He shook his head. "Mrs. Brantley called. Said to take you off the list."

"I have a purse in her trailer. That's all I'm here for." *And… maybe one last order of cheese biscuits from the catering truck.* "Five minutes," I pleaded. "Maybe ten."

He shook his head at me and I wished for the old days. When I could just pull out a hundred and buy the ability to break some rules. "Escort me," I offered. "You can handcuff me to your side if you want. I know you've been dying to use those cuffs." I gave him my best smile and saw him weaken slightly.

"Well…" He glanced toward the shack.

"Five minutes," I repeated. "Just straight to Nicole's trailer and back."

And that was how I ended up handcuffed to an eighty-year-old man.

Just kidding. He didn't use the handcuffs. And he was more like mid-sixties, but that doesn't have near the storytelling punch. He shuffled toward Nicole's trailer, and I trailed behind him, texting Hannah, hoping to get a goodbye in before I left.

I opened the upper cabinet and moved a bag of chips aside, tugging on the edge of the black bag until it fell out. There. Just as beautiful as the day I left it. I clutched it to my chest and turned to Fred. "One last stop," I said. "Joey Plazen's trailer. I just have to drop this off there."

He glanced at his watch. "It's been ten minutes already, Chloe."

Ten minutes because he walked slower than death. I could have hit both trailers *and* gotten cheese biscuits in the time it had taken us to walk here.

"It's on the way back. Two doors down." I jumped up and down a little and gave my best doe eyes.

"Fine," he grumbled, and I swooped out the door ahead of him.

"Shut the fuck up." Hannah stood at the counter in Joey's trailer and gawked at the bag. "You're *giving* this to me?"

"Yes." I smiled. "I know. I'm amazing."

"Seriously?" She ran a tattooed hand over the front of it.

"You quit?" Joey asked the question for the third time and I finally turned to him.

"Yes. And yes," I said to Hannah. "Seriously."

"Why?" he asked, standing from the couch and walking over, the kitchen in his trailer too small for the three of us. Fred coughed from the open doorway, and we all glanced his way.

"Umm… " he said tentatively. "Miss Madison…"

"I'm not allowed on set," I said, filling in the others. "Fred wants me out."

"Here." Joey pulled out his wallet and shuffled through some bills, pulling out a handful and holding them out to Fred. "I'll watch the klepto. Make sure she leaves straight from here."

"With a stop at the catering truck," I chimed in, giving Joey a hopeful smile.

"No," he said. "No catering truck."

"What the F?" I stomped my foot, mostly for dramatic effect. "Why?"

"I'm not shuttling your ass around the set while you complete your shopping list."

"So … I can go?" Fred asked, stuffing Joey's cash in his pocket.

"Yeah," Joey said, and Fred nodded his goodbyes, the door creaking shut behind him.

Joey waited until he was gone, then nodded at me. "Talk."

"Yeah, Nicole was having an *affair*?" Hannah perched on the counter and unzipped the bag, peering inside and checking out the inner pockets. "And she's pregnant?"

"Yep." I said, hoping she wouldn't press for details.

"Who was it?" Hannah asked, looking up from the bag.

"I don't know." I shrugged, opening Joey's fridge. I grabbed a beer and avoided eye contact, shredding the skin on my palm before I realized it wasn't a twist off.

"You don't know?" Joey stepped closer, and Hannah pushed him away.

"She doesn't know. Stop hounding the woman."

"You still with Carter?"

I looked up, the beer finally open, and met his eyes. "Yeah. No thanks to you."

His mouth twisted. "I'm sorry about that. I…" He grimaced. "I was an asshole."

"Wow." Hannah raised her eyebrows. "The truth comes out." Joey glared at her and she giggled, refocusing on her new bag.

"You were," I agreed, tipping back the beer. "Total asshole. You know how you could make it up to me?"

"Tickets to the premiere?" he offered.

"I was gonna say cheese biscuits, but sure, throw in tickets to the premiere. Two," I said pointedly.

He clutched his chest in mock pain. "You won't be my date? I'm heartbroken." He raised his eyebrows in hope. "And forgiven?" He looped an arm around my shoulders and waited for my answer.

"And forgiven," I affirmed, smiling when he pulled me to his chest. "Now, get me cheese biscuits before I change my mind," I threatened.

"Yes, ma'am." He lifted a chin to Hannah. "You coming?"

"Oh no," she said. "I plan on getting some one-on-one time with my new lover." She patted the side of the Balenciaga.

"Enjoy it," I said, waving at her as Joey dragged me to the door. "Courtesy of Victor Worth."

She laughed. "I'm an equal-opportunity slut, I'll take gifts from anyone. Feel free to send that Maserati my way!" she hollered, the words catching me right as Joey tossed my beer in the trash and shut the door.

The Maserati. I wondered what happened to it. I'd signed the title over and left it in the glove box. Had overnighted Vic the keys. And a few days later, it was gone.

"I'm gonna miss you," Joey mused, reaching out to tug on the end of my ponytail.

"I'm gonna miss this place." I held up my fingers an inch apart. "Just a bit."

"And me?"

I scrunched up my face. "A little."

He stopped at the back of the catering line, pushing his hands into the front of his pockets and looking at me, all hints of teasing gone. "I really *was* an asshole, pushing you to date Vic. Carter … I can see you guys together. You're a cool girl. He's got his shit together—always did."

I grinned at him. "So, you approve?"

He laughed. "Yeah. You have the Joey Plazen blessing of approval. It's kinda a big deal."

"Thank God," I breathed. "I can go to sleep happy." The line moved, and we stepped up to the window. I placed my order, almost groaning with pleasure when I got the cardboard box of mini biscuits, steam rising out, the smell almost as good as the taste. Joey walked me all the way out, promising to call Carter and see me soon. I waved to Fred and stepped out the gate.

And just like that, my time at *Boston Love Letters* was done.

January

When I was little, my mom told me you should find a man who loved you more than you loved him. That way, she explained, you would never get hurt. In theory, it made sense. But now, I believed half of the beauty of love was *in* the loving.

I didn't want to be the aloof woman who had a boyfriend wrapped around her finger. I wanted to be terrified of how madly-in-love I was, ready to give up everything for him, for us.

And finally, I was.

98. Chloe & Carter, Sitting in a Tree.

ChloeMadisonNYU
98 likes
ChloeMadisonNYU Dinner.
According to Cammie, I'm
supposed to put M&Ms in it.
But that's rich bitch stuff.

I packed boxes, and he carried them. Half of my life had been moved up one floor and into his apartment. I wanted to finish. Had set aside the entire evening. The girls offered to help, but I wanted, before I merged my life with Carter, the time to myself. He'd be busy anyway, a dinner date set with his mother. Apparently her private investigator had finished his report and she wanted to "go over it" with him. I eyed him from my spot on the living room floor, his arms above his head as he pushed a new air filter in place. "What time's dinner?" I asked.

"Seven." He got it in and stepped off the toolbox, moving closer to me as he wiped his hands off on his pants. "I can bring you back a plate."

"Nah." I busied myself with my DVDs, flipping through five seasons of *Friends* and wondering if I would actually watch them again. "I've got a frozen pizza I can heat up."

"You seem stressed about my dinner." He stopped in front of me, and I set down the DVDs, looking up at him.

"Aren't you?" He seemed ridiculously calm. Annoyingly so.

"Her decision doesn't matter." He crouched before me so that we were eye level. "It's not going to affect us."

"Oh yeah." I snorted. "What's financial security?" I shrugged. "You don't need that."

"I'd rather have you."

I shook my head and pulled a stack of novels off the shelf. "You say that Carter but … you don't know. I know what a sacrifice that is." I looked at him. "I lost everything. It's not easy. It's romantic, but it isn't easy. It *sucks*. And I don't want to be the one responsible for you to go through that."

"You don't think you're worth it."

"Changing the direction of your life?" I looked away from him. "No."

He caught my chin and pulled it to him. "Look at me, Chloe."

I did. His eyes grounded me. I could look at them all day. My calm in the storm, they looked at me as if they knew all of my secrets and loved me for them. They were certain and strong, as if they had never second-guessed anything. "You act like I'm the only one giving up something."

"You are."

"My parents' wealth is the exact same as that Maserati that sat across from our building. You could have had it. You could have had that life, either with him or a million other guys in this city. But you didn't. You stayed with me. You didn't even hesitate."

"That's different."

"It's not." He shook his head. "I love you, Chloe. Everything else fades away from that."

I thought of my mother's advice, how stupid it was when compared to a love like this. There was no room for a safety net with love, not when you had feelings that overrode all reason. I grabbed ahold of his shirt and pulled his mouth to me, scared of the depth of my feelings for him. I wanted to give him everything and was heartbroken that I had nothing to offer, my love seeming paltry in the face of all that he was risking.

Being with him could never be considered a sacrifice. And what he was saying—that I had given up wealth by choosing him—that was crazy. *Nothing* was being given up by being with this man. I kissed his mouth and tasted his love and didn't need another thing from this world.

The cardboard box got pushed aside, my books falling off the shelf as he pulled me down to the floor and kissed me. I got dust in my hair when he grabbed it. His tool belt dug into my hip when he pulled me to him. When his phone rang, we were breathless.

"Don't answer it," I begged.

"I won't." He silenced the phone but saw the time. "But I have to go."

I pouted, and he kissed me. Promised to be back soon, and then left.

I rubbed gently at my swollen lips and stared at the TV stand, a moment passing before I had the sense to resume packing.

I finished the box and tucked over the lid, pushing it aside and moving to the bookshelf, pulling framed photos off the shelves and wrapped them in hand towels. I thought about the night before. We'd been up late unpacking my stuff in his place. He'd wanted to know everything, a story about every framed photo, my favorite shoes, my stuffed zebra, the set of elephants from my summer in South Africa. Some of the stories were Vic stories, but he didn't care. It was another thing I loved about him, his confidence. Times when Vic would have slunk off to sulk, Carter pulled me closer and laughed.

My confidence wasn't as strong. I asked him to pack up the Presa Little art. Offered to help him carry them down to the storage lockers, but he refused, announcing that he was listing them for sale.

"You don't need to do that." I had pulled at his arm, trying to get his cell phone, to stop his call to the gallery.

"Why wouldn't I?" He'd frowned down at me, genuinely confused. "They bother you. And they should. They were from when I dated her."

"But … they're beautiful." And they were. Some of her best. They took my breath away every time I walked in his apartment.

"Not as beautiful as you." He pulled me closer. "We can sell them. Put the money down and buy a place."

"But what if…" *we break up*. That was what I was going to say. He'd never be able to afford to buy them back.

"We're not." His touch had been gentle when he'd lifted my chin, and I closed my eyes to his kiss. Relaxed in his arms and let him work his cell phone out of my hand.

I boxed up the books and then moved to the stack of loose papers, thumbing through receipts, a cable bill, and then, my first résumé. I looked it over, the pathetically sad page that I had brought to Nicole's interview. Thank God she'd never asked for it. I carried it to my laptop and stuck it underneath, updating it another to-do item I needed to knock out next week. Monday, I was going to empty out my savings and pay off my tuition bill. It'd leave me with nothing, but Carter had insisted on it. He didn't want me to get another dead-end job just because I didn't have a degree. So, with a diploma finally in hand, and an updated résumé, I'd hit the employment search again. It wouldn't be easy; New York was hell on the unemployed. But at least I had a place to stay. And a deposit that would be returned to me, if Carter deemed the apartment to be in suitable condition. Maybe a bribe was in order, one of the sexual variety. It couldn't hurt, right? I could wait until he was working in the engine room, all sweaty and hot, then tempt him with some ice water. Get him up to our apartment and then strip him naked.

I lost track of my plans when the door to my apartment opened. Turning around, I stared at Carter. "What are you doing?" I glanced at the clock. "You should have left by—"

"I canceled."

"What? When?"

"Just now. It's pointless, meeting with her." He stepped forward, tossing his jacket on my couch, his hand pulling at the knot on his tie. I loved when he was dressed up. Loved the look of him with neat hair that begged to be violated. A stiff shirt that hugged his muscles perfectly. Dress pants that clung to that fine ass.

I pulled my eyes from said pants. "Pointless? How can it be—"

"I don't care if they approve of you." He got the tie loose and yanked it off. Stopped before me and pulled at the bottom of my sweatshirt, his fingers snagging my T-shirt too, pulling both of them over my head. He grabbed at the front of my sweatpants, his hands dipping inside and around my waist, big palms settling on and squeezing my ass, yanking me hard against him as he kissed me. "I love you," he said, pulling off my mouth and pushing me down on the couch, rolling my sweatpants down the length of my legs. "That's the only thing that matters. We'll figure the rest out." He stood above me, my heart beating hard, and I watched as he removed his belt, pulled his dress shirt over his head, and then his pants unzipped and everything I loved was before me, naked. Then on top of me, hard.

After that … I lost track of thought.

99. Six Months Later - June

ChloeMadisonNYU
147 likes
ChloeMadisonNYU He is my everything.

"What do you think?"

Carter chewed the edge of his lip and examined a stain on the ceiling. "I think it's a shithole."

"Yeah," I agreed happily. "It is." I walked to the window and pushed aside the cheap shade. "But look at that view."

"Trevor thinks this is a good investment?" He met me at the window. "It seems a little … small for him."

I almost laughed. Small would be a nice word to describe the two-bedroom to my boss, a man who bought city blocks and not rundown apartments. A boss who had taken pity and given my skinny resume a chance. A boss who seemed thrilled at the real estate opportunities I had found him so far. "I haven't approached him about it." I turned to Carter. "I found it for you."

"There's no *me* anymore." He turned to me. "Us."

I rolled my eyes but didn't hide the smile. "Okay fine. *Us.*"

His last Presa Little had sold at auction three weeks earlier. I wasn't trying to dig into his business, but I could use a calculator. My poor boyfriend had enough for a down payment on this, plus a chunk left over to remodel it. Especially since he could do the majority of the remodel himself.

He leaned against a wall and crossed his arms, looking at me. "What would you suggest? To flip it?"

"You want my expert opinion?"

He laughed. "Yes."

"I'd keep it. Renovate it and rent it out. It'll more than cover itself."

"Would you want to live here?"

I scrunched up my face. "Not really." Not that the place wouldn't be nice, but our apartment—there was just so much love in those walls. I felt like we had history there. I loved it despite it being owned by his parents, who had cut all ties with him, save for business calls about his job. I don't know if they were mad because of my parent's actions, or mad because he chose to date me despite that, or—and I think this is really it—they didn't like him choosing me over them. Carter stepped toward me and I refocused on him.

"Okay." He lifted his chin. "Make an offer on it."

"Really?" I clenched my notebook and did a mini jump for joy.

He chuckled, pulling me to him. "You've looked at property every day for four months, and this is the first one you've ever brought me to. I think that's a good sign."

"It *is* a good sign," I promised him. "It just had a big assessment and they're redoing the school around the—"

"Chloe." He shut me up with just the word, tugging on the ends of my hair and looking down at me.

"Yes?" I looked up at the man I loved and almost swooned.

"Stop talking and let me kiss my wife."

"Your what?" I pushed against his chest, but then his lips were on me, and they were my weakness, soft and strong, my mouth opening for him, our kiss deepening.

When he pulled off, I tried to speak, tried to understand. Surely he wouldn't propose *here*, not in this filthy condo in Tribeca. Proposals were supposed to be done in grand fashion, with candlelight and music.

But then he dropped to one knee and looked up at me, holding my hand, love pouring from those eyes. And in that moment, I wouldn't have had it any other way.

"Chloe Madison, will you marry me?" he whispered.

I didn't hesitate, didn't need to think it over; the question one I had dreamed of for months. "Yes!" I shouted, his arms wrapping around me. He laughed against my mouth and pulled back.

"I don't have the ring with me," he admitted. "I wasn't … it wasn't supposed to happen like this." He kissed my forehead. "I'm sorry."

I pulled his mouth down to mine. "Don't ever be sorry. It was perfect."

And it had been. A little unorthodox. Not what I had always envisioned. But this entire life wasn't how I had envisioned it.

It was so much better.

<<<<>>>>

Epilogue - Carter

I had seen girls like Chloe before. That's what I thought, that first time I saw her. She was like a baby doe, skittering on her feet, legs and arms spread out for balance in that New Year's Eve snow. My first instinct had been to protect her, to scoop her into my arms and carry her inside. But I'd known girls like that my whole life, and they didn't want protecting—at least not from men like me.

My first mistake was judging her—just because she wore expensive clothes and stepped from a private car, a purse dog in hand. When she smiled at me, I saw every girl from my upbringing—the girls my mother warned me away from, the ones that only saw Prince Charming if he wore the right watch, in the right zip code, with a big portfolio and an intent to spoil. I was afraid of her because of it. Afraid because, in the wobble of her smile, I saw something else. Something that drew me in and wouldn't let go. A hint of a girl who needed saving, and not financially. A hint of a girl who I wouldn't be able to walk away from.

She stuck in my mind, like a dream you couldn't shake, each memory fainter than the last. I should have gotten her last name. Her number. Anything.

And then she opened that apartment door and was there.

I'm not gonna tell you the leap my heart took. Or the way I had to tighten my hand against the doorframe because I thought I might fall. But I will tell you that the fear returned. She was different from my memories. Her hard edges softer. Her eyes kinder. The stiffness she had given me that New Year's Eve night … it was gone. And I almost wanted it back. I needed the reminder of why she wasn't good for me, of why we wouldn't work, of why, in this huge city, I needed to find a simple girl—one who would fall in love with me, and not my trust fund. And Chloe wasn't that type of girl. She was the type who'd look at me and wouldn't want to dive any deeper. Except …

she did. And from the beginning she shook my foundation. She scared me.

And later, she broke me. She found the weak places in me and slipped in, her tiny hands cradling my heart and making it her own. Such a tentative touch, yet one forever imprinted on my heart. Protection is the smallest thing I want to do for her. I want to protect, but also provide. I want to build her a home, and make babies with her, and to open her eyes to everything she hasn't seen. I want to watch the rest of her journey—to see her in a job she truly loves, in a life she truly wants, and I want to give it all to her but I know she has to find it on her own. And that is the hardest, and the most beautiful part.

There is nothing left in me to save. With every imperfection in her I find, I fall farther. Every twist of her head, giggle from her mouth, and shriek of her orgasm … I am more vulnerable. When she found out about my family's money, she was disappointed. When she told me about her parents, she was embarrassed. When she struggled with Nicole's infidelity, she was flawed. And when she spoke of Vic, she was human. And when she looks at me, she is complete. There aren't enough words to express how that makes me feel.

I can't live without this woman. She is my best friend. She is the second half of my heart. She is the blood that pumps through my veins.

She is my everything.

She is my future.

She is my Chloe.

She is my Love.

and then...

ChloeMadisonNYU

♥ 141 likes

ChloeMadisonNYU So... According to Glamour, Nicole and Clarke are still together. Clarke will be such a great dad! #happy

ChloeMadisonNYU

199 likes

ChloeMadisonNYU Quite possibly the first time I've ever been 'excited' to see Nicole... #BostonLoveLetters #releaseday #intheaters

ChloeMadisonNYU
308 likes
ChloeMadisonNYU So incredibly happy as his wife.
#weddingday #togetherforever

ChloeMadisonNYU

209 likes

ChloeMadisonNYU I've never once looked back. #soulmates

The End

From the Author

Thank you so much for reading Love, Chloe. I feel like I have been in Chloe's head for so long now! As some of you may know, this story first started as a Cosmopolitan.com online serial. I would write one episode (chapter) at a time, and the posts would publish three times a week, Chloe's story unfolding over the course of a year. Chloe's story was not nearly as cohesive as it appeared in this book. Since I wrote serial one episode at a time, it sometimes wandered. There were directions I expected her story to go that it didn't head. Thoughts she had which I later regretted. This book allowed me to fix all of my regrets and to properly add to her story (over 80 extra pages of content!), giving it a much better impact and reader experience.

The Cosmo episodes are still live – if you want to check them out, you can visit alessandratorre.com and click on the COSMO tab at the top. There are 156 episodes there, so be careful … you may get swept up and lose a few days. But honestly, don't feel like you need to read those. They may confuse and ruin your image of Chloe. If you do want to check out a few deleted scenes, I have chosen for your enjoyment at: alessandratorre.com/lcdeleted/

If this is my first book that you've read, please consider moving on to another one of my books. Hollywood Dirt is a great fun/sexy option. If you prefer a book with a jaw-dropping twist, check out Black Lies or Sex Love Repeat.

Want to be notified when my next book releases? Preorder pricing will always save you 40%! Visit nextnovel.com to sign up.

Want to follow me on social media and see my writing progress, photos from my daily life, and my embarrassingly extensive shoe collection? Please find me on Facebook, Twitter, Pinterest and Instagram! Also, I LOVE Goodreads! Please look me up and join my group Shh… [Smut, Heroes, & HEAs]! Shh has live chats with four authors every month, plus book chats, giveaways, and lots of fun games! We'd love to have you join the fun!

Thank you so much for purchasing this book and for meeting Chloe. If you enjoyed it, please consider leaving a review or recommending it to a friend.

Thank you again for your support!

Alessandra Torre